# Gone Bodfishin'

## By David Clark Done

It was four in the morning when Luke finished checking the documents assigned to him. The end of the tax season was approaching and it was clear they were running out of work. He knew it wouldn't be long before this job would end and he would be unemployed again. Finding, and securing temporary jobs was a never ending cycle. A cycle he had gotten used to.

To make matters worse he was sleepy, and needed a jolt of caffeine. Most nights he would pour another cup of coffee and fight off his desire to go to sleep. The late night hours were tough. He had been working the graveyard shift for over a month, and his body was still not adjusted. Quitting time was three hours away. He decided to skip the coffee.

Luke was working his way through college. Checking tax forms was just another temporary job taken to keep a roof over his head. It put food on the table and helped him buy books. For Luke, boredom was the worst thing life had to offer, and checking tax returns all night long was boring.

He had two neat stacks of completed returns piled up on his desk.

The small pile contained rejects. He picked up both stacks and headed to the central office. The door was ajar, he threw the rejects into a basket marked for re-examination. The others were ready to be signed and filed. They needed no further attention. The night foreman, a massive giant of a man, picked up the novel he was reading and grunted.

"Did you finish them?"

"Yes, the whole batch." Luke answered wearily. " It had many rejects as usual. One of the rejects belongs to Captain Kirk."

"Captain Kirk?" the big man flashed a grin showing gap teeth.

"Yep, William Shatner. You remember from Star Trek? Sci Fi show? The show was canceled last year. I was sad when it happened. ."

"The one with Spock? The guy with the pointy ears?"

"Right, that's the one. Shatner's return was red flagged. You can check out the total amount he made in his final year." Luke egged his guy on.

"I liked Captain Kirk, he's a handsome son of a bitch. " John lunged toward the basket and pawed through the papers. His gigantic fingers thumbed through the forms looking for the return in question. Luke knew if there was anything John liked to do, it was inspect the tax returns of famous celebrities. And Shatner was famous to those who had watched his ill-fated show.

"What's the problem with his return?"

"I don't know, the system red flagged it! It was way beyond my pay grade, so I left it for you to solve." He teased the big man.

Luke chuckled as John scrambled trying to find the documents. He could hear the blood throbbing in John's brain. "How much does Shatner make? I'll bet it is a bundle."

John found it and gasped! The gross income number was larger than the salary of the President of the United States, not bad for an actor!

Having satisfied his curiosity, John peeked up over the forms and said, "You worked so fast, I haven't any more for you to do. You can hang around here till seven if you want, or you can go home. I'll punch your card and make sure you get paid for a full shift. You should leave."

Overhead the buzz of a lane coming in for a landing shook the building. Luke had been on his feet for twenty hours straight and was dead tired. He wasn't sure he wanted to go home. He didn't have a car, his ride home was provided by his girlfriend. She got out of bed every morning and drove twenty miles across town to pick him up.

She was always waiting for him in the parking lot when he got off work. Since it was so early, she was not due for a while and was deep asleep. He did not dare call her. Not at four in the morning!

"Are you sure? My girlfriend is set to pick me up at seven. If I go home now I'll have to hitch a ride. At this time of night I might as well stay and work. I doubt I will get a ride."

"Nothin for you to do." John was buried in the problem of solving Shatner's red flagged return. The Captain's issues were urgent and now he was on a mission to locate and solve the problem. He was beamed into the document and would not materialize again until the issue was resolved.

"Alright, I might get lucky."

Luke decided he would chance getting a ride and would call her later and warn her. The night air was cold and the moment he let the door of the warehouse close behind him he regretted not having crawled up in some out of the way corner.

"God damn it, I'll stand out here in the cold all night." He resigned himself to the fact. He searched the long stretch of Pacific Coast Highway hoping for a friendly driver to appear. Well, he thought, this is the L.A. airport and cars come and go at all hours. His thoughts drifted off to the school work he had not done. He asked himself why he was bothering with it at all. He was not interested in it anymore and hadn't been for a long time. "I have nothing better to do." He answered his own question out loud. "If I had something better I would do it."

A set of headlights approached, and flashed by him, the car pulled over and stopped a hundred yards down the road.

What luck! He did not believe it, did the car stop for me? But of course, it had to, he was alone, there was no other reason to pull over at this spot so late at night. The road was deserted and no one else was on it.

Luke ran at full speed towards the car, afraid the driver would take off without him. It was a yellow cab with its lights off. Luke ran so fast he was unable to stop fast enough and almost flew past the cab door. Off balance, he reached out and caught the door handle and yanked it open.

He dove into the front seat next to the driver. Gasping and out of breath he could not speak. His lungs heaved in rapid fire. The driver leaned away. The driver had his face buried in a map. A long uncomfortable silence ensued.

Luke caught his breath and leaned back trying to catch a glimpse of the man's face. A full minute of stony silence elapsed, Luke was not sure what to say. He felt a definite tension in the cab, something was wrong.

"Well, how far down the road are you going?" Luke asked, annoyed.

"What?" The voice was shaky but sounded relieved.

"Didn't you stop for me? I was hitchhiking, I thought you stopped for me."

"Jesus," the man let out a long hissing stream and dropped his map. He had a thirty eight revolver pointed right at Luke's chest. "Jesus, I almost blew you in half." The driver's hand trembled as he put the gun away in a pouch on the door of his cab. "I didn't notice you, I stopped checking for directions. What are you doing out here?"

"Sorry, I thought you pulled over for me. I work on the night shift down the road a bit. They let me off work early. I am trying to hitch home. I wanted a ride so bad, I didn't think about it much. Sorry if I scared you."

"Cabs never pick up hitchhikers, man." The guy was getting angry. "You scared the crap out of me."

"Well, at this time of night you can't be sure." Luke shrugged. The driver had a thick brown mustache and was wearing a cowboy shirt. His cowboy hat lay on the floor. Luke was glad he had not stepped on it when he jumped in the cab. "Interesting hat." Luke nodded at the Stetson.

"Shit man. You're crazy." He said and then the driver burst into a nervous laughter. "You're only a kid, Christ, you gave me a scare, but hell you're a kid."

"Well, I will start walking, I have a ways to go.  At least I got warm for a minute." Luke reached for the car door.

"Wait a minute, where do you live?" The driver's voice had become warm and friendly.

"Down the highway in Redondo Beach, about twenty miles or so. I can't afford a cab."

"Sit in the back seat and lie down where no one can notice you. I'll give you a ride, I'm headed that way, but don't pop your head up. If an inspector catches you and I don't have my flag up, I'll lose my job."

Luke did as he was told and climbed into the back where he let his head rest against the leather. He tried to keep down and out of sight.

"Can't stand this job, this late night shift is a bust, not many fares at this time of night. Bars have been closed for two hours. The only chance for a fare is around the airport. What kind of work do you do out here?" He had a bit of an accent but Luke couldn't place it. He figured country but no place in particular.

"I'm a student. I check tax forms for accuracy at night." He nodded towards the building housing his office. The driver stared at him in the rear-view mirror.

"I'm Al, I've been doing this cab thing for a couple of months, I work as a stuntman during the day. Have you ever seen the western fight show at the Circle Star amusement park?"

"Yeah, I've seen it. Are you in it?"

"One of the stars, been one, on and off for five years now, but Christ I hate it." Al glanced over his shoulder and grinned. "Same damn show every day, three times a day. Fake fist fighting! It gets old."

"So, why are you driving a cab late at night?"

"Me and my partner are trying to make enough money to escape this rat hole. That's why I'm driving and working two jobs. I gotta earn some money. We're starting our own movie set, out in the high desert." Al's eyes sparkled. He flashed a wicked self satisfied grin.

"Living in Los Angeles is wearing me down, L.A. has too many people. But a movie set sounds cool. How did you get into it" Luke Al exuded excitemen.

"Yeah that's it, too many people, too much wear and tear, it grinds you down, no matter how hard you try, you will never make it working for wages. I gotta go on my own, gotta build my own empire, it's gotta start somewhere. I hope I will catch a lucky break?"

"You think you can do that?" Luke was caught up in the man's energy. "Build a movie set? Make movies?"

"We're already building it, we got an old Western movie town. I got some partners, but I ran short of money. Needed some money to live on. I figure it won't be long and I will have saved enough to go back and we'll finish. We hope the movie companies will come and rent it, and make Westerns. As soon as I earn a few more bucks together I will move back out permanently. My family is waiting for me."

"That's fantastic!" Luke was impressed. It wasn't every day he met such a big shot. He tried to imagine the odds of it happening! What a long shot.

A call came over the radio and Al picked up the speaker.

"No, I haven't had fare for a while, I'm cruising around the airport lookin' for action but it's dead tonight." Al spoke into the hand-held box. "Yeah, I'm not far, I'll take it." He turned back. "Sorry kid, I got a fare up the road in Hawthorne. I'll take you as far as I can though, we should be close when I drop you."

"That's great, I only live a few miles away. You will put me close. No problem. I owe you one."

"You're a student right? Come this summer if you'd like to come out and help us work on the set. I think you'd like it. You could learn to be a stuntman. Here's my card." Al handed his card over the seat and Luke took it. It read "The Silver City Movie Set and Ranch," Al Johnson, Proprietor. Bodfish California."

"It is beautiful, and has a lake to swim in when it gets too hot to work. Think about it, if you've nothing else to do. I'll make sure you are fed and have a place to sleep. What's your name?"

"Luke". He put the card in his shirt pocket. He was tempted, just maybe, he thought. Why not?

"Well, Luke, I better let you out about here. My fare is waiting in the diner right up the road."

"Thanks a lot for the ride. I'll think about what you said." Luke slammed the door as the cab pulled up to the diner.

"What luck," he was invigorated. The walk home passed in a twinkle. He was disturbed by the barking of an alert dog who objected to his baritone rendition of "Swing Low Sweet Chariot". The dog seemed to be saying "you have no right to be on the street so late at night.

Chapter Two

Luke was bored with his studies and cou;d not focus or find any value in what he was doing. The school term dragged to a close. He shuddered to think his future would be more and more of the same old thing. He wanted something new, something challenging. He had to face it, he no longer pretended he didn't care. Indifference was his enemy. and was holding him back.

His studies didn't matter in the grand scheme of things. Why memorize the exact order of all the Egyptian Pharaohs who had ruled prior to the time of Christ. Who cares how long they lived or what they did? He was studying middle eastern cultures and their history. In a year he would graduate with a B.A. But if he wanted it to mean anything he would need to go to graduate school and earn a master's degree. The idea of teaching others did not appeal to him, the tedious subject at a community college. His motivation to go to school had slipped away.

To make matters worse, he was on the verge of physical exhaustion. All he ever did was work, and when the work was finished, he found some more. Why read some dry old book about people who had lived thousands of years ago and go to work at a meaningless stupid job. He was at the point of total frustration. Why was he doing it!

Luke fingered the card the cab driver had given him and read it for the fiftieth time. He was looking for an excuse to throw aside his old life, and start a new one. The calling card was a little two inch long messenger of fate, The Silver City Movie Set and Ranch, Bodfish, Ca.

"Bodfish. What a name." He said it out loud.

He kept replaying the weird details of the chance encounter that had placed this card in his hands. It didn't matter what was waiting for him, any new life would be better than what he was doing.

"I might be grasping at a phantom, but what if it is real?"

What a glamorous life! It would mean an opportunity to break into the movies! He had taken three years of drama in high school, when most boys were taking woodshop. He had landed the part of Peter in the Diary of Anne Frank in the school production and everyone said he was terrific in the role. Acting had been fun and it was something he knew well. Why not try it again?

Luke had starred on the wrestling team. He was athletic and in top shape. He was not easily intimidated and had never sought out a fight but would not back down from one if he was pushed. He was not afraid of doing stunts. How hard could it be? He thought "I can do any stunt anyone else can do." He wanted a new beginning.

He imagined the dull life he had been living coming to a close. He was doing well enough to enter a teaching program, and it offered a safe,easy existence. But he didn't want to teach. He had been encouraged to pursue a PHD. If he did it meant five more years of study. In his mind PHD stood for piling it higher and deeper. That was not what he wanted. He hated the scholastic life he had been living. He was not cut out for it.

He cut all ties with his current course and found a better one. He wanted excitement! He would become a stuntman and work on camera in the movies. He decided to leave without saying goodbye to a single person. Let them wonder what happened, let them guess where he had gone. A clean break and a new start, he was excited at the prospect of chasing a dream.

"Cut it all off," he said looking into the mirror across from the barber's chair. "Where I am going I will be too hot for all this hair. Cut it short."

"Okay," the barber made a face while looking at the long flowing mane of hair, and began the task of cutting it off. "Don't get many of your type here."

"I suppose not, I was a student until yesterday, I never have money to have my haircut. But I need it done. I'm going to live out in the mountains in the high desert country." Luke waited with patience as more than a year's hair growth fell beneath the chair in clumps and piles.

"Wouldn't live in the desert for anything. I never liked it, it was too hot and nothing to do." The barber became more talkative as he cut Luke's hair and Luke became more human to him. "Funny thing, all this hair makes you seem five years older."

"Well, I met a guy, and I got a job waiting for me. Yes sir, I am going to train to become a stuntman." Luke thought it made him sound important and powerful. In his mind he compared it to saying "I am going to teach ancient history to college freshmen." It made him chuckle.

"Well I guess if you got a job, it's different. Tell me again where you are going?" The barber was circling Luke taking snippets of hair in an effort to make it neat and even.

"The mountains where they border the high desert in Kern County. Town called Bodfish out near China Lake."

"I knew a guy who lived there once. He swore by it, a strange kind of man. Never talked much, I never knew for sure what he was thinking, but he swore by China Lake."

"I've never been to China Lake before, but I'm leaving tomorrow. Bodfish is a little town right by the lake, that's where I am going."

"What do you think?" The barber held his mirror up so Luke could check the back of his head. His hair was all now short and trim. He barely recognized himself.

"That's fine," he had a sinking feeling in his stomach for a minute at the sight of his neck. "I'll get used to it."

His little room was barren now. In the corner he stacked six well sealed boxes all addressed to his father. He had addressed and marked each one with an approximate weight. He thought they totaled four hundred pounds, but he was guessing. He had cash to pay the driver who was coming to take them away.

He wasn't sure he wanted to spend the money. The thought of leaving his books, and accumulated papers for disposal by the landlord had appealed to him, but he was not quite able to do it. He thought someday he might go back to college and pick up where he left off. He decided to send them to his Dad for safe keeping.

He wrote a letter to his father's attention and attached it to one of the boxes. The letter was brimming with feelings of hopefulness for the new life he was about to begin. He imagined the scowl on the old man's face. For sure, every word would be misunderstood.

"To hell with him. I have to please myself." Luke chortled.

His pack was leaned up against the wall. It bulged with all the clothes he owned that could still be worn. He had six changes. He was ready to go. His alarm was set for six in the morning. The truck was booked to arrive early and he planned to leave as soon as the truck left. He flicked out the light and for the first time in months was alive.

When sleep came it was a sound one. the kind of sleep one experiences when a heavy burden has been lifted. Adventure called, and Luke was ready and anxious to answer the
Call.


Chapter Three

Luke studied the map and decided it would be a little more than a day's travel. He expected a short easy trip up to the high country. He did not own a car and hitchhiking was always his primary method of travel. He loved to do it. He read people well and knew how to handle them. Hitchhiking offered excitement, with every ride you met someone new, you had a fresh beginning and then it ended. It was the nature of the beast.

Luke was looking forward to sticking his thumb out and leaving his dull existence behind to begin a new life. He would sleep outdoors under the stars again, and if possible find a new perspective and enjoy a mental freedom he found was rare in the world.

Luke warned himself not to expect a warm welcome at the Silver City. He could not be sure if Al would be there. What if Al did not remember him? He had no way to be sure the old town and movie set was real. It might not be the place Al had claimed it to be! Perhaps it was nothing like what he had imagined. Could he learn to be a stuntman? Was that even possible? He was going to find out. It was a leap into the unknown. He took the leap!

In his imagination, he envisioned himself doing all kinds of dangerous and amazing things. "I will go and give it a chance and see what happens." I see nothing to be gained by indulging in self doubt, he assured himself. After a series of short rides he hooked up with an army Lieutenant who was stationed at a base somewhere in the desert area.

"Going to Bodfish?" he responded to Luke's sign. No one else who had stopped had any idea what the sign meant. The Lieutenant was the first person who offered a glimmer of recognition.

"Yep." Luke was relieved.

"I'm going nearby." The lieutenant indicated he should jump in.

The officer spoke in short crisp monosyllables. He did not waste words or energy. and much to Luke's relief was familiar with the location of Bodfish. He drove them through Los Angeles and out into the desert. Luke marveled at the fact Los Angeles itself was built in the desert and if water had not been imported from Colorado it would still be desert. The thriving metropolis that was Southern California, including the lush farms and orchards of Orange County were man made, and depended on water from the mighty river.

Luke was looking out at a huge vast stretch of dry desert. He saw it had little life or foliage. It is an illusion, he thought. It is teeming with life. Luke had spent a week when he was younger with his scout troop camping in the hot sand. He knew there was plenty of life hiding in the hot sun.

He had experienced how cold it gets at night when the coyotes and snakes and lizards all materialized. He had walked in the desert when it was in bloom with its cactus buds and flowers. He had marveled at how colorful and beautiful it could be.

As they cruised along Luke kept track of the road signs but saw no mention of the town of Bodfish. The officer pulled over and motioned for Luke to leave.

"That's the road to Bodfish." He pointed down a two lane road winding into the distance. The road was unmarked.

"Wow, I'll take your word for it."

Luke's map had shown Bodfish was at the base of the Sierra Nevada's leading up to the mountain range itself. It was the "high desert area", a stretch of land caught between the snow capped mountains and the elevated desert.

"Thanks, again! I never would have found it without you".

The car pulled away and Luke sat and marveled that this tiny town was too small to justify a road sign. What would have happened if he had not run into the Lieutenant?

Luke sat at the junction waiting for a ride. An hour went by and no one stopped. The sun started going down and night appeared in brilliant orange and pink hues lit up the sky. He pulled out his harmonica and started to play. His voice was deep and mellow, with range.

"You get a line, I'll get a pole, honey,

You get a line, I'll get a pole, babe

You get a line, I'll get a pole,

We'll go down to the crawdad hole

Honey, oh baby mine."

He found it an easy bit to play. He had come to believe it was about a country boy trying to seduce his woman. He played it and never got bored with it. The world was a better place when he sang.

Life slowed down, he didn't feel so hurried. The wait for a ride was inconsequential, almost relaxing. Finally a bright red pickup truck stopped and a throaty female voice offered him a ride.

"Goin into Bodfish?" a middle aged woman smiled at him through a half rolled down window. Her eyes had the beginnings of crows feet and her face was framed by light delicate frown lines etched in the corners of her mouth. All the lines got deeper when she smiled. She had a sparkle in her eyes.

"Yea, I'm headed to Bodfish." He smiled back.

"Hop in, I'm going most of the way." She waited as he climbed into the back. "You are the first person I have ever seen hitching a ride to Bodfish. Ain't much traffic in Bodfish."

"I got an invitation, I have a job waiting." Luke answered.

"You can sit up here with me, I don't bite. At least not until I'm asked." She acted annoyed. Luke decided to sit in the cab with her.

The road to Bodfish wound between canyon walls dotted with "falling rock" signs. Little piles of stone gave evidence of partly cleared landslides.

"It has been awhile since a road crew was here." Luke tried to make small talk.

"Our roads are not on the state's priority list for repair and we don't like the government much."

Hardy desert shrubs were growing in the jagged rock making it crack and break apart. The tenacity of the shrubs made a statement about endurance and working against the odds.

"Amazing how plants can take root in solid rock. Makes a person think." Luke tried again to make conversation.

"What kind of job you got in Bodfish? Really not much in town, these days. Never has been." She checked him up and down taking in his young, muscular six foot frame.

"I been offered a chance to become a stuntman at a movie set being built by some friends." Luke's voice was full of enthusiasm.

"A movie set? In Bodfish? You sure? It's a small town and I never heard about any movie set." The woman answered.

"I got the owner's card right here. He invited me to come out and join him." Luke flashed the weathered and torn card at her.

"It's funny, I never learned about it before."

"It's a start-up, getting up and running. I'll be in on the ground floor."

"I believe everyone can use a fresh start." She smiled at him.

Her old truck strained as she put the pedal down. She tried to coax it over a pass separating the high desert plain from the mountains. It moaned and complained as they rounded around a sudden bend in the road.

There was a lake visible in the twilight. A river fed into it from the north side of the lake. She eased the truck off the road and stopped. She nodded towards it.

"That's my turn off. I have an extra bed. You can stay the night. If you need a little money I can find some work for you around my place. I am all by myself.

Been that way for a long time now. I got an odd job or two." She gave him a coy smile and waited for an answer.

"I want to sleep outside tonight, down by the river, thanks anyway."

"Please yourself, I'll make you dinner if you come." She licked her upper lip showing him a bit of her tongue and pouted at him. Her sensuous eyes caused a brief stir in Luke's groin but he shook it off. She was twice his age and he was on a mission.

"Naw I've been looking forward to sleeping under the stars," he got out and hitched his pack over his shoulder and walked off towards the river below.

"Bodfish is about ten miles down the road." Her voice trailed off as he turned his back and left her.

Interesting woman, he thought, she's been living all alone out here for a while. Must be lonely. It can't be easy for her. Her truck disappeared over a hill and he was on his own again. That's what I like about hitchhiking, he thought. You never know who or what might present itself.

The river bank was soft and sandy, the night air was filled with mosquitoes and gnats. He walked along the bank for a half mile until he found a spot that wasn't swarming with insects. He laid his pack down, away from the bank. He was still close enough to hear the sound of the water running. The fish in the moonlight rising to the surface trying to catch insects. One broke the surface, and vanished back into the fast moving water.

"It's a sign, not every river has fish." It affirmed he was on the right path. Everything would work out.

On most days it would be too early to think about sleep, but since he had spent the whole day hitchhiking, he was tired. It had taken longer than he had expected. A lot of the day had been spent standing in the hot dry sun. It had baked his face and was catching up with him.

He unrolled his sleeping bag, took out a bag of beef jerky and removed two long strips. He lay looking up at a clear and clean night sky getting darker. Soon it was filled with thousands of bright blinking stars. He sat munching jerky and the show unfolded. He was happy.

He was filled with a peaceful resolve and hoped in the morning he would find the cab driver who had given him the battered card now crinkled up in his wallet. The fast moving water gave him a sense of well being that helped him fall asleep. His dream mind wandered ahead expecting his future would be bright and without disappointment.


Chapter Four

Luke found the "Movie Set" at the far end of the little village of Bodfish. It was surrounded by a wooden fence patched together from odds and ends of rotting lumber. The planks varied greatly in length and width. It was as if many different kinds of wood had been bought from a lumber yard having a going out of business sale. It reminded Luke of a smile, carved on a Halloween pumpkin that was missing some of its teeth. A dilapidated sign was dangling over the front entrance of a locked gate. The sign read: " Welcome to Silver City".

Luke stood on his tiptoes and strained to peer over the fence. It featured a single street lined on either side by a total of about twelve ramshackle old buildings. Most of the buildings were marked by signs, "General Store", "Livery", "Hotel" , and "Jail". Some were unmarked.

At the far end of the street he noticed a stable and a chestnut brown mare was feeding. Just like in the movies each building had a stand in front to tie up horses, along with a water trough. There was only one horse, so Luke concluded the obvious, it was a one horse town. He laughed at his own joke.

"Can I help you?" a voice asked in a drawl. It came from right behind him and it startled Luke. He hadn't sensed a was person was so close.

"I'm looking for Al, know him?" Luke starred up into the face of a tall dark lanky man in a cowboy hat. His hair was black, slicked back and oily. Luke guessed he was in his late 30's.

"Who is asking?" The drawl was a little lower and slower thistime. He cracked a broken smile showing yellow teeth with a gap where one had gone missing.

"Well, he kind of invited me to come and work here." Luke thought this was a critical moment.

"Did he? Didn't say nothin to me bout spectin no one. " The man was skeptical. He scratched his head. He paused and mulled over the dilemma, debating with himself what to do next.

"Well he's not expecting me, but he did invite me."

"Al's round back, let's go find out what he says. I'm Dean. Dean Kramer, pleased to meet ya." He nodded and loped off with long strides, looping his arm in a circular motion indicating Luke should follow. Dean's stride was quick and nimble, he ate up lots of ground in a hurry.

"Hey Al, I got a fella here says you invited him to come and work here."

Luke did not recognize the grizzled man bent over in a heap wrestling with a rusted automobile engine. He had long straggly hair in need of washing and a prominent bald spot on the top of his head. He was tugging frantically. He kept grunting and tugging but the part refused to loosen.

"Damn it Dean, This damn thing craft shank is stuck, we'll never fix my truck running without the right part. This damn lot of junk needs to be cleared out as soon as possible. I'm sick of looking at it."

"It's comin Al, every day we haul a bit more off and clear some ground."

Dean reassured Al that he was on the right path, and all he needed to do was persist.

"What's this bout somebody I invited here?" He walked right past Luke without a sign of recognition.

"He's this youngin standin rite chere. Say I don't know your name, do I?"

"Name's Luke. Al, we met one night in your cab down near the L.A. airport. You almost shot me, you gave me your card, I got it right here." Luke fished into his pocket for the card, pulled it out and handed it to Dean.

"It's your card alright Al." Dean held it up for Al to take a look.. "You member anything?"

"Wait a minute, one night a young fella jumped in my cab when I stopped by the side of the road. I nearly blew his head off, thought he was going to try and rob me. Can't remember what he looked like. Was that you?"

"Sure was," Luke smiled, letting out a soundless whoosh of air. He was relieved Al had recalled making the invitation.

"Well don't that beat all" he shook his head and extended his hand. Welcome to Silver City, I'm damn glad to have you. I could use an extra set of hands cleaning up this mess." He gestured to the mess of auto parts, stoves, refrigerators and junk piled up in every direction. "This used to be a junkyard but it is soon gonna be a movie set. This area is the backlot. It's all just like I told you."

Luke took in the block long pile of rusted broken relics with a sweeping glance and let it sink in. So this was the future movie set he had set out in search of. Wow! He had a momentary flood of disbelief and disappointment. What a colossal mess!

"We can't pay you nothin, but you can sleep in the Sheriff's office. It's got an old bunk, right from the first days. You can eat your meals with me and my wife. An extra plate's not a problem."

"Where can I put my pack?" The disappointment vanished and he had a sudden surge of relief, this gamble was going to work out somehow. He told himself again he was on the right track, this was the opportunity of a lifetime.

"Dean, show this feller the jailhouse. Young fella, you come on back and give me a hand as soon as you move in." Al nodded at Dean and the matter was decided.

Dean led Luke out onto the street, and to the jailhouse door. It was locked. Dean fetched a circular ring with many keys from his overalls, he located the correct one and let Luke into his new residence.

"Ain't that like Al to invite a stranger into our mix." Dean's voice had an edge to it. Luke feared it might portend problems but the die was cast. He was an official resident and employee and stuntman in training. He walked through the door into a dark dingy room, it took a moment for his eyes to adjust to the lack of light.

The first thing he noticed was a half burnt candle on a metal tray in the middle of the room. It was sitting on an old card table. The windows were shut and barred, so only a few rays of random sunlight made it through the cracks to light the room.

As his eyes adjusted he realized the table had two chairs and a desk in the corner. Everything was covered with dirt and dust. The bed was a box several feet high covered with an old quilt. It had two small jail cells with tiny little bunks in them. People must have been smaller back then was Luke's first and only thought.

In addition to being dark, the room was filled with the musty damp air. He squinted and was able to pick out an empty whiskey bottle sitting on the table. It had cobwebs hanging off to the side anchoring it to the edge of the table.

It had cobwebs in every corner of the room. Some stretched all the way down to the floor. They provided a cave-like atmosphere, almost as if they were underground. A metal latrine was sitting next to the bed. Luke put his pack down, it held all his worldly possessions. He was officially "moved in."

"Is that the toilet?" Luke motioned to the can.

"Yep, from way back a hunnert years ago. Everything's authentic, just liken twas in the early days!." Dean tried to sound convincing. "What you think, wanna sleep here?"

"It's sorta interesting," Luke banged his hand on the bed and raised a cloud of dust. "Must have been a challenge to sit on it."

"You got any work gloves?" Dean asked in a loud voice after seeing the swirl of dust raised from the bed,

"No, I didn't bring any with me."

"You'll need em. Well you can use mine for now, I got to go into town and buy some cigarettes." He tossed his gloves to Luke. "You smoke? Need a pack? I'll pick one up for you."

"No, I might bum one from you now and then. I'm trying to quit and can't afford them right now."

"I'll buy you your own pack. Tell Al I went to buy cigarettes."

Dean left, leaving Luke to himself for the moment. This wasn't at all what he had expected. He decided he had to accept it and move forward. He had no other choice.

As he sat on the bed he raised another cloud of dust. He brushed the bed and debris stuck to his fingers. He had to shake his hand in the air to rid it of the muck.

The place was not "perfect". He focused and muttered under his breath, "Time's a wastin, I might as well make myself useful." Luke went back to find Al still twisting at the engine still trying to remove the part he needed.

"How do you like the place? It's somethin isn't it? Where's Dean?" Al's prominent mustache bobbed up and down as he spoke. Al was beginning to gray, and had some deep lines around his eyes. He was older than Luke remembered, probably close t0 forty. It had been dark in the cab and tense.

"Went to town to buy cigarettes."

"Off to keep from workin you mean. Help me move this engine, I need it up on that platform. I got to tie it down. Then I can apply enough force to break the cam loose. Everything is so jammed and frozen, they might be burned together, can't tell . Let's lift it up where I can tie it down."

Luke bent to help him and together they managed to slide the old engine through the dirt and lift it onto the platform. It was heavy but the two men did it without a problem.

"You and I got a job ahead cleaning this place up, and getting rid of all this junk. This is going to be the parking lot. We are going to need space for all the customers who are coming soon." Al was excited as he gestured to the heap of old autos that were stacked two and three high.

"A parking lot? Doesn't look like a parking lot. More like a junkyard." Luke nodded towards the mounds and mounds of rusting useless waste.

"It was a junkyard, but we are gonna change all that. It's gonna be a movie set. And this area will be the parking lot."

"Are you going to take the junk to a junkyard?" Luke mused at the idea.

"Ain't no junkyard anywhere nearby. Nearest one is in Bakersfield, three hours away in one direction. Costs a lot to dump it. We gotta find a ravine or place to set 'em down and let nature take its course. She'll wear em down sooner or later. We already got a spot and got rid of a couple of loads."

"You're going to dump em outdoors?" Luke's eyes widened, he didn't like the sound of it.

"Got to, ain't no harm in it. We won't put em where they are in anyone's way." Al's body stiffened up and hardened. "You got something to say about it?"

"I guess not." Luke backed off. He was on his first day on the job. His inner voice was whining at him for being a ninny.

"We ain't alone, we got a partner. A retired contractor, we're all working' towards making this a movie set. After the movies are a success, we'll open it up to tourists and sell tickets and give tours." Al was bubbling with enthusiasm.

"Well to do that, you do need to haul all this junk out of here." Luke tried to be agreeable.

"This is going to be a regular gold mine. You're on the ground floor. I expect you to work hard and do like I say. In time I'll even teach you how to be a western stuntman. Did I tell you I was in the stunt crew at Five Stars Theater in Los Angeles?" Al's blank beady eyes focused on Luke.

"Sounds fantastic! It's why I came. It'd be cool to be a stuntman and work in the movies.The old Sheriff's office is interesting. It'll be a challenge. Does it have water and electricity?"

"Not yet. But one day soon."

"That's gonna make things interesting." Luke was stunned.

"Shower is at my house, my wife will set an extra plate, you can clean up as you need to. We do have an outhouse. It'll be for guests someday. You can use it when you need to go at night. Most times we keep a roll of paper around. I'll Have to make it your job to keep it stocked."

"Okay, you have many visitors now?"

Luke's eyes drifted down along the row of old buildings. They were all leaning a bit in different directions as if they were all standing on borrowed time and might collapse into a heap at any second.

"It's gonna be a hard task to make this place right, but we got twelve buildings, each over a hunerd years old sitting on this property. The sheriff's office is the original one in this county and dates to around 1850. We got an old Post Office building we're gonna move soon. You can help us move it." Al painted a bright future. These antique buildings were the proof. They were a testament to the truth of the vision.

Dean appeared in his old Ford pick up truck and drove right up to them.

"Need some help boys?" He grinned out the driver's window. "Have a smoke." He held the pack out for Luke to take one.

"I'm ready to haul a load out of here!" Dean backed up.

Dean sat as the two men struggled with the heavy job. He was busy chewing, and smoking and never lifted a finger.

The sun climbed in the sky and was beaming straight down at them. By noon it was well over one hundred degrees. Al motioned for them to stop.

"Can't do hard work in this heat." Al was dripping sweat. "Got to find some shade. And I want a cold one. It's no use working here now."

"I'll say," Dean says. "I'm plumb tuckered out."

"When did you ever do any hard work? No wonder I decided to find another partner." He winked at Luke.

"Shit that was harsh." Dean pretended to be hurt.

"Had anything to eat today Luke?" Al wiped his forehead and stared at the sun overhead. "Come on over to the house and meet the old lady, She should have something ready for lunch about now."

"You boys will need to drive out to the canyon and dump this stuff. Here's my keys, I'll need my truck back in the mornin'." Dean threw Al the keys and sauntered off. It was time for lunch at his house as well.


Chapter Five

Al led Luke through an open field, turned by several empty lots, and followed a dirt road lined by eucalyptus trees. He stopped in front of a rickety, tumbled down picket fence. Its' gate was swinging in the breeze. Luke surmised this was home. Al pushed through a flimsy screen door and stomped his feet to shake off the dust on his boots.

"Hungry, I'm honey. What's for lunch?" he shouted out.

A slender brown haired woman appeared for the first time. She stood and stared, unable to say anything. It made for a long awkward moment. Her hair was tied in a ponytail. She was without makeup of any kind. Luke thought she was plain but had pleasant features. She relaxed and flashed a bright warm greeting smile.

"Who's with ya?"

"Never mind who I got, where's the food? I'm starved." Al took off his hat and threw it on the table. He had two plates already out.

"Set on the seat of honor! And bring out an extra serving for our new hand here. His name is Luke, he'll be working and eatin with us from now on."

Peggy nodded her acceptance. Luke thought she was used to accepting and following Al's lead. She rolled her eyes and carried on nimbly following her husband's orders. She never asks any questions.

"That's my wife Peg." Al shrugs as if to say, "I am in charge.

"I'll make some extra sandwiches, baloney and cheese alright? I heated up some tomato soup too." Peg motioned to the meal waiting on the table. The soup still had a little steam rising up.

Al motioned for Luke to sit in Peg's seat and eat the lunch she had already laid out.

"We need someone to sleep in the Town at night, to be a kind of a night watchman?" Al bit into the sandwich with vigor. He fanned the soup and took a sip testing it .

"Have you had any trouble?" Luke asked.

"Not yet, only a few broken windows so far. Ever use a shotgun?" Al's voice was edgy.

"No. The only gun I ever had was a BB gun."

"Well it ain't hard to use. I got an extra one, you can have it while you're here. I sawed the barrel down to half size so it will be effective close up."

"You want me to carry a gun?" Luke was incredulous. The idea had never entered his mind.

"Everyone in this county carries a gun." Al fired back. " A sawed off shotgun is the gun of choice. But you can only shoot someone close up. If you do, you'll blow a hole right through them."

"Is it legal?" Luke was a little worried.

"Shooting someone or carrying a gun?" Al chuckled.

"Of course shootin' someone is illegal."

"No law against carrying, not around here." Al nodded to his wife Peg. "Honey, bring me my sawed off out of the closet, and I want to check it out. Make sure It's clean and ready."

"Sure thing babe." Peg went to fetch it. Luke became aware he was eating Peg's lunch.

"A couple of the old boy's up come down on social security check day and go on a drunk. Next thing you know they are bustin things up. It'll be a help to have someone working on the movie set to warn us. You should have a gun to protect yourself."

"What do you want me to do if they do show up?" Luke sensed trouble ahead. His warning lights went on. What was he getting into?

"No real need to worry about them, they're alright. They get a little ornery now and then. All the buildings we got are original. Can't be replaced. The sheriff's office you're goin sleep in is way over a hunert years old."

"Is that right?" Luke was impressed, perhaps the dust wasn't a problem. What if the bed bugs had a sense of history?

Peg reappeared with a double barreled shotgun and a box of shells. "It's ready." She held it out. The barrels were no more than two feet long.

"This is yours as long as you work here." Al handed it to Luke and waited for his approval.

"I never had a gun before, how does it work?" Luke took it, it was heavy but he liked holding it in his hands. He shook it a little. It was not that heavy, he decided.

"You got two barrels, two shots, did you load it honey?"

"Yep, it's ready to go." Peg flashed a little smile.

"So. You can cock it if you want or just pull the trigger, either ways it will shoot. So all you have to do is aim it and decide to fire. It blows out a circle of pellets in a tight circle and they expand as it moves out to a foot around or so. The further away it gets, the bigger the circle the pellets make."

In an instant Luke had become an armed man and he liked it.

"Thanks." Strange how the sudden acquisition of a loaded gun made him stronger and more in control of things.

The front door flew open and Dean burst in a huff of excitement. "Guess what I saw? Guess what I saw?." He was too excited to let them guess and so he burst out with the news. "A Sssssss- slide, a water slide." His face was aglow with joy.

"A what?" Al tried to manage surprise.

"A slide, and it was almost like the one they used to have at Frontier City back in Kentucky. Not as tall, not as winding, but it's at least two stories high. Don't know what in the hell it is doin in Jarvis' yard, but I saw it for sure, as large as life and twice as purty."

"Well la ti da ain't life grand. Okay, what's a slide got to do with the price of tea in China?" Dean's overwhelming excitement had baffled Al. He refused to take the bait. He leaned back unimpressed. "Who cares about an old slide?"

"On a hot day back in Frontier City the slide was about the most popular thing in the whole county. Kid's ud climb up and slide down into the cool water until they are shrunk up like prunes." Dean made a long dipping motion with his arm.

"Ya don't say." Al was catching Dean's feelings of excitement.

"If we got a holt of that thing with a refreshing pool and put it out in sight of the road so as it can be seen as you drive by, the kids will go crazy and just naturally come to use it. We would sell a million tickets." Dean was elated! He had experience with kids, and the hottest days were straight ahead. The slide was a god send and he was sure it would solve all their problems.

"It sounds costly." Al gave Dean a gesture of distrust.

"It's not any old slide mind you, it's a two story slide and it is in Jasper's yard. I think we can take it! Winner! Winner, chicken dinner!" He clapped his hands together. Life was about to be a walk down easy street and he was already strolling down Broadway!

"Well that does sound interesting" Al warmed up and chimed in. He figured it was impossibe to guess what Dean was goin to come up with but this had all of the makings of the best thing ever.

"Couldn't keep them away if we tried, and it's so tall everyone will catch sight of it from the road, and wonder bout it, and come to check it out!." Dean grinned .

"Might be worth takin a drive out to see it.." Al wondered where this slide was hiding. " By the way I gave Luke my shotgun he's gonna be our new night watchman."

"Ya don't say? Well I'm glad we got one. I tell you I don't sleep right at night for worryin bout it. What if someun came in and burned it down. What'd we do? Not a board can be replaced."

"You think someone wants to burn it down?" Luke sensed real fear in Dean's voice. Warning sirens were screeching in the back of his mind.

"Well anything might happen, couldn't it?" Al jumped in.

"I suppose, but do you have any reason to think someone is going to try to burn down your town?" Luke stared into Al's eyes. What was he getting into?'s

"Honey, tell him the truth," Peggy came back from the kitchen.

"Someone might want to," Al tried to hide his eyes by takin a sip from his lemonade. "We're not sure what is goin on."

"Who?" Luke didn't like the sound of this, with a shotgun in hand, he asked. "Who?"

"We don't know, if we did, we'd beat the shit out of em. But we don't." Dean answered.

"Ain't nothin cept a few broken windows and cut locks." Al changed the subject. " You got money for a six pack?"

"No, Liz got my pocket money today." Dean stared down at the floor.

"You are in luck, I Can cover a couple of six packs, we got a new pard now so we need at least two, or three of them before we go back to work. Let's buy some beer and check out this slide." Al motioned for Dean to lead the way.

Al's old truck fired up with a roar and the three of them packed in the front seat, with Luke squeezed in the middle. The center street in town was a two lane road. The three men found themselves squeezed together, forced to rub elbows and bump shoulders and legs.

The cab was full of the odor of beer. The fumes came from Dean who had already started drinking early in the morning. He leaned his head towards Luke and burped in his face.

"You're kind of large for a kid." Dean had not expected such cramped quarters. Luke decided if the situation came up again he would hop in the bed in the back.

"A bit over two hundred," Luke answered. "Hard muscle."

Al stopped and Dean went in for beer. A storefront sign in the window offered fresh bait for the fisherman, and seeds and equipment for the farmer. Behind the counter a blinking sign offered hot dogs and draft beer. The off colored paint on the walls was chipping in places. Dean disappeared and came back with a case of beer.

"Got some cold ones for a change." Dean tore open the box and flipped one to Luke. He handed one to Al, and popped one for himself.

"What's up? Isn't this illegal?" Luke was uneasy drinking with an open can in the car.

"Only one sheriff in this town and he's got a broken arm. Broke it the other night down at the saloon trying to stop a fight. He ain't been out of his house since." Al took a swig from the can and chugged it down with gusto. " Sides, he don't mind us drikin a bit."

Dean reached across the seat in front of Luke and began to honk the horn. He stuck his head out the window and let out a howl of approval. A shapely young woman turned her head and the truck load of men pulled away.

"She didn't wave, what a bitch." Dean sounded upset. " I guess she didn't see me."

"You got a wife and kids at home, you shouldn't be honkin at Darla." Al gave Luke a knowing glance.

"She's bout the only thing in this town that's under fifty and still got a pussycat worth petting." Dean was always on the prowl.

"She's way too young and good looking for you." Al put the emphasis on "way too young".

"Hell she's twenty five, ain't much difference tween twenty-five and thirty five." Dean pretended the age difference between them was ten years but in truth it was fifteen.

Luke opened his beer. It gushed and foam drenching his pants spilling everywhere. The spurting lasted many seconds forcing him to hold the can away from his body. He was soaked. It was Dean's fault, he had shaken it up!

"She's workin, came out of that room with a load of towels, damn I want to get into her pants." Dean made it clear that Darla was the target he was aiming at.

"You got no reason to chase after her." Al took another swig. "She's way too special for you. I think she even went to college and hell, I think she might have a degree. And what in the hell were you doing shaking up Luke beer and messing up my truck?"

"I'm makin her my business. She is ripe and ready. What more reason do I need? Sides being book smart ain't nothin. Being bed ready is what counts and something tells me she is." Dean thought most women were on the lookout for a man, even if they themselves didn't think so. He also figured they were looking for him even if they didn't know that yet either.

"Something tells me she is out of your league." Al liked tossing cold water on Dean's boasts. "You made a mess again."

"I think it is just a matter of time till she comes around. Sorry bout the beer. Luke, you opened it too quickly."

Dean indicated that Al should turn up a dirt side road. Al hit the gas. They were jostled and bounced over potholes cut by the previous winter's rain. The dirt road twisted out of town and back into the hills. They kept on until they reached a point high above the lake, where Dean motioned for them to come to a stop.

"Right natural wonder, ain't it?" Dean opened another beer. He waited for Luke and Al's approval.

Luke took in the panoramic view of the lake and thought what a beautiful sight. It was sweeping and grand.

"Yeah, it is a beautiful lake." Luke answered.

"Not the lake you moron, the slide." Dean nodded towards a grove of trees. Luke saw nothing but a grove of old growth tangled up and twisting out of control. Try as he might, Luke didn't find a thing.

"It sticks out four feet at least." Dean was annoyed. It was too beautiful to miss. "You found it, right?"

"Real fine," Luke answered. But he didn't see a thing. He was tired, and the bumpy ride gave his stomach a thrill it didn't need. Baloney and tomato soup drenched in a foamy beer chaser was turning in his stomach. Al had hit every available pothole until Luke was queasy.

"Don't see nothin but treetops." Luke didn't and refused to pretend that he did.

"We can sneak up on it. We'll need to take the  trail down yonder. It's right out back of old man Jarvis's house. It's blocked, but you can still see it from this angle. The platform is at the top. Can you now?" Once again Dean pointed to a spot in the tree line.

Luke picked a spot on the tree line. "Yeah I missed it at first, but I found it."

"I asked old Jarvis who it belonged to but he claimed he had no idea." Dean said. 'Problem is it's on his property."

As they walked, the slide appeared and came into full view. It stood a full two stories high, towering above Jarvis's house.It stood imposing, anchored and strong! The slide promised a ride that twisted and bent along a looping course. It had a platform wide enough for kids to wait for a turn to ride down the ramp. The slide had been outside a long time and was dirty. It was covered with rust and had not been used for a long, long time.

"It is a site to behold. Mysterious, ain't it?" Dean said in wonder.

"If'n we clean this up, it will be usable again." It brought joy and excitement to his voice. "I think we ought to take it. It don't belong to no one. "

Al's mouth hung open in disbelief. He was hooked. He wanted it, in fact had to have it.

"I'll bet the kid's will flock to this idea. Just imagine a sparkling cool clean pool waiting for them to swim in. What a thrill! We'll need a pool for sure. Once they get a hanker for it. It will sell it's self. The parents will have to come.to to see what the fuss is about." Dean saw himself as a visionary.

"Wouldn't do that if I was you boys. It don't belong to you. Stepping out from a clump of bushes was an old man, with a long rifle, a bushy beard and caterpillar eyebrows. He was heavy and round with an unkempt white beard, He had on a pair of blue overalls, and a red bandana. If it wasn't so hot he would have been the movie double for frosty the snowman, minus the snow.

"Jarvis, I asked you whose it was and you didn't know." Dean blurted out.

"Well I member now, it belongs to me, my brother owned it and he gave it to me. Don't think I want you to have it." Old Jarvis squinted at them from bloodshot eyes bringing up his hunting rifle to show them he meant business. "You sure better not try to take it."

"Hell, what is it to you?" For the first time Luke realized he wanted the slide as much as the boys.

"None of your business Sonny boy. I don't want it in that place of urin." He waved the gun in the air and spit a little bit of mucus out of his lungs. "It's on my property and it's mine. I intend to keep it."

"I can handle this old coot." Al was annoyed with Luke for having stuck his nose in it. Al knew how to deal with old Jarvis. It was easy.

"Jarvis I can bring up a case of Jack if you like, it is the finest whiskey Jack Daniels has to offer. Deal? Will you trade the slide for a case of Jack?"

Al had hit Jarvis at his weakest point. Jarvis backed off, scratched his beard and hesitated looking for all the world like he might take the offer. But his momentary weakness didn't last long.

"Me and this slide have a history, an I don't want lots of people comin to this town. I like it, like it is." Old Jarvis spit out a wad of tobacco juice aimed right at Luke's feet. He missed by a fraction. " I like it quiet. Most people hereabouts want it that way."

"You got it all wrong Jarvis, we want it for our kids, so as Dean's kids can ride it." Al countered.

"Don't sound like what I heard a minute ago. Swinmin pools, people stopping, coming to ride your slide. Nope. Don't like it." He cocked the rifle for effect.

"You think I'd lie to you? What for?" Al tried his level best to act hurt.

"You fellers come on back some other time and bring your whiskey and I'll think bout lettin you have the slide." The old man's hands started to shake. Luke wondered if he was angry or in need of a drink.

"Let's do the deal now." Dean stepped forward and begged the old man. Jarvis answered by pointing the gun to waist level. He waved it back and forth letting them know that he was aiming it at them. They backed off.

"Scoot, rite now, I told yah I'd think bout it, but for now git! I don't like havun so many people on my land at one time. Git."

They were afraid the old man was about to become nasty.

"Damn ornery old coot." Dean muttered under his breath while looking back at Jarvis. Jarvis had a reputation for sudden violence and it was hard to guess telling how much of it was true.

"You cannot ever be sure what he is goin a do." Al pulled on Luke's arm.

They piled into the truck and Al pushed down hard on the gas causing the tires to spin. The truck lurched forward with a burst of speed and lunged around the corner of the unpaved old road. For a moment Al lost control, and the car pulled into a shallow ditch. Old Jarvis howled with laughter and taunted them. They fled in fear before him. He laughed with ghoulish delight. He had scared them for sure and it made him powerful.


Chapter Six-

The early evening air was hot and dry. They sprawled on the porch with their shirts unbuttoned hoping the faint breeze might somehow cool them. Cold beer had flowed all day. Luke kept silent and listened to his new bosses. It had been a long first day, he was tired and found it hard to concentrate on what they were saying. His mind wandered to the dusty cot in the jail, it was filthy. How was he going to be able to sleep in it?

"Sleep on it, not in it" he said to himself, "Hell it couldn't be any dirtier than the ground" but then he thought, "What if it has mold in it or bugs." His mind drifted through a range of negative possibilities about the dusty old bed.

"I want the damn slide!" Dean's harsh voice snapped him back to the moment.

Dean was rambling, ranting, and working himself up. He convinced himself the slide was the key piece to creating a lasting future for his family. Damn it I have a right to it.

"If we leave it up to old man Jarvis it will waste away until it rots." Dean was saving it from ruin. Giving it a purpose.

"Slides are natural! I say we should go up one of these nights, take it apart and just plumb steal it. Old man don't own it." He banged a beer on the table for emphasis.

"Hold on, if we steal it he'll figure it right away and press charges." Al attempted to calm Dean down.

"Old coot's got no right to stand between me and that slide!" Dean's face turned a bright shade of red. "Once it's ours it will belong to us. Possession is ninety percent of the law."

"Be mighty hard to steal in the middle of the night. He'd hear us and come out shootin." Al reasoned.

"I say we get him drunk. If anyone can drink old Jarvis under the table it's you."

"Drinking him under is not goin be easy. Jarvis has a hollow leg." Al answered.

Al had first hand knowledge of just what it entailed. He had had a bout of drinking on his first week in town Jarvis had shown up with bottles in hand claiming to be the official greeting committee of Bodfish.

Jarvis meant well but he launched the two of them on a whiskey drinking binge that lasted for days. It left Peg angry and disgusted for a month. Since that day, Al had kept his distance from Jarvis. Peg's anger when unleashed was a thing to behold. But this was different, this needed to be done for the betterment of all involved, they all shared in the project of making the movie set a prosperous success.

"Perhaps you could put something in his whiskey." Luke piped in.

"Whatcha talkin bout?" Al perked up.How about a strong sleeping pill? If you give him one or two, it won't hurt him, only put him into a deep sleep." Dean and Al nodded at each other. They liked it. Yes sir, they liked the way this boy thought.

"Do you have some of those?" Dean was excited.

"Not sure, my girl used to use them. I might have some in my pack." Luke shuddered as the possible negative consequences of giving the old coot a sleeping pill seemed dangerous. Warning sirens sounded in his mind. He wished he had kept his mouth shut.

He had two of them in his pack, but he didn't want to risk it. Luke was filled with regret for having been so thoughtless.

"No I don't have any. I did a while back but I think I took them. It was a stupid thought. Forget about it." Remorse was nagging at him.

"Old coot is tougher than nails." Al was on it. "My wife's got some pills, I think one of them will do the trick."

"If you and Luke went up with a case of whiskey in hand, he'd drink with you for sure, he couldn't resist. You ever member Jarvis to say no to Jack Daniels?" Dean slapped Luke on the back. Luke had become one of the boys.

"You're right! It'd be easy if Luke was along. Jarvis ud drop his guard. And Luke could slip him the pills, and as soon as he is out cold, we'll grab the slide. I just know it! It's ours!" Al was on fire with the vision. His mind was reveling in it.

"Jarvis will never suspect what hit him." Dean clapped his hands together in gleeful anticipation, the slide was his destiny. In his mind's eye he saw the peaceful face of old Jarvis lying on the ground passed out and defenseless, unable to defend the slide. It was perfect.

"Hell, we got to do it. I can just imagine the slide standing tall and proud in the center of the movie set. The kids laugh, splashing, while their parents are taking pictures to show the folks back home. Damn! We got to do this, " Dean was ecstatic. "We'll teach that old coot a lesson. He shouldn't be so selfish!."

"I agree! We gotta have the slide." Al chimed in!

Luke pondered his first day on the job. He had become a stuntman in training and was now a slide burglar charged with drinking an old man under the table and drugging him. Things had changed in a flash.

"Can I take the shower you promised?" Luke was grimy, and thought perhaps a shower was just the thing to put him back right.

"Sure thing." Al slapped him on the back, and yelled at his wife. "Peg,  toss the boy a towel, he needs to clean up."

Luke let the hot water wash the desert dust off his back. He wondered what kind of pill Al's wife had on hand, and how strong they might be. It was his plan they were following. What if something went wrong?

Chapter Seven

Luke's dinner consisted of some potatoes and a little meat that might have been meatloaf, plus some soggy overcooked green beans. Luke wolfed it down the meal with gusto.

"Don's got a job lined up. You can help us move a building." Al dropped the news on Luke.

"Another building?" Luke perked up.

"It is an old blacksmith's or post office or something. Hell it don't matter, It's an original and it's old. It'll help make our site better for sure."

"Move it?" Luke wondered how that was done?

"It's outta the ground and up on blocks. We gotta move it onto a moving plate and transfer it to the movie site." Al explained.

"What am I going to do?" Luke asked.

"You'll help out as called fer."

Al's head jerked up with a sudden start,"Someone has broken into the movie set." His breath was quick and short. He motioned towards the old town, and signaled for Luke to listen.

"Hear it?" Al's eyes dilated with excitement.

"What are you talking about?" Luke couldn't hear a thing.

"We got tin cans strung on a wire above the fence.. They're banging together. Someone's climbing over the fence. Grab the shotgun, we'll catch the bastard." Al was deadly serious.

"What is it? What are you talking about?"

"You deaf? They're clanging like chimes, Someone is up to no good. Haul your ass over the back fence and I'll come in the front. We'll trap em between us. Catch 'em in a crossfire." Al waved his pistol in the air motioning Luke to hustle. "Grab your gun!"

Luke ran to the back of the fence. The rickety old boards wobbled and wavered as he vaulted over them. For an instant he thought the fence might collapse, but he cleared it and began stalking the intruder. No one is in sight. He edged up the street.

 A black fuzzy presence came shuffling out of the dark night. It was a threatening figure armed with a pistol raised and pointed right at him. Luke realized it was Al, who was now visible standing rigid in the moonlight.

"Stop right or I'll shoot." Al's voice rang out in the night. Luke could hear the slur in Al's voice brought on by a day of heavy drinking.

A long tense silence followed. Al kept the gun pointed straight at Luke. giving him no sign of recognition. What to do?

"Al, it's me, Luke." His shaky voice broke the stillness.

Al kept the pistol pointed at Luke for a long time. Without responding, "Luke?"

"Al, it's me, Luke." Luke shivered.

"Second time, I almost shot you." Al lowered the gun to his waist. "I'm glad you had the guts to come over that fence. I needed to find out if you had grit." Luke guessed he had passed a test of some sort.

"Night Luke." Al patted Luke on the back and left him to his dusty bed.

Chapter Eight-

Luke unrolled his bag, crawled in and tried to go to sleep. His imagination churned away. The dank dusty room played havoc with his breathing. The dust in his nose and lungs nagged at him, and kept him awake.

The night dragged on and on. There was no clock, and no electricity; he could not judge the passing of time. The wind was blowing hard making loud whistling noises that filled his ears. It came in through the many cracks in the planks that made up the walls. He drew the bag up around his neck trying to relax, and drifted off to sleep.

"You killed my Pa! you killed my Pa!" a tiny figure was standing at the end of the cot, crying, and shouting. "I want you dead! I am going to kill you!"

Luke raised his head and located the source of the sound was at the foot of the bed. It was a little boy, he was young, perhaps less than three years old. Luke thought he might have a gun in his hands.

Luke shook his head, his mind resisting and at the same time accepting the image, he tried to clear it from his mind's eye. Was it a real fleshh and blood boy? With a real physical body. The boy was in turmoil, shaking, and crying, and threatening all at the same time. He radiated energy and Luke was not sure. Did he imagine a gun in the figure's hand?

"Sheriff, you are going to die in your bed." The figure's tiny hand made a menacing gesture.

Luke hoped he was dreaming, but it all seemed real. In a flash he was awake and sitting up in bed. Somehow there was light in the room, and the tiny figure cowering in fear and anger, crying and shaking. The vision had remained even though he was awake.

"I am not the Sheriff." It was all Luke could manage to say.

"You killed my Pa, he's gone. I am going to kill you."

A wave of sorrow and regret flooded through Luke's conscious mind.

"I am sorry you lost your Pa."

With that the little figure vanished, and Luke was alone in the room. "I am alone, sleeping in the sheriff's office from the 1850's, I wonder what happened here?"

He got up and went outside, a million stars covered the high desert sky. The moon was out and three quarters full. The visitation had been amazing and vivid, the boy's face was wet with what felt like real tears flowing from his eyes. It had been a child's voice, cracking and shaky. Luke felt his entire body become icy cold and once again realized that he was all alone. How could he explain it? Did he need to? It made him shiver.

He asked himself, if it wasn't a dream, what was it? The only answer that made sense to him was that he had been visited by a ghost, one that had suffered a loss in this town a long time ago.

Chapter Nine

"Rise and shine! Time is wasting sleepy head!" Al was pounding on the door. He had a half eaten egg sandwich in his hand. "Hurry, we're late. Don's already up and has been working for hours. Get your lazy ass up."

Luke shook his head as bits of the night's strange dream slipped away. He remembered the child, but did not imagine it had anything to do with him. He thought, If it was a message it had to be connected with this place. The child is haunting this place, not me. It couldn't be personal. I am just the one who happened to be here.

"Is the sandwich for me?" he asked, eyeing the food in Al's hand..

"It is." Al said, giving him what was left of the fragment of nourishment Peg had provided.

"Any bacon on it?" Luke took it gladly. Even though Al had taken several bites from it.

"I'll tell Peg to make some bacon just for you next time. Nah, you moron, be happy, and take what you get. We gotta hurry, Don is waiting."

"When does he start work?" Luke was curious and anxious to meet Don.

"Whenever he wants to."

"What's my job?" Luke asked again.

"We're moving a new building. We already dug a hole in the lot." Al pointed to a plot of ground with a hole six inches deep in a rectangular shape.

"What was it used for?" Luke asked

"It's a blacksmith's shop or a post office! No one's sure. But it's one or the other. It's old and we got it. Don't matter much do it?" Al hustled to the truck, and Luke followed right behind.

Luke grinned it seemed Al thought one old building was the same as another. Luke tried to picture a building over a hundred years old, standing up on stilts of a sort, and still intact. It strained his imagination.

"Come on, Dean's got his truck all hooked up. We can't keep Don waiting." Al's voice crackled with urgency.

Dean was towing a metal plate that was twenty five feet long and five inches off the ground.

"That's gonna hang out and take some space from the oncoming traffic." he called out.

"It'll fit." Dean was curt

"I think it will block two lanes. I am afraid it will be dangerous". Luke worried.

"We'll balance it on the platform. We've done this a lot. Got it down, real scientific like. We secure it as best we can and go slow. Don will go ahead and clear the way."

Dean was hunched at the wheel waiting. A cigarette hung from the side of his mouth. "Come on, we're late. I don't want Don to get upset."

"If I'm late, it's all Peg's fault, blame her. She needed me mornin. She likes to start the day off with a hard poke, and I try to give Peg what she wants. She was in real need this morning." Al basked in the glory of conquest. "Married Life, someday you'll mind out." He patted Luke on the back.

Luke sat in the middle of the seat. Once again Luke was aware of just how cramped the seat made him feel.. He made a note to himself in the future to remember to ride in the back".

"Damn there's Darla again." Dean honked the horn and stuck his arm out the window and waved. Darla was an attractive woman who was annoyed at the unwanted attention she was getting.

"Liz ain't goin like you chasin after her like that." Al did not approve of Dean's constant philandering.

"How's Darla goin figure out I'm interested if I don't tell her?" Dean grinned a toothy grin that showed one of his front teeth on the right side of his face was missing. "Girls got to know she is wanted."

They cleared town and turned down a dirt country road that fed into an uninhabited valley. Deserted farmhouses and dilapidated barns marked spots where people had once lived and prospered. The fields were untended and wild growth had taken over where once crops had been planted and flourished.

The scene repeated for a few miles until it was nothing but open country. They traveled through land that was unspoiled by human hands. The Kern river flowed past frosty white crests of fast moving water.

"Used to be a town out here, it's been forgotten. No one cares about it anymore." Al nodded. "A lot of the buildings came from this old town."

"They belong to anyone?" Luke asked.

"Naw, they're all unclaimed. We're savin em. Don puts em back together as best he can, and then we move them. They belong to us now. No one cares, no one remembers."

"You never worry about the original owners showing up?" Luke pushed the point.

"They'd all be ghosts if they did." Al laughed as if the thought was funny. "Ghosts with ghost deeds."

When they arrived they found Don walking around the building pounding nails into planks and making a last minute effort to tighten the structure before they rolled the platform under it. He hoped it was ready to be hauled off but transport was always a risky business. He saw Luke for the first time.

"Who are you?" Don eyed Luke up and down. "City Kid", he thought, must be soft. Don had just turned fifty and had done hard physical work all his life. His hands were hard and full of calluses.

"Name's Luke," he extended his hand. Don's grip was tight forcing Luke to squeeze back hard. Don was shorter than Dean, and was rail thin with a paunch around the middle. Luke imagined Don was tired and a little worn out. His thinning gray hair had gone white in several spots. Luke decided he had friendly eyes.

"How'd you end up here?" Don was pleased to learn how firm and strong Luke's handshake was.

"Al invited me and I decided to come." Luke said with a shrug.

Don began to question Al's sanity. Why bring another mouth to feed into this venture he thought? And why a kid? In truth Don was already sure Al was a bit crazy.

"That so?" he waited for Al to confirm.

"Yeah, it's a long story, I am surprised he came, but a ways back I did invite him. I'll tell you about it some time. He's sleeping in the sheriff's office and Peg and I are feeding him. He's goin help out. He's an extra set of hands and eyes. Our new night watchman. We might teach him to stunt fight and ride western style."

"You're a handsome kid, I bet one of those movie director's will put you in a show." Don cracked a grin.

"I want to learn. Being a stuntman sounds like fun. That's why I came here."

"If you're lucky someday you'll be in the movies, but today we're moving a building. It seems like this is an old post office, but after checking the records I can't be sure about it. It's had more than one use over the years. I'm hopin it'll hang together long enough for us to move it." Don grinned nodding toward the old wooden frame tottering up on stilts swaying in the breeze.

"How are we gonna move it on the platform?" Luke asked..

"Dean's gonna back up on it and we'll prop it up with levers and put rollers under it one inch at a time, then I'll tie the bastard down. Once it's rolled on and tied down, we'll take it to the movie set and roll it off. Just you wa

"What will I do?" Luke asked.

"Just try to be helpful, we always need some extra muscle."

Don was also aware Dean never tried to carry his weight when it came to physical labor, and hoped a strong young kid was the answer.

"Sounds like how they built the old pyramids in Egypt. You can count on me".

"Not sure about pyramids but we can always use some more muscle." Don had warmed up to Luke.

It took considerable pushing and lifting to bounce it onto the rollers and slide it. It took a lot of work, but between the four of them they had just enough muscle to do the job.

"For a moment it shook like it might collapse." Don noted, but luck was with them and now it was steady and ready for its journey. He signaled Dean to drive.

"I've got the lead." Don hung out the open window and swung his lantern. The lantern was a signal to alert traffic that a load was coming. He drove down the road trying to block oncoming cars and force them to stop. Drivers stopped in bewilderment and let him pass.

"Luke, you climb in the back of Dean's truck and hold tight to the ropes. If you think the building is going to roll, pull hard, and holler out. We are going to go real slow and hope it don't break loose. I want you to be careful. It will be a nightmare if it starts sliding and rolls off the platform. Hold tight and yell if you think it is slipping."

Luke got up into the back of the pickup and grabbed the rope and pulled on it. It was tight, and had no slack in it. He wondered what would happen if the damned thing did break loose and started to slide off the back. Could he hold it? He braced his feet against the truck door determined to try it if disaster reared its head.

Dean inched down the road and the rope tightened up even more. As it tightened Luke got an idea how much tension was involved. The rope was straining and it was likely to get much worse. If the thing got loose it would be a mess, that was for sure.

The trip out of the valley was slow and tortured. It took forever, far longer than the twenty minutes they had spent that morning. Dean was taking it slow and easy. The truck began to angle upward. They were climbing a hill! The ropes holding the building in place on the platform drew tighter and tighter. The grade in the hill had become a threatening monster. It was a very heavy load and the steep grade had put a real strain on the old truck.

Dean's face was tense and distorted in the rear view mirror, The engine whined and screamed. It complained every inch of the way. Steam and water vapor appeared and rose under the hood. The midday sun blazed down, and the truck was overheating fast.

"We should be using Don's damn truck, it's newer and stronger than mine. I want to stop and change trucks." Dean yelled at Al.

"We'll do it once we reach the top. If we stop on this incline it will be a real shit show." Al was right. If the building got rolling it would roll back to the bottom and crash.

"Damn we should have thought about this before we started." Dean was afraid that his truck might have exploded. But Al was right, it was impossible to try and re-hitch it now. Dean pushed it forward. Worry was etched on every wrinkle of his face.

"We're almost there! Keep going! Just a bit further! Shut it down!" Al was shouting above the sputtering rage of the engine.

The truck jerked and the road flattened out. Dean shut off the engine! He let out a cry of relief, opening the hood quick as he possible. He reached for the water pump. It burned his hand and he screamed in pain.

"It's red hot!" He shook his burned hand in pain. "Can't get the water cap off, I got gloves on the floor!" he yelled at Al for help.

Al appeared at the side of the truck bed. "Luke give me the water jug." Al grabbed it.

"Careful, a little at a time," Dean had gotten the cap off the radiator and Al was pouring water into the opening. A hot hissing steam issued forth and the engine sounded strained and made a high pitched whiny sound. It belched and gurgled. "Be careful, too fast and she'll seize up."

"Bitch is plumb out of water. I shoulda checked it before we started out." Dean complained fearing the engine had been damaged.

"Is it still running?" Don parked and joined the group.

"I think so, I need you to hook up for the rest of the ride. We never should be using my truck."

"Can do," Don moved to the back of Dean's truck and pulled out a couple of wood blocks. He wedged them behind the tires and began unhitching the trailer. "Luke jump down here and help me, we have to re-rope this baby."

"Damn she's been overheating a lot." Dean threw the empty water jug back into the truck. "Lucky she is still running. Gage is almost back to normal, Damn heat. It's so damn hot out here." Dean relaxed knowing his truck was saved for today.

"Shit my truck's brand new. Plenty of power. Nothing to this haul for me. Sorry Dean. Damn stupid idea to use your truck." Don and Luke finished the tie downs and were ready to head back to the movie set.

Dean and Al rode ahead with the lamp waving at and redirecting the only that approached.

Don popped a beer and handed one to Luke.

"Back home no one ever rides around with an open beer can." Luke took a sip.

"Sheriff is a pal. He drinks with me all the time." Don winked and smiled at Luke as he toasted their success. "He don't mind a little beer behind the wheel."

They drove into town guzzling beer and pulling the "new" old building for everyone in town to admire.

Getting the "Post Office" off the platform and in place as planned. When it fell off the end of the platform it shook and creaked for close to five minutes. It was in need of a lot of repair. The project had taken the better part of a day, but it had been exciting. Luke had a deep personal satisfaction, his chest swelled up with pride.

"That was a lot of fun" Luke grinned at all of them, damn he had never moved a building before. He liked the newness, the experience of doing something new. I am going to become a stuntman and now I have helped move a building. It was a lot of fun.

"Al, you still got that old sheriff's badge?" Don winked at Al.

"It's up at the house. Why do you ask?

"I think we should give it to Luke, appoint him the official sheriff of Silver City."

"Sheriff Luke". I like it. It has a strong ring to it." Al agreed.

Luke added "became a "Sheriff" to his resume."

"How about we go up to the house, and have a bite and have a beer or two?"

"Sure thing Boss." Luke belonged. He was home.

Chapter Ten

Dinner was hot dogs, fries and a beer. Luke was so hungry that he ate three dogs with buns hoping he was not making a pig of himself.

"Honey, I think you need to start buying bigger grocery orders as long as this horse is here." Al ribbed Luke.

"Reckon that's right", Peg cleared the table and started washing the dishes. Luke and Al went to the living room  and watched the black and white television.

"Don't like color T.V. I watched one once but the colors did not seem real at all." Al turned on the Central Valley news station. "I like black and white best."

"I have seen some color tv's that are okay, but most are not life like. The colors are too pastel. Black and white is better. It has shades of gray and white but that can be mighty fine."

Luke had never owned a television, but his family had a black and white. Color televisions were for rich people. Normal people had black and white ones.

Al gulped down his beer.

"Woman, we need another beer out here."

Peg appeared with two fresh foamy Buds. She had her own open can waiting, but she had learned that girls don't drink with the boys when the boys tried to talk business.

"What's on the news?" she asked.

"Not sure " As Al spoke, the newscaster's voice became deadly serious.

"Motorcycle gangs have been spotted traveling in caravans heading south on Interstate Five. They are thought to be armed and dangerous."

"That sounds bad, what if they're coming here?" Peg challenged Al for reassurance.

"Reliable information is limited but some speculate they are heading for a remote location, perhaps in the high desert area. Rumors are circulating that they are planning a national gathering. State Police have been caught by surprise."

"Don't that beat all? Well I got news for them. They better stay away from Bodish." Al made a threatening gesture at the television.

The anchor spoke straight into the camera and added with real concern,

"Folks, this sounds like a bad situation. We will keep you advised as more information becomes available."

"Damn, ain't that somethin." Al took a swig of beer and pulled out his pistol. If they are coming here I got 'em covered." He waved the gun in the air and laughed. "What you think bout that Luke?"

"It's strange. Never heard of so many traveling together at one time. Be a hard group to tangle with that's for sure."

"You know I heard they share their women. If one has a woman he shares her with the other men. How's somethin like at sound to you Peg?" Al winked at Luke.

Peg turned and left the room without a whisper. Luke thought he might have heard a choking noise, but it was muffled and indistinct. The room went quiet. Al grew sullen, almost angry. He stared at Luke through narrowed eyes. It was as though he was sizing him up.

"Can I trust you?" Al's mood was turning deadly. .

"Well, I guess, I mean sure., of course. Why do you ask?" His tone put Luke on guard. What was wrong?

"I mean it. I need to find out if I can trust you." Al was staring hard at him. Luke thought he might be angry but could not fathom why he would be.

"Well sure, of course."

"I gotta a Map. I got a treasure map. It's a secret. Wanna check it out?" Al was getting drunk.

"Treasure?" Luke's interest was sparked. "What kind of treasure?"

"It's a map to a gold mine, an old miner give it to me. He come down from the hills and into town for a couple of days. He was all worn down, real sick and tired, all the life was goin out of him. He'd been up in them hills a long time. He gave me the map." Al squinted with narrow eyes.

"It's real hard to believe!" It gave Luke a cold chill up and down his spine.

"Told me he searched for years before he it. When he struck it rich he was too sick to mine it. Dug out a few feet and had to quit. Came down looking for help and then gave me the map. He died that night, right after he gave it to me."

"How long ago was that? Have you tried to find it?" Luke played along. If a con of some kind was about to unfold, he was ready.

Al got sloppy drunk but judging by his goofy grin he was being truthful about the map. He is sincere, Luke thought, but his moods were flighty and unpredictable.

"Well I don't blame you for being doubtful. It does sound a bit crazy." Al drained the last liquid out of his bottle and shook his head. "But it's true."

"Honey I need another one." Al called out to Peg. "I'm dry."

"Yeah, you're right. it's quite a story, I don't know what to think." Luke was skeptical.

"I'll bring it and show you." Al went into the back bedroom.

Peg came out of the kitchen the moment Al left the room.

"Whenever he gets like this he starts talking about his "gold mine." You must humor him, and listen, he can become angry if you make fun of it. He takes it personally, just keep quiet and listen." Luke decided Peg herself might be two sheets to the wind.

"Woman, what are you doin out here? This is man's business." Al gave her an angry gesture as if to strike her. "Mind your business woman."

She left with her eyes warning Luke. "Beware" he is in a volatile mood.

"Here's the little beauty, one day this is going to make me a fortune." He unfolded and spread the weathered old document out on the table treating it gingerly as if it was of immense value. Luke thought it was ancient and fragile, as if it had been folded and unfolded many times and was on the verge of breaking apart when handled.

"Trouble is I don't have all the keys to decipher it. I think this river shown here is the Kern, and if you follow it north you will get to the right territory, but nothing is marked. It is an unnamed river on his map. He put no names to the landmarks. No starting point, nothing I can be sure of. So I'm just guessing, but it's got to be right here."

"Have you tried to follow it and gone looking for the mine?" Luke shook his head and thought it's not much of a "map."

"That's the problem. I am too busy. I need time to go back and search again. I got too many distractions. Running the movie set and my family take all my time right now. If'n I had a partner I trusted, I might let him try to find it for sure. I need someone I can trust," Al looked at Luke with expectations.

"What's wrong with Dean and Don? They're your partners." Luke asked.

"Naw, I tried and they always treat me like I'm crazy. They don't believe. They have even laughed at me." Al's face twisted for a moment in anger, "They're fools!"

"Do I understand this right? You want me to hike up into the mountains using this map, and try to locate an old lost gold mine? And if I find it you want to split the profits? Do I understand you right?" Luke's eyes narrowed, the beer was making his head swirl. The warning voice in his head made a choking sound. It fogged up in his brain.

"You make it sound cold. You make me sound greedy. The only reason I can't do it myself is I have a family and this here movie set project here to develop. I would go up with you if I could. I have the map, and some money for a grubstake, for equipment, food and a mule to carry the goods." Al was anxious! Had he found his man?

"Well I'll be," Luke whistled out loud, "I'll bet there's a whole bunch of deserted old mines up in those hills. How could I find the right one? I'd be lost trying."

"Edward spent a year working his mine. He had been working on it right up to when he got sick. I'm thinking he left lots of signs proving his recent activity. Open digging areas are easy to spot. He was digging and then got sick."

"That seems real thin. I'd have a tough time deciding if someone had been working it or not."

"I got a book on it. I'll show you."

Al went back to his bedroom and came back holding a hardbound book. "Gold Mining In California". It was a library book. Luke read the barcode.

"It's got ten pages of pictures. Pictures of mother lodes and rich veins." He handed Luke the book.

"Al, this is from the Bakersfield public library. It's not your book is it?"

"You're right I stole it, but I needed it. These pictures show what an open vein of gold looks like!"

Luke examined the pictures of granite and rose quartz lined with streaks of gold. The pictures had long streaks of yellow cake showing what pure gold looked like.

"Yeah I guess if I found a lost mine with huge deposits of quartz and long gold streaks running through it, I would be on easy street." Luke thumbed through the pages of the stolen book searching for something to say.

"Give me some time to think on it." Luke winced. Al's body went limp in disappointment. " I came here to be a stuntman, not a miner."

"Well you'll never have a better shot at getting rich." Al tried to hide his disappointment.

"Say where's the badge you are supposed to give me ?" Luke changed the subject. Al relaxed and let the tension drain from his hands.

"I forgot bout it. It's in the bedroom." Al returned with a silver badge in hand. "It's real silver, a full ounce. Yes sir, real silver!"

Luke pinned it on his chest and grinned. "It's official! About your map, gimme some time to sleep on it. I'm not sure."

"No need to rush, mine ain't going nowhere, we got time." Al's voice sounded flat. Once again he had failed to close the deal. No one believed in his map or the lost mine in the hills. Luke was not sold. Al put the map back in its case.

## Chapter 11

With his shotgun in hand, Luke went to the front gate of the town, and let himself in. His mind was tossing in turmoil.

"Shit!, I am not letting Al get a bead on me with that pistol again. He might just shoot me." He was alone in the hot, still night air. The memory of Al pointing the pistol at his head was disturbing.

"Fucker was so drunk he might just shoot me." He repeated his thoughts out loud.

"Hell! He might just slip up. All I want to do is learn to gun fight like a stuntman and fall off a horse. That guy is dangerous." Luke was starting to wonder what he had signed up for. Where was it all going?

As he walked down the street he checked each building to be sure no one was around. The town was empty except for the lone horse standing in his stall.

Luke had almost no experience with horses. His parents had taken him on a holiday to Bryce Canyon National Park and put him on a rental mule. That was it. He stopped in front of the horse's stall and the stench of fresh manure was overwhelming.

"No one's cleaning your stall ." The horse was silent. If the stench was bothering him he wasn't telling.

"I'm going to have to learn to ride you, before I can learn to fall off." The horse kept silent.

"I'm Luke, I understand your name is Charlie, Charlie Horse. I like it! How's your knees?" Charlie kept his head down, he was eating.

"I'm the new sheriff", I guess you'll be my horse when I learn to do stunts." Charlie lifted his head and turned it sideways as if to acknowledge Luke for a moment.

"This conversation is one sided. I'm going to start being the one to feed you and care for you. Dean added it to my duties." Charlie kept his head down and kept chewing.

"Okay, well I hope we can be friends. I need you to remember to help me when the going gets rough."

Luke thought Charlie snorted agreement but wasn't sure. He wondered and hoped that Charlie had given confirmation he was a willing ally but he had his head down eating.

"I'll be back to muck out your stall in the morning. For now just try to relax and enjoy yourself." Luke shrugged, and laughed at himself, and resumed walking down the street.

The pungent odor of horse shit followed him right up to the front door of the new "Post Office". The latest resident of the old town was standing in its place of honor.

"There's nothing postal about this building. It's just four walls and a door, with a couple of boarded up windows." Then he saw it. Don had hung a sign on it. It said "Post Office".

"I like your sign, If the sign says you're the post office then by God, you're the new post office. Where do I buy my stamps?" Al wasn't the only one who had gotten drunk. The beer had done him. He was talking to animals and empty buildings.

"I guess it's okay since no one is talking back." He thought, if they do I better start worrying.

He picked his way through the treacherous piles of rusted cars trying to make his way back to the dust filled room he now called home.

"If I close my eyes and concentrate real hard I can imagine an asphalt parking lot right in this spot. A place where all the future tourists will park". He opened his eyes, nothing had changed, it remained a long line of rusting metal junk.

"What a gig, I haul off the junk and then I bring it in. Right now it's hard to tell the new junk from the old junk." He had opened his eyes just in time to avoid cutting himself on a sharp, broken, rusty tailpipe jutting out in the pathway.

"No telling what slithering creature might come out of these at night. I'm glad I had a tetanus shot last year." He took one last glance at the piles of junk reflecting the moonlight, and shook his head. He had arrived safely at his electricity free home. He opened the door and stepped into the darkness.

"Might as well go to sleep. If I am lucky I'll dream, I hope it is a beautiful dream."

Luke's shoulders ached, he had done some heavy lifting and pulling during the move. He was sore. He tried to ignore the pain. Luckily the many cans of beer were making him sleepy.

He took a couple of cautious steps and put his hand out trying to find the bunk. The jail was small and so was the bunk. It was dark, he had to let his eyes adjust to the lack of light".

The bunk was filthy and full of dust. The maid must be off duty." He laughed. "Even if I had a vacuum cleaner I couldn't run it."

Luke took his shoes off and curled up in his sleeping bag. At least the bag was clean. It was getting a little cold. The temperature shifts were extreme. Far greater than what he was used to in the beach towns. Luke decided sleeping in his clothes was a practical idea. He was warm and it took him a long time to fall asleep.

"I'll change in the morning. I hope Peg will let me wash my clothes. I need some clean clothes." Luke liked to play the harmonica when he was alone. He kept it in his backpack. He reached down and searched for it. It was hard to locate his pack in the dark. Once he found it he raised the harmonica to his mouth and started to play.

He had learned a few riffs and bits of famous songs but had never mastered anything. In seconds he let recognizable pieces of popular songs free to dance in the night.

"You got me runnin, hiding, runnin, hiding everywhere I go." His voice had a resonance to it that people seemed to like. He sang out loud and let it rip. After ten minutes of blues, Luke style, he was happy and was ready to sleep. Some people like to meditate, Luke liked to play the harmonica and sing.


Chapter Twelve

Luke tossed and turned in bed dreaming fitful dreams. Knock, knock, knock! Someone was pounding on the jailhouse door!

"They're coming, wake up, I got a wire they're coming."

Luke struggled to respond, his mind was hazy, he figured he was awake but in truth he was asleep.

"Who's coming? Who are you?"

"Listen Sheriff, a wire came in saying "Outlaws were comin this way. I came right away to warn you. We all rely on you to protect the town!"

Luke opened the door and found himself staring into the eyes of a thin faced man with a hawk-like nose and spectacles. He had a visor on and wire rimmed glasses. Luke had never seen the man before.

"Outlaws?" He was having a dream. He shook his head and like magic the door was no longer open, it was an illusion, the hawk nosed man vanished.

Instead he was sitting up in bed as the knocking intensified. Someonewas banging on his door. Confusion engulfed his mind. Sleep and the dream mind had met in the night and for a moment he wasn't sure what was real.

"Wake up!" the two voices haunting him belonged to Al and Don.

"What's up?" Luke asked, peeking his head out.

"Dontcha hear them? They've been rolling through town one after another for over an hour. Loud as hell. Some night watchman you are, you'd sleep through a tornado." Al gestured to the street. There was a loud noise roaring through the night, it was the sound of motorcycles speeding by.

"What the hell?" Luke tried to remember the face of the man with the long hawk nose and wondered what it had to do with any of this. Nothing, he decided it was another bizarre dream and shook it off. "What's going on?"

"We have a state park up the road a bit and they're all going to camp. I counted over a hundred of them so far, and they keep coming." Don was excited. "I'm worried for the safety of the set."

"What in the world would they want with this place?" Luke could not fathom the threat. "It's just a string of old shacks ready to fall over.

"I went over to the Sheriff's house and woke him. He don't want to do nothing. Nothing! Can you believe that?" Don's hands were shaking. Don had a high powered rifle in his hand, Luke was afraid he was ready to use it.

"Calm down, anyone got a clue who they are? What are they doing here?" Luke had seen motorcycle gangs around Los Angeles now and then, and for the most part they always kept to themselves.

"Their jackets say "Hell's Angels". It's them, the ones on television, they're here." Al piped up. "They're everywhere."

"If their jackets say Hells Angels, they're from Northern California. The most violent gang in L.A. is Satan's Slaves." Luke spoke up.

The pack of bikes passed through town and the roar subsided. Luke stopped in mid sentence realizing they had been shouting at each other.

"Damn they were loud." He grinned in the moonlight.

"Sheriff wants us to become deputies, he is all by himself here. He's called the state police for help, but he wants someone to back him up if they come down into town tonight. We got to face them." Don was nervous.

"He wants me to be a deputy? Are you kidding?" somehow Luke found the idea exciting. He was about to become a real law man.

"He wants all of us, he thinks us stuntmen will be up to it. " Al knocked Luke hard in the shoulder. "What do you say, are you ready to go up against the Angels? "

"No, not today, not ever!" Luke thought about the fifty or so bikes that had just passed through town. Hundreds had already arrived and more were coming.

"Sounds nuts to me. How long before the state police can be here? Luke asked.

"No word on that as yet." Don interjected. "We don't have to do anything unless they come down here. I hope they will stay up at the park. But, if they come down here we will need to protect Bodfish. This place is all I have."

Bodfish was quiet at night. It had a coffee shop that stayed open until ten, a gas station with a garage, a small grocery that sold alcohol, a bar, a church, and a motel. Outside of Al, Don and Dean no one had a clue what was going on at the junkyard. It was in transition and was becoming a movie set. To most of the town it had always been nothing but a lot full of junk and old buildings that had seen better days.

"Everything's closed up now. They would have to break in to steal anything." Luke mused.

"We got to go over to the Sheriff's house and be sworn in to make it legal, I told him we would do it, so come on." Don tried to hustle them off to do their duty.

"You promised?" Luke hesitated, he had been okay becoming a pretend sheriff but now only a few hours later he was to become an actual lawman?

"It'll only be for the night, until the state police are here. If the Angels come down here tonight looking for trouble, we will have to stop them. You can do it, right?" Don expected a man to be ready to fight. What kind of a night watchman had he hired?

"Well let's go. What about Dean?" Luke decided to step up. Duty called. He answered the call.

"Damn where is Dean?" Don was suspicious and full of  disappointment.

"He went to play with his old band. They are out from Tennessee on a tour of some sorts. He has a gig playing drums and won't be back till Sday."

"Dean plays the drums ?" Luke couldn' picture it. He tried to imagine Dean playing the drums. He couldn't. Country boy Dean driving a beat?

"Yeah, he used to be with a country band back in Tennessee. They weren't much. But they have caught on a little, and are on tour. The band leader asked

Dean to come up and join them. Dean is hoping to pick up a few dollars," Al explained.

Don gestured to them to hurry. Soon the three of them were standing in the sheriff's kitchen with their guns in hand. The sheriff was fifty five with thinning gray hair. His arm was up in a sling. He was a used up man who had seen his last bar fight. His arm was broken, and now he needed the stud stuntmen to save him.

"Sorry to put you boys through this. They just started arriving. It's scary. I counted at least ten groups and they just keep coming. I am all alone. I called the state police office in Fresno and they will have as many state cops here as soon as they can. I expect them sometime in the morning. But I just want to think I am not alone." The sheriff's eyes flitted from face to face, Luke imagined he had fear in his eyes.

"Do you have any idea of what is going on?" Luke asked. "Why they're here?"

"The state police think they may be having a meeting or something like that. Rumors are everywhere claiming that they must have picked Bodfish."

"Well I don't want any trouble with them, I just want to be sure they leave the set alone." For Don nothing else in the world mattered.

"I got my wife to protect her and Dean's family too." Al thought for a moment.

"If they break into the liquor store, I'd just let them do it no sense getting killed over someone's else's booze."

Luke thought that for once Al made sense. Hell, why die for some else's booze?

"They are arriving in the middle of the night. Nothing to do, and if the state police are here by morning I reckon it will work out. Hell, if I have to fight, I'll protect myself." Luke patted his shotgun and gestured that he was ready.

"I need to swear you all in. Woman, fetch the Bible! "

She hurried off to get it.

"I hope things will not get out of hand. I'm glad to know I am not alone."

His wife appeared with the family Bible. A short ceremony followed, during which they all swore to uphold and honor the law. The sheriff's wife held the bible, allowing the sheriff to conduct the ceremony with his one healthyarm. At the end he tried to pin a deputy badge on their chests. The attempt was awkward, Luke saved the day by pinning himself and the others.

Damn he thought. "I am now a lawman."

They all hurried out of the sheriff's house. It was two in the morning and the night air was chilly and cold.

"I am going to load my guns. I'll come over and help guard the set. Don had a stockpile of weapons and he intended to load them all. He was committed to protecting his investment.

"I'll be damned if I am gonna stand by and let them destroy my town."

Luke thought by the tone of his voice that Don was itching for a showdown and might even ignite like a powderkeg if he was pushed.

"I'll round up Dean's kids and let em all into our house. We'll board up for the night." Al took off towards Dean's house. "At least we'll all be together. Peg and Liz can shoot and I got plenty of guns." If the bad guys were coming he was ready. They would come to regret any invasion of Al's little kingdom.

"Well I'm going back to sleep." Luke did not expect trouble. And did not imagine that a gun fight was imminent.

They split up and went their separate ways. Luke started the short walk alone down the jail house road that led to the town and set. He heard a roar coming up from behind, it was the sound of approaching motorcycles, he counted a score of them and they were all approaching at once.

He spun and faced them. Their bright glaring lights forced him to cover his eyes.The light was blinding.

Luke squinted between the cracks of his fingers and made out the face of a bearded man with long stringy blond hair. He was wearing a black leather jacket and flying the Angel's colors. Luke guessed he was about six foot two with long lanky legs and arms.

"I'm Sonny, we're from the Oakland chapter." said idling up and gunning the engine.

The leader had a long jagged scar on his cheek that flashed in the light of the bike.

"He has been in a knife fight". Luke kept it to himself.

"It's late. How come you are out on the road alone?" The man growled in a raspy deep voice. "That's a big gun? Are you expecting trouble?"

Luke's was surrounded. It was scary. Damn! He took his hand down from his eyes and stood exposed in their beams. He was not able to make out anyone except for the lead rider. The others were all hidden in the glare. He sucked in a gulp of air and faced them. The man smiled, but it was not a warm friendly smile.

"Damn you are young. Is that a real badge?" Luke took a deep breath and decided to listen and not take offense.

"I am the sheriff and because you guys came to town I am now a deputy. " Luke cracked his boyish grin and winced. "I volunteered".

"That right? You have a movie set in this one horse town?" The shaggy man was the leader.

"Yeah well we're building it now. You can see the sign from here." Luke swung his gun allowing the point of the barrel to crossover the leader's body. He flinched. Had it gone off it could have killed someone. Luke realized he would have torn him in half.

"Is your gun loaded?" The biker asked with a twitch. "You pointed it right at me. You shouldn't have done that. It wasn't a friendly thing to do."

The lead rider was upset.

"Yeah it's always loaded. Sorry, if I was careless with it. I carry it all the time." Luke's eyes were locked on the biker's boots. "Sometimes I forget it remember might go off"

"Are you armed because of us? It seems like you are looking for trouble."

"Nah, I always got my gun in hand. The townsfolk are scared! No one was expecting you. No one had any idea you were coming." Luke stared him straight in the eye. "So they made us stunt men into deputies. I was just sworn in."

"We don't broadcast our business, and we go where we want." The leader's eyes narrowed to slits. "How are you planning on dealing with us?"

"I believe you're staying up in the park. Is that right?" Luke tried to talk calmly and carefully. "You've scared a lot of people in town. I need to find a way to calm everyone down.""No one needs to worry. We aren't gonna bother anyone, we are having a convention to choose a President. We have never had one before. I'm Sonny, from Oakland. I'm running for President."

"You're having an election?" Luke was shocked.

"Yeah and everyone has a vote. We are a brotherhood." Sonny was in charge so Luke wondered how the "brotherhood" thing worked.

"No one will cause any trouble, I give you my word. We have called a truce covering all old grudges, so we won't allow fights."

"That's welcome news, people can relax. How long do you plan to stay?"

"Can't say, we need to elect a President and we never done it before." Sonny spit as he finished his point.

"I'll catch you around." Luke hoped he wouldn't.

With that said Sonny gunned his engine. He waved his mob forward leaving Luke to choke in the exhaust. It was late. Luke decided not to worry. Groups of Angels kept arriving all through the night.


Chapter Thirteen

Luke's attempt to fall asleep was interrupted by a loud banging on the jailhouse door. Don was back armed and ready to defend his property. He was shouting at Luke to wake up.

Luke opened his eyes and fingered the badges stuck on his chest. It had all happened. He wasn't losing his mind, the badges confirmed it. Luke pulled on his pants and went out to face Don.

"The California State Police are all over the place, all the roads are blocked with checkpoints, ya can't drive around town without goin through a roadblock. Must be two thousand of them devils up in the hills. No one's sure what they are all doing here." Don was jittery.

"You seem ready to fight, but I don't think that will be needed." Luke tried to calm his boss down.

"What do you mean? Why do you say that? The town's full of em and their Harley's."

"Yeah we have a whole lot of them here, but they promised not to make trouble. I don't think they will. They have a truce in effect." Luke told Don what he had discovered.

"A truce? What are you talking about?" Don was astounded.

"They got a lot of grudges they often fight about. But they are here to elect a President, and they have called a "truce" and I think they'll honor it."

"What are you talking about?" Don was astounded.

"Just so you know, the bikers have come for a convention. They're here to elect a President." Luke spoke with calm authority.

"A President?" Don stopped in his tracks.

"I ran into a group of them as I headed home last night. They surrounded me and Sonny explained it to me. Sonny is running for club President."

"President? Do motorcycle gangs have Presidents?" Don was doubtful.

"Yeah It's strange they think they need one, but that's what they're doing. Sonny told me they would only come down to buy stuff and would mind their own business. They promised to be trouble free."

"Who's Sonny?"

"Sonny was at the front of the pack. An impressive dude with a scar on his face. I believe him. He had a gang of about twenty of them." Luke motioned to the street."They had you surrounded and you weren't scared?" Don let out a whistle.

"No, There was something about Sonny that made me trust it was alright."

When morning came the town of Bodfish was crawling with police. Luke headed up to Al's and had some breakfast. He wanted to stay out of the way. No use attracting attention to himself.

Al was sitting on his porch with a cold beer in hand. He had a pile of weapons up against the wall. Luke guessed he had been standing guard all night. The stack of empty beer cans right next to him was a dead give away. Al stared out into space, and then he caught sight of Luke.

"What the hell you doing here? You should be guarding the town."He snarled.

A little blond head peaked out the door and recognized Luke.

"My friend." The little voice called out.

"Bubba stay back inside. It is dangerous out here." Al snarled.

Bubba rushed Luke and if there was one thing Bubba could do it was close on a leg that needed hugging. He clamped on tight.

"Help" Luke called to Al.

"Bubba stay back inside. There's bad men lurking everywhere." Al grabbed the child and yanked him off Luke's leg. "Mind we for I tan your hide."

Bubba was a whirlwind and slipped from Al's grasp managing to reattach himself to Luke like glue.

"He's Dean's oldest boy. Dean lets him do what he wants. Spare the rod." Al took hold of Bubba and pulled him off Luke for a second time. "I mean it or else." He tossed the boy through the door and closed it behind him.

"You gotta show him you mean what you say. Why aren't you guarding the town?"

"Don's on duty. I came up to bring something to eat."

"The kitchen is full up, we got Liz and Dean's kids over here, lots of mouths to feed, but I think Peg can find you a bowl of cereal. I'm staying out here on guard in case the hoodlums show their faces." Al went back to his beer.

"The bikers ain't gonna do nothing. They'll keep to themselves."

"How you know what they are gonna do?" Al squinted at him.

"Cause they told me so." As Luke spoke, Bubba got the door open and reappeared. He swarmed Luke and reattached himself to Luke's leg for a third time. Bubba smiled, he was losing his baby teeth.

"He always like this?" Luke asked.

"Just ignore him. Now git." He swatted Bubba on the ass.

Luke found Peg and Liz sitting on the couch sipping tea. Bubba lost interest in Luke's leg and started playing with his younger brother.

"I told you, didn't I tell you." Peg gave Liz a meaningful nod. "He's sleeping in the old town. Guards it at night." Peg winked at Liz, her lips formed a wolf whistle.

"You weren't lying." Liz gave Luke the once over and winked at Peg. She licked the corner of her mouth with her tongue. Women tended to like him on sight. He was used to it.

"So who told you and what did they tell you?"Al had followed Luke in, and interrupted the women's talk. "When did you talk to the gangs?"

"Last night, out on the street after I left the sheriff's house. They will be keeping to themselves, they have private business to attend to." Luke let his revelation sink in.

"They told you their plans?" Al was stunned.

"They don't want trouble. They are under a flag of truce." This was crucial, it meant Al didn't have to stay up all night again.

"That so? Peg we got any cereal for Luke?" Al let the news sink in. "Well I'll be."

"So they want this to be a peaceful week so they can conduct their business." The women were impressed by Luke's cool head and calm demeanor. He had made some new friends.

"So you weren't scared?" Liz was impressed.

"They didn't seem all that bad."

Peg poured Luke a bowl of cold cereal and gave him a cup of coffee.

Liz stared at him intently. She was evaluating him. What in the world does she want? She wanted something, but what? He felt her eyes boring into the back of his head.

It occurred to Luke that things might not be smooth in her marriage. It made him shudder. The last thing he needed was to be entangled with a married woman. The little voice told him to run away as fast as possible. He left and headed for the old town. He told himself to make sure he was never caught alone with her.


Chapter Fourteen

As Luke approached the set he found four Harley's parked at the front entrance. Don's voice cracked as he greeted Sonny and his crew.

"Luke, these men came looking for you."

Sonny and a few of his friends were surrounding Don who looked frightened and small. Sonny was overweight with long flowing hair and a full beard. The whole group were strung out having spent the night outside on the ground. They flew their colors on the backs of their leather jackets. They were impossible to miss.

"Morning Sonny, what can I do for you?" Luke said it in his deepest voice trying to sound manly and confident.

"Ya member us? We have a long wait at the café, so we decided to come here. Your sign says you offer tours. We want one."

Luke had read the sign many times before, but somehow he had not taken it seriously. No one had asked to give one before.

"I guess now is as fine a time as any to learn." Luke winged it. He tried to glance over some notes Don had prepared for an occasion just like this. They were terrible.

"How much does the tour cost?" Sonny asked.

"A dollar a head." Don popped up and thrust his hand out. "I wrote the script myself."

"Okay," Sonny took out a five and handed it to Luke, " We are a total of four. I need change."

Don reached for the five, but Sonny pulled it back and placed it in Luke's hand "You got change don't you?"

"Sure." He gave Sonny a buck. "I guess I can read this to you, it's a list of the buildings, how old they are, and where they came from. You'll have to be patient, I haven't done this before. But first let me tell you that these are all the original first buildings in the county from around the 1860's, some are a little older."

Luke led the group down the street. He stepped into the role of being a "tour guide." Don tagged along, keeping within ear shot. He was close enough to be able to hear the lecture being given for the first time. His chest swelled with pride as Luke pointed out the buildings one by one, and read from the text.

"How many movies you made here?" one of Sonny's friends asked.

"As of now, none, but we will one day. That's the plan." Luke answered. "We're getting ready."

" I bet no one has lived here in a long, long time. It is kind of spooky." The man was razor thin with arms covered in tattoos. A bandana was wrapped around his forehead, hiding his hair or lack of hair.

"I'm the only one living here right now." For the first time Luke sensed how deserted and lifeless the place was.

Charlie snorted as the band approached. Luke thought "that horse is always watching everything."

Ping, Ping, Ping! Luke was shocked in disbelief as puffs of dirt in a line rising on the street. Luke realized someone was shooting at them, a line of bullets hit the dirt one after the other and they threw up a small cloud every ten feet. The line was coming up the street straight at the bunch of them. Ping, ping, each puff was marking a path, and the shots were converging on them.

"Hide behind the sheriff's office." Luke yelled, motioning them all to head for shelter.

When they all ran, Luke stood in the center of the street and picked out at a spot on a nearby hill where he imagined the shots were coming from. He stared for a long time hoping to pin down the exact location where the shots had originated. The onslaught stopped before he was sure.

"What you goin to do Deputy?" Sonny was demanding help.. "Someone took shots at us."

"They came from back in the hills. I'm going to go catch the son of a bitch." Luke answered.

Luke headed off towards the hill with his shotgun in hand. He was determined. The old town movie set went silent. The firing did not start up again.

"Come back, it ain't worth the trouble," Don tried to call Luke back.

"You gotta finish the tour."

The hill was heavily forested. The trail was hard to climb so Luke made his way from tree to tree. Don's kept calling for him to come back. Luke kept moving, determined to move forward. He  waited around to catch anyone who might be in the area.

"Damn" he thought. "He must be long gone by now!"

He found an active deer trail and it led him to a level area. The trail deserted. He saw no one, heard nothing. He began to feel foolish.

"Damn stupid. But since I am here I might as well check around." The thick brush scraped his legs as he walked but the path widened and cleared. "Someone has been here a lot," he said to himself. "This is more than a deer trail."

He came to a clearing. Standing in front of him was a strange structure. He approached it carefully. It was a hut or a small cabin. Was it the home of the sniper? He called out but no one answered.

The roof was made of corrugated steel and it slanted to let the rain flow off. The walls were glass, but they were not flat sheets like windows or sliding doors. Instead they were round and curved and had many different colors. As he got closer he found they were bottles of glass joined together by clay or dried mud.

A realization came to him that they were wine bottles and they were being held together by an adobe-like substance. The unbroken bottles were stacked to form a wall that was four inches thick. They were opaque. Luke found himself unable to penetrate the interior of the cabin.

"It's a wine bottle hut." he shook his head. "Anyone at home?" Luke called out and got no answer. He edged his way around the small building and found an opening. It had an opening and a heavy duty wool blanket hanging over the door. The blanket had tightened and sealed from the inside. He poked his head inside, "Hello".

The room included a sleeping cot, plus a stack of books, and a small writing table with an oil lamp. Whoever lived here had a gas camping burner to cook as well as a gas lamp to read by.

"Damn, a hermit lives here."

The wine bottles allowed light to come in during the day. The light was filtered through the bottles, some were dark green, others were orange or yellow, and still others were clear or white. The hut maker had not taken the labels off the bottles, they let in patches of light stream in. It created a patchwork effect. It was a lot cooler inside the hut than out.

"Someone's made this to be cool in the summer and dry in the winter. Cleverhandiwork" he thought and shook his head. "To each his own" he said out loud breaking the silence.

Luke realized he was trespassing. He had no evidence that the shooter was also the owner of this strange hut. He backed out and let the blanket fall back into place covering and closing up the entrance. He couldn't help but think the owner of the hut was the same man who had been firing at him. "But he couldn't ever be sure."

He shook his head and went back where he found Don in the process of finishing the tour. He had stepped in and picked up where Luke had stopped. Sonny and his boys were all laughing and acting like Don had become their best friend. Luke was amazed at the transformation.

"You're back." Both Don and Sonny spoke in unison. "Catch the guy?"

"No, I found an old hut, made of wine bottles. Weird, it was deathly quiet with no one around." Luke shrugged his shoulders.

"The hut must belong to Jake, best to leave the hut and Jake alone. He comes down every once in a while and gets his government check. I almost never visits anymore, not since his wife died and his children moved away." Don spit out a yellow fluid as he finished speaking.

Sonny held out a wad of tobacco offering it to Luke. Don was enjoying a chaw. "Old Jake don't like new folks coming around. Makes him grumpy. He ain't alone, he has a few others like him in these parts. They ain't social, can hardly stand each other. "

"Well sheriff it seems like the tour's over. You missed it." Sonny patted Don on the shoulder hard and they both grinned at each other. "Must be about our turn for breakfast. Damn stupid to pick this place for a meeting. Too small. One Café, two thousand Angels waiting to eat. One Liquor store, we'll drink the town dry by sundown."

Sonny and his group headed off to breakfast.

"You made the first dollar anyone ever made at Silver City." Don was jealous and green with envy.

"Chalk it up to blind luck." Luke waited for Don to demand the money back, The demand never came.

"If Jake was doin the shootin, he wasn't tryin to hit anyone. If he was tryin to shoot some, he would have done it. He was a sharpshooter in the war. "

Found his hut did you? Wondered where he was hiding it. It's just like him to make it out of wine bottles. He used to drink a lot of wine Had a woman with him, she liked wine, he picked up with her when his wife died but ain't seen her in a long time."

"Imagine that." Luke was sorry he had trespassed. If a man goes to so much trouble to be alone, you should leave him alone.

The state police took over running the town and the Angels stayed in their camp only venturing down to buy booze or food. They caused no trouble in the town and the police let them do as they pleased. In three short days they picked the shelves of the liquor store clean, spending more money in Bodfish in three days than was spent the previous year.

When they pulled out they left a mess. After the campsite was cleaned up, a naked body was found. The dead man was in his twenties, with no identification. He was listed as a John Doe and no one ever came looking for him. The story about finding him went around the town but no one had any idea of what to do, and so nothing was. The body went unclaimed and the matter was seldom discussed. The Sheriff forgot about the badges he had given his deputies. Luke was proud to have been a lawman for a day.

Chapter Fifteen

Don bought Luke a high beam flashlight to use when he made his nightly rounds.

"Can't have you out in the dark tryin' to protect something you can't see."

The light had enough power to blind anyone caught in its laser-like beam. Luke appreciated having it. He was sure that his often inebriated bosses would never confront any real danger.

Al was in the habit of trying to sneak up on him, and made a regular effort to catch Luke off guard. When Al was on the prowl, his heavy drunken footsteps always gave him away. Luke had plenty of warning of his impending arrival, and started hiding in waiting for him.

"Gotcha, you bastard!" Luke would spring out of the dark and flash the beam into Al's heavy drunken eyes. The blinding power of the beam always stopped Al in his tracks and forced him to blink away in pain. After a couple of sessions of blindness, Al stopped checking up on Luke at night.

Don was a different story. He was sneaky and quiet. He was driven by fear, and was convinced that danger lurked around every corner. He was compelled to keep Luke on his toes to protect his investment. His nervous mind suffered from frequent recurring nightmares always involving arson and fire. Picking on the night watchman had become a source of pride for him. He liked to jump Luke and startle him when he got the chance.

"If I can sneak up on you just imagine what a bad man with evil intent might do." He would say and shake his head in disapproval. "Gotta sharpen up boy!"

Tonight as he made his rounds Luke was on his toes. He imagined he heard Don's baleful voice nagging him without mercy.

"A business can earn its "first" dollar only once. You got mine." But it was only Luke's imagination..

Somehow it never occurred to Don that he was the boss and if he wanted to he could just demand Luke give the five dollars to him. Luke figured fate had put the money in his hands and it was his until it wasn't.

As a result, Luke kept the precious five dollar bill separate from his other money, it was something he tried he had to keep track of. Every night after finishing his rounds he would retrieve the historic bill out of the dirty sock. The bill had become wrinkled and worn.

"When I spend this it will be for something he wanted." That was unless Don ordered him to hand it over. For now it would remain his to spend. "Fate," he said to himself. "This . Bill was fated to be mine. I'll spend it on something important"

When he fell asleep that night he dreamed he was back in the old west, sitting at a card table, playing poker. He was winning and a fabulous young girl was flirting with him. She was a barmaid in the saloon and had a penchant for sitting on his knee. He would often stop playing cards and kiss her. She made sure he got a winning hand of cards every time

"You're my lucky charm." He told her.

In his dream she always kissed him back. He kept winning, and was happy, floating in a warm pool of her loving charms. Luke believed a unique bond was growing between them.

"Bam! Bam! Bam!" A loud noise interrupted his dream, was it gunshots? Was he in danger? He sat up, and his body was on fire. He was aroused, a sexual energy was flowing through his groin. For a moment the dream became clear. He had fallen in love with the barmaid's face. He was certain the dream was important.

He listened and it was quiet, only the usual moans and whistles of the wind filled the cracks of the town. Frustrated, he tried to go back to sleep and restart the dream. It was no use, he could not recapture a firm memory of who she was. She became a ghostly mystery.

That same morning Dean returned from his week of playing drums with his old band. He had missed the biker invasion but was full of stories about life in the limelight of music.

"It was just like old times." he bragged.

The truth was the band was doing well without Dean and was now making records. During Dean's heyday all they had ever done was play cheap honky tonks. Now they were booking shows all over the country and traveling all the time. They were making money!

Johnny, the band leader, was Dean's childhood friend and he brought Dean back to play whenever he could. He made it an important deal by always introducing him as a "founding member," with a stake in their success.

Dean returned from his adventure with Johnny "flush" with cash. He flashed a wad of hundred dollar bills in the air with a flourish. It was a veritable fortune considering one of the shows had been at a prison and had been done for free.

"Johnny is a talented man, and he asked me to come back and play full time again. It is mighty tempting. One of the hardest things for me to do movin' here was to give up my drummin'. I would like to play with Johnny again but Liz won't hear of it."

"Got me a barmaid in one of those little towns." A grin broke on his face as he delivered the revelation of his sexual conquest.

"You gotta understand that's why Liz don't want you trapsin' all around." Al was jealous of the "easy money" and women. He could imagine Liz ripping Dean a new one if she ever caught wind of it.

"Don't say nothin" Dean said frightened at the thought of one of them blabbing out of place to Liz about his conquests. Luke figured Liz knew her husband well and everything he did. If Dean thought he was getting away with cheating he was kidding himself.

"I think she already suspects you. If she don't, she's dumber than I think." Al spoke up.

Luke shuffled his feet and kept his mouth shut. Liz had come off as as flirtatious and trouble. He kept silent, determined to stay away from her and out of her sight if possible.

"You know all the time I was gone, I was thinkin bout that slide. Well.... Not all the time... but a lot of the time. We gotta grab that slide and set it up in our park. It's goin to waste, just sittin' with moss growing on it. It's a shameful waste!" Dean's obsession with the slide had grown while he was away.

"I agree," Al chimed in. "We should go up with a case of Jack Daniels and make the old boy sloppy drunk and make him an offer!"

"He said he wanted to keep the damn thing." Luke reminded them.

"If he agrees to let us have it he gets a case or two of Jack. If he don't, we'll slip him one of Peg's pills and we'll just take it." Al laid out his plan.

"Jack Daniels is expensive" Dean was intense. "We'll all pretend to drink. Make him take two or three to our one."

"How do you pretend to drink?" Luke asked.

"We all pour one but just take little sips. If we do it right he'll drink three or four to every one of ours. I hope he'll pass out and we'll just take the slide straight away." Dean slapped Al on the back. " It's a plan that might work"

"Stealin' it is a bad idea. It would be best if he gives it up of his own free will. What does he need with an old slide?" Al was determined. He had a bead on the old boy. All it would take was some Jack!

They decided to do the deed on the following day. Al would buy the booze and they would take both trucks to be sure they had room to fit the entire disassembled slide. They agreed to be at Jarvis's house by ten.

"If we start too late in the morning the old boy will have started greasing himself. He'll be half in the bag when we arrive". At that moment they spotted Don's wife, Sue, coming down the road. She was walking with deliberation and heading straight toward them.

"Boys, I need to talk a moment." She called out. "Don sent me."

"Whyn't he come hisself?" Dean did not like Sue, she was brutally honest and never hid her feelings. She also thought poorly of Dean, and did not bother to hide it. The feeling was mutual.

"Well, he don't like to be the bearer of bad news. He leaves that job to me." She narrowed her eyes and focused. "We got a letter from the Bank in Bakersfield. They raised up the interest rates on the banknotes covering the properties Don's been letting you live in. They have done the same to the set. He's gone to town to talk with them about it."

"What's it all mean?" Al asked.

"It means we have to pay a lot more to float you boys. I don't want you livin' for free no more. This whole damn thing is way too expensive. We can't do it no more." Sue had been smoldering ever since Don had swallowed Al's story about bringing movie companies to Bodfish. It was killing her.

"The houses where we live are key to the deal. We are investing our time and sweat in this place." Dean spoke right up.

"Well I never liked it, and I don't think it is ever goin' happen. Don keeps thinkin' one day it will pay off, and movie companies will come here to make Westerns. Damn foolish idea if you ask me." They all knew how she thought, she had made it clear many times. The boys were silent.

"I want him to start charging you boys rent right away." Sue said it again.

"How long will he be away?" Al hoped a reprieve was possible.

"Not long, a few days. He has an old friend in town, he's gonna try and help." She glared at them. "He's thinkin' the only way to survive is to bring in some new money to help out." Sue no longer seemed angry, only desperate and sad.

"We might have an answer that will solve everything." Al let out a hint about the commercial potential of the slide.

"What you talkin bout?" Sue perked up.

"Just be a little patient, we got a little surprise all planned out." Dean doubled down, certain the slide would provide the future success they all craved.

In his mind's eye he heard the excited squeals of the happy kids propelling head first into the cold clean water. He could smell the cotton candy and thought about selling cotton candy! Why the hell not? It's perfect. He was back in Tennessee at the Fronter water park!

"If I were you boys, I would start thinkin' bout how I was gonna make some money and quick. Al, you might be headed back to Los Angeles and that cab."

Then she zeroed in on Dean.

"I got no idea what you can do. Sweat my ass! I don't think you have worked up a sweat since I've known you!" In frustration she wheeled on her heels. "I'll let you know when I hear from Don. You are on notice. I am expecting some news soon. You should expect to start paying rent!"

"Well I'll be damned, the woman don't have a kind bone in her body." Dean shook his head as she vanished from sight.

"We best take the slide before Don gets back. We'll surprise him for sure." Al was shaken. "We'll need somethin'."

"You live here for free?" Luke guessed the problem, and it was ominous.

"Yeah. We are living on what we have saved." With Al's admission the grim reality became crystal clear for Luke.

"Better put our hands on the slide quick. We need a real "attraction" right now." Dean brought their focus back to the task at hand

"For now I think I'll stay have to put. We're close to cleaning out the junk. Soon enough there will be room for a pool. No other place for it." Al improvised on his feet. "One thing at a time, first we acquire the slide."

"Next to the line of old rusted autos? I hope we don't have to do that for long." Luke did not like it. "Not a safe spot for kids to play."

"One problem at a time. I'll go buy some Jack and we'll deal with Jarvis tomorrow morning."

They all agreed it was the best thing to do. First things had to come first. Jarvis was still standing in the way.


Chapter Sixteen-

That night Luke dreamed about the gorgeous barmaid whose visits brought him luck. She shined with a glow and everything she touched in every moment of every dream seemed to come alive with the promise of new love. He liked it, and was intoxicated by the promise. This time, when he woke up he remembered he had been dreaming about Darla and this knowledge was firm in his mind and did not slip away. Darla was the barmaid frequenting his dreams. She had become the highlight of Luke's dreamlife and was starring in it nightly.

"I don't know her, I never even talked to her. But it's her, she is the one in my dreams." his inner voice whispered it.

"How strange. I have never talked to her and have never been close enough to her to find out what she is like. Yet, I am dreaming about her every night."

That settled the matter, she was his lucky charm. She was in his dreams and he hoped she might be in real life as well. His mind returned to what lay ahead.

They were going to go up to Jarvis's, and drink him until he is blind. Once he was inebriated, and vulnerable they would convince him to part with the slide in exchange for a case of whiskey. If they couldn't bargain for it, they would take it by force.

The future success of the project depended on it! So if it became the last resort, they would steal it. Luke dreaded that idea. He had never stolen anything in his life, and didn't want to start now.

"That old thing's a piece of junk! It's worthless." His intuition told him it had been sitting out in the hot blistering sun for years! It had endured many harsh winters! It had to be in terrible shape!

"If they force you to steal it you need to figure out how to sabotage and ditch the plan."

The thought of sabotaging the plan caused his stomach to knot up in a bunch. Luke was in an inner turmoil, and he was still debating with himself when he arrived at Al's door. What was he going to do?

"Al's not here." Peg called out. "I made you some eggs and a little bacon. It's sittin waitin on you." she nodded at the table.

"Where's Al?" He started eating.

"Gone to buy some whiskey. Be back soon though, he said you'd understand."

"Yeah, we got a plan." Luke was nervous. He was worried Al's plan was too risky.

"What brought you to a place like this?" She asked.

"Well I realized how tired and bored I was, and I decided to try something new. Al offered me this job, and it sounded like a fit, So here I am. What about you? What brought you two together?"

"I first saw him when he starred in the stunt show. During a fight, he fell backwards and bumped into me. Knocked me on my butt. But then he was kind and friendly. He had a grip like a vice. After the skit was over he found me and told me again how sorry he was and well… that's how it all started."

"He knocked you down?" Luke shook his head. "Wow."

"Then after we dated I found out he had been in the movies with John Wayne and I fell for him even harder." Luke saw a sparkle in her eyes.

"Interesting." Luke visualized Al knocking Peg on her butt.

"It was meant to be." Peg said.

"Are you worried about what is happening with Don and the bank?" Luke changed the subject.

"What are you talking about?" Peg's face was blank.

Al had not shared the news. The girls were in the dark about the pending problems with the bank. Luke backed off. He always tried to not meddle in the business of husbands and wives.

"Dean ain't gonna come along. He's staying behind." Al thought it best if the two of you handled it.

"Did he say why?" Luke was surprised.

"Something about Dean being too pushy and irritating to Jarvis. What are you planning on doin' with old Jarvis?" Peg prodded him for details.

"Jarvis has something we all want. We're gonna try and get him to give it to us. Well not exactly, more like trade for it."

Luke could still see Dean slamming his fist and shouting that he would take the slide by force if old Jarvis wouldn't give it up. He imagined long tall Dean wrestling and rolling on the ground with gimpy old Jarvis. Not a fair fight, Luke sensed Jarvis had a mean side. If it got that far Luke's money was on Jarvis. That old bear would roll Dean in the dirt in a heartbeat.

"Changin the subject, we're having a picnic on Saturday, we want you to come." Peg asked.

"A picnic? Where? Who's going?" Luke was often bored and alone. Bodfish was small and didn't have much going on.

"There's a wild water site by the river. It has a barbeque pit and tables. It has a small wading area for the kids. "

"Sure I'll come. I love to swim." Luke perked up.

"You need to be a strong swimmer. It is quick out towards the middle. Dean and Liz and their kids are comin'. Sue invited Darla from the motel. I'll grill up some hamburgers. Al is bringing a few beers." Peg saw that Luke perked up at the mention of Darla.

"Sounds like fun, I'm in". As Luke answered, Al barged through the door toting two full cases of whiskey.

"Woman, you got those pills I asked for?" Al saw Luke, "Bought two cases to be safe. After all, no use goin short on the deal. One is backup if we need to sweeten the pot. We get Jarvis drunk enough and show him the second case, and it will be like fishing in a barrel with a shotgun"

"So far Jarvis is noncommittal." Luke reminded Al that Jarvis had not agreed to relinquish the slide.

Peg appeared with a bottle of pills. "Here's the pills you asked for. They are strong. What are you going to do with them?"

"What kind of pills are they?" Luke asked.

"I use them to lose weight. They take away my appetite and twenty pounds."

"Diet pills? You are going to get him drunk and give him diet pills?"

Luke was incredulous. "You know what that is likely to do?"

"No, don't care much either. I want that slide. I need the slide to help save the town. We got to try everything. No use holding back now."

Al was a determined bull.

"Peg says Dean ain't comin? How come?" Luke asked.

"I told Dean to hang back until we call for him. No use overwhelming Jarvis The old coot ain't keen on Dean. You and I can close the deal. Dean would just be in the way. "

"The pills don't seem like a smart idea any more." Luke pointed out the obvious problem. Giving him diet pills. Diet pills would not put the old guy to sleep. It would be just the opposite. Al cut him off in mid sentence.

"It was your damn suggestion." Al was annoyed. "Why are you having second thoughts?"

"I suggested sleeping pills, not diet pills." Luke no longer liked it at all..

"Diet pills, sleeping pills, pills are pills." Al was in charge and he had made up his mind. The plan was set and as far as he was concerned, it was time to put it into play. "All we got is diet pills so diet pills it is going to be."

He motioned Luke it was time to go, so they scurried out the door and piled into the pickup.

"We'll need Dean's truck to help haul the slide away. Especially if Jarvis passes out and we end up takin' it. We gotta get it in one trip." Luke was afraid a second visit would be a disaster. It was all or nothing.

"Dean won't be far off. He'll be waitin' for my signal." Al had downed several beers that morning and was floating.

"What's the signal?" Luke asked.

"Never you mind, when I give it, you'll know it. It will be obvious."

The boys were armed as usual. Al was carrying his rifle and pistol while Luke had his trusty sawed off. They were all set for a visit with the menacing Jarvis.

"You think Jarvis will let us on his property?" Luke asked, recalling their previous send off.

"For sure once he gets his hands on the  case. I never seen him turn down free Jack! Not bloody likely he'll start now."

Al had a history with Jarvis and all he had to do was show up with the booze in hand. Al believed he was weak and was an easy sell.  When Al eased up to Jarvis's front door he found the old man sitting on the porch with his dog. He had his rifle propped up standing against the front wall.

"Hold it right now." He swung the rifle around to his knee pointing it above Al's head.

"Hell Jarvis I brought you that case we talked about. Got it right here." Al held it above his head with both hands careful not to drop it. "You have a clue how much this costs. Well I brung you one."

Jarvis lit up with Joy! Al had come through! His face lit up.

"I need a slug of Jack bout now." He grinned at Al, "Come on over right now, both of you."

The first bottle opened and was emptied in a hurry. Al opened the second bottle and poured Jarvis another drink. Luke sipped on his. He marveled at the speed with which these two had powered through the first bottle.

"Heard you had some long haired girls visit your town a while back." Jarvis slurred the words "long haired girls"and spit out a wad of chaw.

"What girls?" Al gave up rationing the flow of drinks and instead began to keep pace with Jarvis. Luke sipped on his first one and watched the two dueling drunks.

"Those motorcycle girls. They toured your town. Young one here was guiding them around for a while." He sneered showing his yellowed teeth.

"You know about that?" Luke asked.

"Jake told me how he dusted their skirts." Jarvis spit out another bit of chaw and squinted, narrowing his eyes. He laughed as he said "dusted" their skirts. "I hear they danced like girls in a french chorus line." Jarvis broke into an even deeper laugh.

"Someone shot at all of us. Was it your brother Jake?" Luke still wanted to get to the bottom of the shooting scare.

"Let's have some more Jack." Jarvis held out his glass and Al filled it again. This time Al dropped the crumbled powder of two diet tablets in the glass. The act was stealthy and went unseen.

"Give the youngin' some more, he ain't had much." Jarvis took several gulps and then drained his entire glass. "More please." He swallowed the powder without noticing a thing.

"Naw, gotta keep the kid sober. We came up here to dismantle the slide. I need the kid to help me take it down. He's gotta stay sober." Al guided the conversation back to his objective. "You said if I brought you booze you'd trade me the slide."

"Said I'd think about it, how about a refill to help me think?" Jarvis kept holding out his glass. "You gonna help me think or not?"

"You got no use for that old piece of junk. It's been sittin for a long time, doing nothing. I am willing to take it off your hands as is, flaws and all. Can't be worth nothing to you." Al was closing in on getting the deal done.

Al poured the refill, and at once Jarvis's hands began to shake and his eyes twitched.

"I am a little short of breath." Jarvis's lungs were heaving.

He gasped and gulped, taking in huge quantities of air. He gazed off in the distance like he was floating away and then snapped his head around in a half circle. His eyes began to blaze. "Don't recall Jack making me react like this before, my hearts pounding. Racin' like a speed boat."

"Do you know what's happening?"Al questioned Luke, holding him accountable.

"My heart's pounding out of control." Jarvis grabbed his chest.

"Do somethin youngin'" Al demanded that Luke fix the crisis.

Jarvis had one hand on his heart and the other was holding out the glass he wanted to be refilled. Al gave him another fill up. Jarvis started to hiccup and his breathing got heavier and heavier, and faster and faster.

"Don't understand what is going on." His eyes darted from face to face. Sweat appeared on his brow. "Damn my bloods racing. It's like I'm running a sprint." He said downing the shot Al had given him.

Jarvis tried to stand up on his feet but only staggered and lurched against the wall. He was able to grab hold of his gun which he pointed into the air and fired three times. The shots echoed back from the surrounding hills.

"What the hell you doin?" Al began to panic, realizing the situation was becoming dangerous. Jarvis was always unpredictable.

"Called Jake." Jarvis was hyperventilating now. "If he is nearby he'll come. Got to do something. Take some action! I wish I had a cow to milk. If I only had a cow! Need somethin' to do with my hands. Damn ain't squeezed a cow's tit in a long time." Jarvis was in a panic, his breaths were coming faster and faster.

"Do something!" Al commanded Luke to help. "This is your doin."

"Ain't cleaned the house in a long time, it's important to clean the house top to bottom. Got to begin at it right now. Whole house could use a scrubbing and vacuuming. Can't recall where I put the vacuum. You guys got a vacuum in your truck?" His eyes were bouncing from object to object.

"Jake? The rifle shots are a signal to Jake? Why call Jake?" Al was terrified of Jake. Everyone was.

"Try to calm down, breathe deeply and relax." Luke moved to Jarvis's side.

"I want to dance cept I can't dance. Haven't danced since my wife and I did at our wedding'"

Jarvis wanted Luke to provide an answer. "Or was it Jake's wedding? It was someone's wedding for sure."

Luke thought Jake was the hermit whose wine bottle house he had stumbled on. It was Jake who had opened fire on them. He was like a ghost living in the back hills, coming and going in unpredictable ways. Everyone was sure he was dangerous and mean.

"Need my brother," Jarvis belched out the words and held out the glass for still more whiskey. "The slide belongs to him. He had it here for his kids. My heart feels like it is riding down a slide. I need to move around but I can't do much. Jack never did this to me before. Strange. I feel strange. I can't imagine what is happening to me."

"You need to hold off on the whiskey for a minute." Luke encouraged Jarvis to slow down..

At that moment a squat round muscular man came hustling up the driveway at full speed like a rhino in heat. He was waving his rifle motioning for them to back off. As he approached, Luke saw how much the brothers were alike. Jake was coming full throttle and was all steamed up.

"Stay away from my brother. What did you do to him?" Jake was full of fury and anger and vitriol flying from his eyes. He shook with wrath. "What is going on here?" He bellowed.

At the sight of Jake, Jarvis started to calm down.

"You know Al here and this young un has been stayin with them. They brung us a case of whiskey. Don't know why but my heart is actin up. Beatin like a drum! It's a mystery."

"Don't say? A case of Jack? What fer? Yeah, I been watchin the young un in particular. Always hangin' round those old shacks in that fake town down below." Jake said. "Been keeping an eye on all of them. What you done to my brother?"

Jarvis began again to wheeze and cough. His body shook for a moment, his face got queasy, and he vomited. It was enough to send a stream of yellow liquid splashing on the wall. "I must have drunk more than I reckoned. That helped, I feel a bit better now." He put his arm up on the wall to help him stand and keep his balance.

"Never seen you so unsteady." Jake put his hand on Jarvis's shoulder.

"Never had Jack come on me so sudden. It was like a bolt of lightin but it is calming a bit now." He held his belly and wiped the drool from his lips on his shirt. "Supthen got to my tummy bad."

"Throwing up helped." Luke saw the mess it had splattered on the wall. It was going to stink for a longtime.

After a long pause, Jarvis steadied himself and put forward the case for the case, "Jake, these boys want to trade for our slide. They brought us a case to trade for the slide, what do ya think?"

"Two cases, I got another in the truck! I brought two cases." Al decided to go all in.

"It seems you have already made the trade. I see two empty bottles and a third one open. And it's just now noon." Jake shook his head. He felt saddened that he had been left out so far. "Why do you want the slide?"

"We're gonna put it up in the movie set to help bring in the tourists with kids." Al laid it on the line. On an impulse he decided to trust telling the truth. He believed Jake could smell a lie in a half hearted fart.

"You mean I'll have crowds of kids runnin and makin' a racket at all hours?" Jake shook his head in instant disapproval.

"Your kids loved it Jake." Jarvis argued. He was starting to hiccup in between shakes. They were coming one after another and Jarvis was having difficulty getting out full sentences.

"My kids ain't the problem. It's hoards of other people's kids swarming below, that's the problem." He waved his hands in the air. "I won't have it."

Jarvis wanted to make the trade. On that issue his thoughts were clear. It was just a matter of getting Jake on board. A few drinks and he hoped Jake would understand his point.

"My kids wasn't a crowd, and I wanted them to use it. Don't like no crowds, don't like long haired girly men neither." Jake spit a long stream of chaw juice.

"Aw Jake, have a drink with us and think on it." Jarvis motioned to Al to pour a Jack for Jake. Jake knocked back another shot of Jack in one sweeping motion, and then put the glass out for a refill.

"Heart stopped fluttering. I'll be better for sure if I have another shot." Jarvis wasn't about to loose pace with his brother.

"I'll have another." With that drink, the master negotiator, Jake tipped his hand and succumbed to the trade.

Jake figured no one had come down the slide for a long time. The Jack was going down real easy. One drink called for another, and each one was a slice of heaven greasing his parched gullet.

"Bam, bam, bam." It was Dean's truck backfiring as it roared up the road.

Dean popped his head out the window, conscious that the sputter and backfire that accompanied him interrupted the drinking festival.

"Heard your shots. Got your signal. Are we ready to tear down the slide?" Dean called out to Al.

"Naw, We got our signals crossed. Jarvis was calling for Jake." Al suspected the brothers didn't like Dean. Al expected an explosion. But it never came.

"What the hell, what's one more," Jarvis was so drunk could tolerate Dean. At least for a while.

"Damn boy come on down and have a taste."Jarvis was flowing and was generating a warm welcome.

The boys understood that a deal had already been struck.The five of them continued on for another hour, until Jake decided it was time to say goodbye to his slide. He did so with an empty bottle of Jack in hand. He made his way to the base of the slide and patted it like it was an old friend.

"Mighty fine slide." He peered bleary eyed at the ancient edifice that had stood for three decades in his brother's yard. "To the slide!" He raised his bottle to the sky in a salute.

With an inebriated grab he pulled the railing and stepped onto the ladder. He was determined to climb up to the top and take in the view one last time. Jake was so old and fat he caused the old slide to creak and groan. He put one foot on each step and tried to pull himself up. Al feared supporting Jake was a lot to ask.

Jake stood up and started waving the bottle in the air. He tried to dance a jig in time to a fiddle that only he heard playing in his mind. The crystal blue lake seemed enchanting and near. He was Inspired, and pirouetted gesturing with joy enjoying the expansive country below.

"I can see for miles and miles and miles." he called to his brother Jarvis.

"You old fool." Jarvis bellowed back.

Jake pranced on his toes, and for a second, Al thougt he might be calling for rain to fall from the heavens. Then with a whoop and a shriek, Jake lifted the bottle to his lips and let its contents pore down his throat. The fast influx of liquid caused a spasmodic jerk, and Jake began to choke.

"It went down the wrong pipe, I can't breathe!" The liquid was burning in his windpipe. "Help!" His voice was faint and weak. The alcohol kept on burning.

"Help," Jake's voice was a whisper.

"You damn fool, common down." Jarvis commanded his incapacitated brother.

Jake threw his head backwards and lost his balance. He stubbed his toe and lurched forward. Windmilling his arms he tried to regain his composure but instead tossed the empty bottle off the platform. Jarvis rushed to catch his brother, certain he was about to plunge over the side of the rail.

Then with a bit of luck Jake caught hold of a sidebar. His overweight body dangled off the edge of the platform poised to fall. It was a long way down and Jake panicked. But instead the old coot summoned up a heroic effort, and pulled himself upright.

"Fooled you didn't I?" Jake burst into the wild maniacal laugh of a man who had just stared death in the eye and won.

"Serve you right to die by falling off, you nasty old bastard." Jarvis laughed up at his brother. "Crazy old bastard."

"You'd like that wouldn't you?" Jake fired right back at him. "You were always jealous, cause I came out first."

He had steadied himself enough to climb on the mouth. He sat down and pointed his feet outward and pushed off.

"Geronimo," he called out. Nothing happened. The surface was sticky with a thick gooey resin. He rolled forward a few feet and came to a halt.

"Damn I'm stuck." He was like a fly in molasses. "Damn thing is covered in gunk. It's all gooey and getting all over my britches."

"Must be pollen, it'll clean up, and be like new again, all we gotta do is polish it up." Dean came to the rescue. The slide was his answer to all his problems and a little pollen was not going to change that.

Jake strained to push himself down but the surface was caked with years of gooey pollen and pine needles. After several minutes of hard effort he was only a third of the way down.

"This is hard work!"Jake had climbed over the side and was  calculating his chances of jumping.

"It's a twenty five feet down, you got to slide down." Jarvis called up.

Jake's arms were tired and limp from the effort to climb down. He wanted to close his eyes and go to sleep. He lay back in the pollen and he let it grab hold of his hair.

"I want to take a nap." was all he managed to say. "Damn, the stuff's gettin in my hair."

"Pull yourself together. Try to bounce and bump your butt up and down. You'll be at the bottom in no time." Jarvis encouraged his brother.

Jake hit a patch where the pollen was not too deep and he made some real progress. That gave him the courage to continue.

"It's easier." He called out joyfully.

Jake got down and stepped off the slide unharmed. He was out of breath.

"Damn thing is a menace." Jake was befuddled and scared.

"Hope you boys ain't havin second thoughts." Jarvis stepped in. "A deal's a deal."

"Hell no! We'll have her fixed up in no time. A little spit and polish and she'll be alright." Dean was a true believer. Nothing could shake his faith.

"It's yours then. It's a fair deal." Jake mumbled, and took what remained of the case under his arm and stuck out his hand.

"Shake on the deal." It was a contract. The brothers burped in unison and the negotiations were closed.

"You boys start to work. I'm gonna take a little nap in the truck." Al headed for his truck, climbed into the cab.

" I need a little nap myself." Dean left Luke to face the project alone.

Luke grabbed the tool box and began taking the ancient edifice apart. Piece by piece he broke it down and filled the two trucks with the load. Rust and age were his enemies but two hours later he finished.

The two brothers had partied till they dropped. They were on the porch snoring under the eye of the setting sun. Jake had rescued the second case from Al's truck before he lost consciousness and had it under his arm for safe keeping.

"Wake up!" Luke roused Dean from sleep."It's all done but I need you to drive back to the town. I can't drive both trucks."

"Just like I imagined it." Dean yelled out the window in triumph as they pulled out.

Luke climbed glancing back one last time at the two sleeping brothers.

'Sleeping beauties" he said as he laughed out loud. The sound of Luke's laugh woke Al who sat up startled.

"What's happening?" he asked through his haze.

"The plan came together, It's all loaded up!" Luke gave Al a thumbs up sign.

"We are gonna be rich!" They exclaimed in unison. "I'm obliged to you for seeing it through to the end." Al punched Luke hard in the shoulder to acknowledge his gratitude.

Chapter Seventeen-

Once the trade was made and he had been given the go ahead, Luke took the slide apart in a systematic and methodical way. He wanted to be able to reassemble it with care. It was a battle. Once he was back at the ranch he unloaded both trucks, and laid the parts out to bake in the sun.

"Sun will kill off the moss and I can have them all cleaned and polished up in no time." Luke assured the boys. "I'll make that slide slip til it's fast and quick.".

"It was real lucky us getting Jake to give up his rights so easy. I can't wait until it's standin' tall and proud. It'll be the most impressive thing in town."

"We're nearly done," Al said.

Luke laid out all the pieces and got to work at cleaning and assembling the centerpiece of the waterpark. He swelled up with pride believing they had accomplished something important.. Luke smiled realizing Jarvis and Jake were passed out on the porch surrounded by empty bottles of whiskey.

"Just imagine all the kids that will come riding once we have the pool all ready for 'em to use." Dean was fixated on the future that was coming.

The job was far from done. Converting a junkyard to a movie set was a challenge. Now the project had morphed and had become a movie set and a waterpark.

"It all seems a bit odd." Luke was wary that he might be rocking the boat.

"What you talking about?" Dean jumped in ready to defend his vision.

Luke was focused on the slide. It tilted to the right about eight degrees. It is wobbly,

"It's nowhere near operational. A lot of the bolts are rusted. I don't think it can hold much weight." Luke spoke up, he had taken it apart and put it back together single handedly. "Plus it's bent."

"Ground must be uneven," Al commented. "We'll have to work on the base. It's okay for now. It's in the only spot we got till you clear out the last of the old car frames."

The water slide was christened  and reassembled standing tall above the sea of rusted metal car frames. Cleaning up and disposing of junk was the number one priority on the list of projects to be tackled.

"We gotta make the slide operational so we can begin to sell tickets." Dean was convinced he had found the "key" to future success and wanted to keep the momentum going. He was on the right path and there was no turning back.

Dean's toothy grin beamed each time he revisited his vision which was full of dozens of happy kids plunging in the refreshing water under the hot sun. First the whole family would tour the movie set and then stop and swim at the pool.

No one had seemed to have the slightest concern they were still missing the key ingredient to the formula. They still needed a pool and all that went with it. Al wanted to believe that if you have faith in the goodness and truth of life, the details would just fall into place. Things would naturally come right.

"I believe it belongs here, it has come home." Dean admired the towering slide as it sat in the glistening sun. "It's gonna be just like back home at Frontier Village in Tennessee."

"Did they make movies in Tennessee?" Luke tried to picture how things had been in the town that had given Dean his "vision".

"Nah, it was a frontier park with waterslides. No movie stars.The kids loved it. Your hard work is paying off. This place will be clean as a hound's tooth in no time!"

Luke and Al had finished loading Al's truck. A bit of space had been cleared. It was becoming less a junkyard and more a movie set everyday.

"One more down, only a couple hundred more to go." Al's voice was always encouraging, he was an optimist. "We're making room for the future."

"I calculate if we can haul off three loads a day we'll be done by the end of summer." Luke offered his homemade calculations.

"Luke, Peg tells me you're coming to the picnic tomorrow." Al changed the subject. "You are coming, right? I got an extra fishing pole, you can go fishing with us. We got a spot." Al's voice was glowing with genuine friendship.

"That tomorrow? I forgot about it. Who else is coming?" Luke enquired.

"Well Don's still in town rounding up some dough. But Sue is coming and she'll be bringing Darla. Have you met Darla? I think you'll like her."

"Just seen her from a distance. Never talked to her. I don't fish though." His heart had jumped into his throat! Damn right I want to meet her. She has been haunting my dreams. She's my lucky charm.

"Not a fisherman?" Al was disappointed.

"Never been one. I do like to swim. I hear there is a swimming hole." Luke answered Al, but his thoughts were not on swimming, if a girl gets in your dreams before you even know her, well it must mean something. He was sure of that. But what?

"Dean is bringing old Charlie along, you might have a chance to ride." Al winked. "Sue always brings horseshoes. Darla plays shoes. I'll bet she'll teach you. Meet me at my house at 11:00 and you can ride with us."

Chapter Eighteen

Luke, Al and Dean with his family in tow were the first to arrive at the picnic grounds. It was already in the mid nineties, when they unpacked their blankets beneath the shade of an old oak tree. They had picked a secluded spot away from the cooking venue. They had the place to themselves.

Sue, with Darla riding shotgun, was the last to arrive at the picnic grounds. Sue was a short but imposing woman. She was heavy set, perhaps even a bit stumpy. Luke had not spent much time with her but he was impressed. She possessed an intensity that drew eyes to her like a magnet. She commanded attention.

She had grown up the daughter of a successful dairy farmer and was the only girl and oldest child in a family of seven. She had six younger brothers who had all answered to her when they were growing up. She knew how to talk to men. Everyone knew she was the power behind Don. Dean and Al knew it too and did their best to keep out of her way.

The dirt road leading to the picnic area was dry as a bone. Sue pulled around the last bend and skidded on the loose gravelly surface. Her tires threw up with a cloud of dust announcing her arrival.

"It's like she's late for church or somethin." Peg jokes.

Darla poked her head out the window. Luke's eyes were drawn to her. He got his first taste of her. She was stunning. Luke took a deep breath and marveled at how fresh and sweet she was in the sweltering heat.

She had on a loose fitting light summer dress. A breeze had caught the edges of the dress when she climbed out and treated Luke to the sight of her long trim bare legs. His heart fluttered.

Sue's truck was equipped with a gun rack. She came well armed. Luke had gotten used to carrying his shotgun everywhere he went. It no longer seemed odd to him that everyone was armed all the time. It was normal because Sue was always armed. She took a backseat to no man.

On arrival the wives unloaded and set up camp, allowing both the men to disappear down the river with six packs in hand. It was that if they didn't catch any fish it was not going to matter much.

Luke wore his cut off shorts for a dip in the river. He shepherded Dean's kids to the riverside. It heatured an indented shallow pool of water that was roped off for wading. Gingerly he waded into the stream, he  took time to get his feet wet.

His body adjusted to the cold. The river went from six inches to three feet deep in a hurry. He wondered how deep it was in the middle.

All three kids were laughing and splashing and wading around in the ponding water. The bottom of the shallows were covered with smooth polished rocks that were easy to walk on. Some were covered with green moss, others dazzled the eye with bright quartz crystal colorings.

Luke passed a yellow buoy that served a warning indicating where the shallows ended. Moving past the marker Luke discovered the strength of the current was increasing. Ropes divided the shallow wading area from the river with its faster current. He was the only swimmer, the area was deserted.

Luke got acclimated, it was icy cold, but his body got accustomed and he was able to stroke out to the middle.. Once in the center, he felt the strength of the current, it was much faster than he had anticipated.

He would have to work hard to prevent being swept down the river. He swam upstream vigorously. At first he was doing an overhand crawl and then flipped over on his back and swam, enjoying floating beneath the cloudless blue sky overhead. His mind relaxed as he worked hard to combat the current.

"Bubba, Bubba?" Liz's voice was loud, and shrill until it became a shriek.

"Bubba? Where are you? " She and Peg had been getting the picnic barbeque ready and were watching the kids from a distance while preparing lunch. She had lost sight of Bubba.

"Help, Bubba's missing!" She was frantic. Luke barrel rolled from his back stroke to a crawl and swam frantically toward the shore.

Bubba was the tallest of the children and as Luke stroked he became aware that Bubba was not visible. He was not in the wading area. As he took his breath he kept his head under the water and tried to locate Bubba. The water was clear and the sun was reflecting off the rock bottom. The water was about six feet deep, and got more shallow until it was three feet.

Up ahead and to the right he saw Bubba. He was floating under the water with his back to the bottom and his face to the sky. Luke was windmilling his arms and swimming as fast as he could. He was hovering over Bubba and looking into his open pale blue eyes.

Bubba blinked when he saw Luke above him and held out his arms. A line of bubbles came out of Bubba's mouth as he tried to call out to Luke for help. He was in the current and drifting towards the raging water.  Bubba kept opening his mouth trying to say something. Luke came to a halt, grabbed him and stood up with Bubba in his arms about thirty feet from shore.

"I got him." He called out. "He's okay." Bubba was okay, he was coughing and spitting out water, but he had not been under long and had swallowed only a small amount of water. Luke held him tight in both arms helping him to shore.

Liz came running to the stream and in her haste she lurched into Luke knocking him off balance. She managed to calm herself enough to grab Bubba while sobbing and gasping for air at the same time. Tears filled her eyes as she stared at Bubba and then at Luke.

"Thank you, thank you." she sobbed in a shrill loud voice.

"Nothing to it! I was close by and I came to him quickly. He was ace up and drifting, floating, choking and spittin water."

Luke pointed to the spot in the water where he had found Bubba floundering. Bubba was small and it had been easy. By luck he had found the boy early before it was truly dangerous.

"Well I am sure glad you were there, another ten feet and he would have been caught in the stream and heading down river." It was Dean standing on the bank. He heard the scream and came running back. "Damn if I ain't beholden to you."

Liz made her way back to shore and soon they were all standing together in a circle. Liz and Dean were taking turns hugging Bubba and looking at Luke. A quiet came over everyone, no one knew what to say and for a while there was a silence.

Luke was embarrassed, it had been an easy thing to do, something anyone would have done. It wasn't much. Just being in the right place at the right time. Nothing much he thought.

They all went to the tables and sat without speaking while Bubba began to romp around willy nilly as if nothing had happened. He grabbed onto Luke's leg just as he had the night they first met and held on tight.

"My friend." That was all he said the rest of the day but he said it and he kept repeating it. Everyone saw Bubba was devoted to Luke.

Bubba had guessed how close to death he had been. Luke felt a little sheepish as the women wanted to make a fuss over him. He felt like anyone would have done it, but they hushed him.

"No one but you could have done it, you were the only one close enough to get there in time."

Al cooked up the hamburgers and dogs. The ladies brought chips, fruit, and pie. Luke asked Darla to play horseshoes and they had a game at the pit away from the others. She had played before and she knew the rules so she taught Luke.

She beat him several times with ease. Up close he noticed how right he had been about her beauty. He guessed she was a little older than he was. As time passed, he started to feel comfortable with her. She was relaxed and calm even though they were alone together for the first time. He felt excited but did not feel awkward. That was unusual, and had never happened before when he was first getting to know a girl.

"Are you from around here?" he asked.

"Naw, I came here awhile back." She smiled at him coyly. Luke sensed she had a secret. What was it?

"Where are you from?" He had figured that she hadn't grown up in Bodfish. She had no local family anyone knew about. Why would a beautiful young woman move to a place like this?

"Why did you come to Bodfish? Bakersfield has a lot more to offer? "Why Bodfish?"

"Why did you come here? Where are you from?" She turned it around on him. Whatever she was hiding, she wanted to keep hiding it.

"Los Angeles, but I think you already know that." He always said he was from Los Angeles, but in truth he was from a small beach town. Huntington Beach. Everyone knew where Los Angeles was so it made it easier. He wondered if she was playing a game with him. What are her rules he wondered?

"Los Angeles, now that's a sprawling  city." She smiled again. Expressive waves of joy radiated out of her face when she smiled. It made him feel like getting to know her. It was like she was always happy. Luke felt the conversation warming up when a woman's voice interrupted.

"Everyone come down here, I got something to say." It was Sue.

She was standing on the top of the park table and yelling at everyone through cupped hands. "Come on Down!" They all joined her, after all she was Don's wife and that commanded respect. They all believed it was her money keeping everything afloat. If Don was the King, then Sue was the Queen.

"I wanted you all together in one place to save time. That's why I planned this picnic."

She had her hands on her hips, and was looking rather grave, she had something important to say.

"Don will be back in two days. He is bringing a banker and a potential new partner. So far this project has been nothing but spending. All the money has been going out. No money is being made, and I am not sure that any will ever be made the way we are going." She paused and waited for the gravity of the statement to fill their minds.

"We are in trouble. Having no money coming in is a problem. Don and I got monthly payments going out and we been gettin tight."

The stuntmen exchanged glances, they shared the same thought, "thank God for the slide. It will solve everything. "

"Don, bless his heart, is set on making this town a spot where people can come to visit and spend their money. But to me it's just an old junk yard, now an old junkyard filled up with old buildings. I don't think Don's vision will ever happen." She paused, and turned to Al. "But I am committed to help!"

"Al, he wants you to perform the Western show you promised together and stage it in two days. Can you be ready to do that?"

She tapped her foot and snapped at the two "stuntmen" waiting for an answer.

"In two days?" Al stammered. "An act ready in two days?"

"You been talking bout it for two years, so now is the time. We need to have your show now. You got these two boys, plus I know Darla would like to be part, and of course your wives must help. And you got Charlie. Damn horse gotta be able to do something other than eat."

As far as Sue was concerned the matter was settled, there would be a western show in two days when the money men came to visit.

"That's bout it, I will let you know when I hear more from Don." When she was finished she climbed down and left, leaving the hardy little band to contemplate their futures in Bodfish.

They finished eating and cleaned up the waste from the picnic, but not before Luke managed to ask Darla out to dinner with him. He had the five dollars from the tour in his sock. It was saved for an event like this and he was lucky to have the chance to treat her. Darla smiled bewitchingly , and said yes, with a little twinkle in her eye.

"I'll meet you at the café at 7:30. " he managed to say without anyone else hearing. She just nodded and his heart skipped a beat. Her hand brushed against his every so lightly and he felt like an electric bolt had gone through his body.

"7:30," was all she said and nodded in the affirmative.

Chapter Nineteen

The hardy band of stuntmen watched as Sue and Darla left the picnic grounds. Sue was in a huff, she didn't like confrontations and it had been hard for her to deal with the problem. The situation was desperate and she had done her best to make that clear to everyone. The ball was in their court now!

"Don't that beat all. Don wants a western show, can you believe it?" Dean was irritated and resented he was being held accountable. He had always been along for the ride. This was foreign territory, producing a western show was Al's domain.

"I think I still got the script for the one we did at the Circle Star. I'll find it. It ain't complicated." Al shook his head knowing it would not be easy. These guys were green.

"Okay. I'm in." Luke was sky high. It was what he had been wanting all along.

It was a chance to break into the movies! It was why he had come! It had begun to happen. It seemed to be heaven sent.

"The script was real simple. I done it a thousand times. We had a Sheriff- Luke that'll be you, I guess. Dean and I will be the bad guys. We'll come into town and rob the bank."

"You don't think I'm too young to be the sheriff?"

"Naw you'll be fine, besides we only need to do one performance. If we can pull it off everything will be fine, and Don don't know bout the slide yet. That is our ace in the hole. Once he sees it and hears Dean's plan, just imagine what he'll say. Our lives will become real easy again."

"What's my part?" Dean chimed in.

"We rob the general store or the bank or somethin'. Luke rides into town and catches us in the act. We take Darla hostage. Luke, you can ride ole Charlie can't you?"

"Yeah sure," Luke said with bravado, knowing that the only riding experience he had was a mule excursion at a state park ten years back. "Sure thing."

"We'll exchange fire and you'll shoot Dean dead. Then you and I will hand fight. I'll knock you down but you will keep getting up. Somehow we got to work Darla into it. You got to save her and then she falls in love with you." Al was waving his hands in the air illustrating as he spoke.

"That sounds kinda complicated. You say I die?" Dean asked.

"It's been awhile but that's kind of what I remember from the Circle Star script." Al answered.

"How does Charlie fit in again?" Dean had begun to worry, Charlie was his horse and he didn't want Luke to ride him.

"Two outlaws can't ride into town on one horse, or escape on one horse. So the sheriff has to ride in on the horse." Al defended the developing the plot line. It was clear to Al that the sheriff had to ride the horse. They only had one horse.

"Darla falls in love with me after I save her?" Luke guessed..

"Yeah, of course you're the hero. The hero always gets the girl." Al responded.

"Sounds simple, do I have to do anything to make her fall in love with me?" Luke asked, trying to be on board.

"Start by not asking stupid questions." Al snapped.

As Al was outlining the story, Luke imagined himself with the shotgun in one hand and Charlie's reigns in the other. He and Charlie burst on the scene at full gallop! He pulls up in a sudden stop and leaps off. There is a gun battle, he shoots Dean and then wins a fist fight to save Darla's honor.

"What does Darla do while I am busy shooting Dean?" Luke asks.

"She's standing rooting for you. You're the damn hero." Al was irritating poor Luke.

"Do you ride well enough to come in at full speed and jump off Charlie shooting?" Dean interrupted, sounding fearful, he had never seen Luke ride, and Charlie was getting old. Luke nodded his head yes.

"Charlie, don't move that fast anymore. He has gotten a bit lame." Now Dean was worried about his horse. "I had Charlie a long time, he is like family."

"We all got to do our part. Charlie has to charge up like he means it. Can't have him limp up either, won't be convincing if he acts like he's a hunnert and one year old." Al was annoyed. His "script" called for an urgent rescue and nothing less could be considered. "Why are you all asking so many questions?"

"It ain't up to me, Charlie has to do it, and Charlie don't read no scripts." Dean glared at Al but it was to no avail.

"We'll give it a dry run. See how it goes. For now, I say he's charging in. It's a start. I got a script somewhere at the house. Just gotta find it." Al motioned it was time to leave so he could get to work sculpting his upcoming masterpiece.

Luke's little voice kept reminding him that he had never ridden a horse, a mule in a state park did not count. He ignored the voice. Hell's bells, he told the voice, you gotta start somewhere and life is about taking chances. The whole reason he came to Bodfish was to find out what he could do with his life. He was not here to listen to his fears.

They gathered up the remains of the picnic and headed for the trucks. As they did, Bubba chased after Luke wanting to ride in the back with his hero. Bubba clamped his arms around Luke like a squid about to devour its kin.

"My friend." Bubba repeated his mantra.

Luke tried to shake him loose. But it was no dice, the kid's grip was iron tight. To make matters worse, Bubba's was wiping a continuous river of snot all over Luke's pants. Luke reluctantly had to accept his fate. Only a crowbar to the side of his little noggin could free him.

"You're Bubba's new best friend." Liz laughed.

"The pants needed to be washed," Luke smiled weakly at Liz.

Getting across the parking lot was slow work. Bubba was a dead weight and had become a forty five pound peg leg. Luke had to hop the entire way. It was nothing compared to the challenge of climbing into the back of the truck itself. Even with the gate down it was a matter of difficult logistics. Luke calculated the various angles of entry with Bubba attached to his leg. One wrong move and he feared he would bash the little guy's skull on the truck gate. Luke settled on swinging his leg gingerly onto the bed of the truck and crawling up into the back while dragging Bubba with him.

Al pulled up alongside and stuck his head out the window and shouted,

"Let's meet tomorrow morning at seven at set, I'll have the script done. You'll all need to learn your lines and I'll show you how to stunt fight cowboy style."

"Alright,Yippee-Ki-Yeah!" Luke let out a howl. He was closing in on his goal to perform in the movies.

As Dean pulled out Luke and his new best friend sat in the back joined like Siamese twins.Together, they headed home, bouncing up and down in unison as Dean hit pothole after unrepaired pothole. Luke suffered in silence.

When Dean pulled up to the front Bubba was still latched to Luke's leg and thigh. Luke struggled to stand upright.

"Dean, he's your kid, do something!" Luke was nearing the end of his rope.

"Bubba, Luke doesn't have a refrigerator in his room. He has no ice cream in the jailhouse and if you don't let go you won't get any tonight." It was a bolt of inspiration!

Bubba gazed around in a panic. This was bad news. It was a difficult choice. Reluctantly Bubba let go. In the end ice cream saved the day.

Luke hopped out of the truck. He was a free man. In desperation Bubba stood and whimpered with his arms open hoping Luke would return and submit to his loving grasp.

"My friend, My friend," Bubba called out from the truck. Dean pulled away with his engine backfiring and muffling Bubba's whimpering. Luke waved goodbye, and savored his escape.


Chapter Twenty

Luke made his way to the jailhouse to change his clothes. His imagination shifted ahead to his dinner with Darla. He gave each one of his shirts a quick sniff, they were all dirty. He had to decide which one was his cleanest dirty shirt and slipped into it. He felt the need to shower. If his clothes could not be clean, at least he could be.

"Only decent thing to do." He said to himself. He retrieved the sock with the $5.00 bill, if he was lucky it would cover dinner. He had a bit extra in case it didn't. "Can't ask Darla for money."

When Luke arrived he found Al digging through a stack of boxes. Paper and documents were littered everywhere. Al wasdesperate.

"What's up?" Luke asked.

"Looking for the script. It's in one of these boxes, I think." Documents were scattered everywhere. "Don't remember which one it is in. Wanna help me?"

Luke realized it was an order not a question. He shuffled his feet and focusedat his shoes,

"I need to take a shower."

"A shower? What for? I need your help now." Al growled.

"He's got a date tonight." Peg came from the kitchen. "Ain't that right Luke?"

"How did you know?" Luke was taken back.

"Darla told me." Peg had on her apron. She had a dish towel in her hand. "It's okay. I understand." She had a sly smile on her face.

"Well I thought I should clean up a bit." Luke kept looking at his feet.

"That's a real fine idea, go right ahead." Peg motioned him towards the bathroom.

"A date with Darla?" Al was still looking for his script. "Tonight? I thought we'd make an early start on memorizing the script."

The sheriff only has a few lines and the bad guys have even less. Then the sheriff shoots Dean. That leaves you and Luke to fight." Peg had en it dozens of times when she was first dating Al

"Yeah, but he needs to do it right." Al would not give in.

"Luke will learn it quick." Peg recalled how simple it all was, and added, "he will do fine." She nodded for Luke to go take his shower.

"I ain't worried bout the lines. It's the shooting and the fight scene. But I guess we will have to do that tomorrow." Al knew he had to give in on this one. He nodded towards the shower.

"I have to shoot Dean? With this gun?" Luke held up the rifle he had been carrying with him all summer. "I ain't never fired this. Had no reason to shoot it off."

"Don't take much. Ya aim and pull the trigger, give it to me I'll show you." The long afternoon of fishing in the hot sun and drinking beer had affected his judgment. Al grabbed the gun, pointed it at the wall and pulled the trigger.

"Bam" Al staggered backwards, stunned by the recoil.

A shock wave shook the house. They all gasped in stunned surprise! A jagged hole eight inches had been torn open in the living room wall. The hole became a tunnel stretching from the front wall all the way into the adjoining backbedroom. The line of sight continued through the room all the way to the back wall of the house.

There was a gaping hole over their bed exposing the backyard to the street. Luke could see the picket fence in the yard.

"Geez those are thin walls." Al gasped. He walked up and peered down the line of sight.

"Woman, I thought I told you to put blanks in Luke's gun." Al said, shaking his head as he surveyed the damage.

"Why would I do that?" Peg had loaded the gun back when it was first given to Luke. "no one said anything about blanks. Besides that was months ago."

"Well that's what I wanted." Al had to blame someone, anyone. Why not Peg? In desperation Al tried to make It clear, she would have to answer for the damage done.

"Wanted, shmanted, you think I read minds?" Peg would have none of it.

Luke had always assumed the gun was loaded. Why would it have blanks?

"Damn glad I didn't shoot Dean with it." He checked the wall, whistled and shook his head. Then he remembered Darla was waiting. "I'm goin to take that shower."

"What in the hell am I goin to tell Don? " Al kept looking at Peg waiting for her to come clean and admit it. Shit! Why didn't she admit it was her fault he had blown a hole in the wall.

"Better yet, what are you gonna tell Sue?" Peg reminded him who the real boss was.

"You're a woman, better you tell her. She'll go easy on you." Al felt like begging.

"We'll tell em the truth, you thought it was not loaded but it was." Peg insisted. "Or you will fix the wall before anyone sees it. Then you won't have to tell them anything."

Luke left them discussing who was responsible and how it was to be resolved and took a steaming hot shower. He borrowed Al's razor. It was then he realized he hadn't been shaving or bathing all summer. Funny how a girl changes everything he thought. "Got into some bad habits."

Luke's "clean" clothes now seemd much dirtier since he had cleaned up. He wished he had washed them. Al kept looking for his long lost script. The hole in the wall loomed and Al was sweating, and swearing to himself. The pressure was building.

 "Got to be here somewhere, I didn't throw it away." He glanced up at Luke. "Tomorrow, first thing. Be ready to go."

"Sure thing." Luke headed out to meet Darla.

Bodfish was a small place. The center of town featured a diner, and the local bar that got considerable action due to its being the only one in town. There is a gas station, with a mechanic on duty and the country store that sells bait for the visiting fisherman.

If you walk a couple of blocks in any direction you will find the residences where the people of Bodfish have lived for generations. Most everyone knows most everyone else, and people think it is normal and right to know everyone else's business. It is simple to follow what everyone else is doing. So everyone always does.

There is a small church and its bells rang every Sunday morning calling the faithful to worship. The church is tucked off at the side of town, and it does double duty by serving to house the school. All classes sit in the same room, and one teacher gives all the lessons. There had been some talk of getting a bus to cart the kids into Bakersfield. Bakersfield was a long drive and the plan was not practical. As a result the small school has served the town of Bodfish as long as anyone can remember.

The motel where Darla changed the bed sheets, and ran the front desk was only busy during the summer months. Tourists did not flock into Bodfish, but if someone did visit, the motel was the only place to stay. The "Vacancy" sign was almost always blinking and it was again tonight.

Luke's walk from set to the cafe took five minutes. He was excited as he approached the front door. He had never eaten at the diner and had no idea what they served or what it cost. But he had learned that if you were going to arrange a date in Bodfish you had two choices. The diner or the bar. He picked the diner. He had been warned  the bar food was terrible.

Luke walked in and noted how empty it was. There was a line of swivel seats where a person could sit by himself at the counter. The only patron in the place was sitting at the counter with his back to the door and did not react when Luke entered.

Luke sat at the dining room with its red naugahyde booths and shining black mica table tops. Ceiling fans were turning and they made the room feel ten degrees cooler. Luke's booth had a streaked bay window. He wondered what would happen if he asked to have the window cleaned. Nothing much he figured, so he sat down and said nothing.

Most of the paintings featured cowboys and cows on the plains.  Luke's table featured a velvet painting in a black velvet canvas  depicting dogs playing poker. The dogs wore visors, and were smoking cigars.

Luke checked out the cards in their hands. A bulldog smoking a huge cigar was holding the dead man's hand. It was the same hand Wild Bill Hickok had when he was murdered by a child in a bar in Wyoming. Aces and Eights! The bull dog was "all in." It was the most prominent painting in the place. The Bulldog was about to score a huge pot!

Darla had not yet arrived and Luke saw from the clock on the wall that he was early.

"Better a half hour early than a half hour late for a first date," was his thought.

He allowed himself to realize how anxious he was, and how much he was looking forward to this chance to be alone with Darla. His life would be better without Bubba hanging on his leg or Sue watching and lecturing from the table top.

"Want some coffee?" The waitress approached him.

"Coffee. I'll have some, black." He picked up a newspaper on the counter, and opened it. It was a Bakersfield paper, the farm section was on top and open. He read a story about a local pest infestation that was causing the cotton crop to have a major problem.

"Damn bugs are everywhere." The waitress commented.

"I am expecting a friend so I will wait for a while and order when she comes."

She nodded, "I have the sports page, do you want it? It has all the scores. The featured article covers the Bakersfield football team. They are doing well as usual. So is my team, the Dodgers."

"Sure, why not. Got to be better than the cotton crop." Just then Darla pulls up in an old Nash. She was early too. She parked right in front, and waved to him as she got out.

"On second thought There's my friend, don't bother with the paper."

Darla was wearing some tight fitting pants and a sweater that hugged her breasts. Luke liked how curvy she was. Other than her legs, he had not formed much of an impression of her figure which was now minted in his mind like a shiny new coin. "Damn" he thought. "She's sexy!"

She came straight to his table and sat down.

"Hi! again," she smiled..

The waitress brought the menus. It was 'country' prices! He was relieved he had enough, and it would not be a problem. He exhaled a little tiny breath,

"Do I make you nervous?" Darla asked. She was used to being given the once over.

"Not at all, but working at the movie set, I have limited funds so I am glad the menu prices are reasonable."

They surveyed the menu and each decided on having a chicken fried steak and the waitress appeared and took their order.

"Do they pay you?" Darla asked.

"No, I am working for room and board. This will be the first meal out since I got here."

"I was surprised when you showed up. I never thought they would hire an employee. They are all struggling to get by, so it did not seem possible."

"That so?" Luke had not thought about it much. "Struggling?" Until Sue had appeared with her ominous news their lack of funds had escaped his notice. It had been obvious to Darla all along.

"Yeah Peg and Liz are always worried. They have a little help from the county welfare relief and they stay for free, but that's it. They gotta cover the food and gas and booze. They're running out of savings." She was still looking at the menu. Since they had already ordered Luke wondered if she was trying to avoid making eye contact.

"Are you from here?" Luke makes small talk. She didn't respond so he tried a different line,"You sure know a lot about what is going on in Don's operation."

"Heavens no, like I told you, I came here from Bakersfield. I been here a little over a year but there are no real secrets here. Everybody knows what goes on in Bodfish. I don't know any more about the movie set than anyone else."

"Why come here? There is not much here."

"That's why I came here. There's not much going on here." Luke thought she was being mysterious.

"I heard you went to college, what would make you come to this place?" Luke persisted.

Darla let out a sad wistful sigh.and shook her head. She lowered her voice so no one nearby could hear what she had to say.

"I need to be honest with you. I'm married. My husband was in the army. He went off to the war and when he came back he wasn't the same. At first in the early years they didn't draft married men so I think he married me to get out of the draft. But after we got married, they changed the rules. They took him away screaming and clawing."

"Really?" Luke was disappointed to hear she was married.

"They let married men with children stay deferred but they started drafting married men without kids. So he started tryin to get me pregnant. He tried real hard but it didn't work. I think he blamed me for letting him be drafted. I couldn't get pregnant. I didn't want to be with him. So he got drafted and went off to fight."

"I have always avoided married women. Been careful not to get involved with one." Luke regretted saying it the moment it was out of his mouth. Her red hair and green eyes were intoxicating, and he did not care at this moment if she was married or not. "Why did you marry him? Sounds like he was using you."

"I kind of blamed myself for not getting pregnant. He tried real hard. He said it was my fault it didn't happen. He was a different man before he went off to the war. A much better man, I would say even a man I respected. But when he came back he was crazy and I was afraid of him. He was insanely jealous. So I ran away."

It occurred to Luke she was an "older woman". Judging by her face he thought she might be ten years older than he was. He knew she had been through a few rough roads.

"Why not file for a divorce?" Luke asked. He had not even considered the idea she might be married. A shiver of doubt ran through his mind about getting involved. What should he do?

"I was afraid he might kill me. I didn't do anything to cause it, but he was so jealous. So I came here, he'll never find me here. I don't want to talk about him. It makes me sick. Can we talk about something else? He is crazy jealous." Her voice shook and she turned away and stopped making eye contact again. A long uncomfortable silence ensued.

Luke remained silent, unsure of what to say. Then Darla started again.

"I got papers filed and I am waiting for them to become final. When they are, I can leave the area. Right now I gotta stay out of sight but close to Bakersfield.

Luke took a deep breath and paused for a moment. He was captivated by her, even if she was married. He sensed she had been looking to end her marriage long before he showed up.

"I heard you will be a part of our show? Do you have time? I mean with your job and all?" He changed the subject.

"I am going to try. Do you think there is any chance tourists will ever come here to visit that old place?" She wrinkled her nose signaling how doubtful she was about the idea.

"Not sure, never thought about it much. I came to learn to be a stuntman and have a shot at the movies. I think that might work. I hope it happens."

"All the boys have to do is drink beer and whiskey all day. Don thinks Al has some movie producers but he don't. Peg told me he was once in a John Wayne movie. He got shot off a horse. They put his name on the screen as an extra. That's about it."

"Yeah, I've been waiting for the training he promised." Luke feared she might be right. " I believe I am going to get it."

"He got fired for drinking on his job at the Circle Star. Can you imagine him driving a cab around Los Angeles picking up fares in the middle of the night drunk? That's a scary picture." Darla grimaced as she described the scene.

"Yeah that's how I met him. I jumped in his cab one night." Luke felt a little sheepish.

"Sue has some money but Don has almost run through it. That's why he went to town." She frowned and gave Luke a "I am sorry to break the bad news" to you shrug

"I guess I haven't been seeing this at all." I now believe the whole operation has been run on a shoestring with little or no funds behind it. His inner voice spoke up: You see what you want to see and disregard the rest.

"If Don can't come up with some money, real money, it is almost certain you boys will have to find outside work. Al will go back up in the mountains and try to find his lost mine. He is always talking about it."

Darla had a lot to say and was determined to say it. "Has Al asked you to help find it?"

"You know about the lost mine?" Her revelation surprised Luke. "I thought it was a secret."

"Not to anyone who knows Peg and Al. He went up there for a week a year ago. Left Peg alone. She and I became friends when he left searching for it. "

"When he told me the story he was shit faced drunk. I figured it was more fiction than fact." Now Luke realized Al had been right on target. Up to now he had written it off as a crazy fantasy.

"Well this time you should have taken him seriously." She put her hand on Luke's and stroked it. "It is a fact! There is a gold mine out there with lots of gold still in it. I know it for sure." Darla had his attention.

"It seemed crazy. Wild talk." Luke was surprised.

"I'll bet there are a lot of abandoned old mines in those hills. Finding an abandoned mine is easy to do. Finding the one with gold still in it, that's the trick." Darla had his hand in hers and squeezed it. "Al found the wrong ones."

"You mentioned that you know something about it? Why?" Luke heard the sincerity in her voice. He wondered if the story of the gold mine was real. What did she know?

"You need to be careful." She was concerned and was trying to warn him. "I like you. I can't see you spending your life here sleeping in that dirty old jail working for free. You can do more with your life." She continued rubbing his hand as she spoke.

"Coming here began an opportunity. It might still be. My stuntman training is about to start." He stared into her eyes.

"Al told you about Edward, the miner with the map. I knew Edward better than Al knew Edward." Darla changed the subject in a voice just above a whisper changing the subject.

"Edward? Who is he again?"

"Edward is the old miner who gave Al the map. Did he show you." She had a calm intensity and a deadly serious side to her.

"When Edward came down out of the mountains he had the "valley fever." He stayed at our motel and tried to recover. He had no one, so I tried to help him."

"Valley fever? What is it?" Luke was paying close attention now.

"No one knows, but many people catch it and die. Edward had it. It affects the lungs, making it difficult to breathe. It's a virus, breeds in the valley." Darla's head shook remembering the suffering it had inflicted on the old man.

"Why didn't he go to the hospital?"

"It's like the flu but it gets worse quick. I had it once and it was hard on me. I was laid up but if you're older or a child it can kill you." Darla answered.

"So, how did Al take possession of the map?" Luke wondered.

"Al met him in the bar on the day Edward died. He asked Al back to his room and told him about it and showed him the map. I think Edward must have known he wasn't gonna make it through the night." She paused to let the story sink in.

"Wow, so it was an old miner in town. But how do you know there was gold there?"

Darla motioned for Luke to come closer. She whispered in his ear.

"After Al left Edward's room that night, Edward called me to come in. He gave me a sack and told me it was mine to keep. He asked me to stay with him. I stayed until he died."

"What happened then?" Luke asked.

"I held his hand while he was awake. He told me he had hit a mother lode. But then he went to sleep and never woke up." She paused. "It was the first time I saw someone die."

"He gave you a sack of gold ore?" Luke was engrossed in her story.

"When I opened it, it was ten ounces of gold nuggets and shavings." Darla whispered.

"It was real?" Luke said, amazed.

"Yeah, he said he wanted to thank me for being there. I took it to the essayer and it was real." She went silent. "Worth a lot of money. Still got some of it."

The waitress brought them each a chicken fried steak. They ate in relative silence. Luke tried to absorb the many viewpoints that Darla had expressed. He noticed she was always looking at him when she thought he was looking away. "I wonder if...." his mind had jumped ahead to ideas of making love with her.

They finished and Luke paid the bill, He had enough left to leave a small tip. "There goes the first and perhaps the last dollar to be made at Silver City." He shook his head. It was not a hopeful thought, was he projecting the future of the Town?

"Let's take a ride out to the Lake. I know a spot." Darla offered. Luke agreed instantly. As they headed off she put on a country station and soon the voice of Patsy Cline, singing "I go out walking after midnight" was filling the air.

Darla pulled down a narrow dirt road lined with woods on either side.

"There's a quiet spot just up ahead. We'll be alone and it has an expansive view of the lake."

"My Dad had a Nash when I was growing up." Luke made small talk. some conversation. "He always said it was a reliable car.""

"It still runs, kinda old and they don't make em anymore." Darla responded.

It was a cloudy and moonless night, and there was little star light. The road was black and difficult to see. Darla had to concentrate to keep the car from sliding off into the brush. She pulled out onto a flat ledge with the lake laid out below. Luke saw the lake shimmering ahead in Darla's headlights. When she parked and turned them off the shimmering vanished.

She turned down the radio and it got quiet. Some clouds moved and the lake reappeared in the star light. He could see the water line in the distance. A sliver of moon appeared from behind the clouds. It wasn't as dark a night as he thought.

Darla slid over on the seat and was on top of him in an burst. Heropen mouth was wet and clamped on his. She put her tongue in his mouth, and they began exchanging tongues, darting in and out. He responded by kissing her hard and then soft, and then hard again. His blood began to boil and he felt his penis getting hard between his legs.

She searched for his zipper, found it, and soon his manhood was out and she was stroking it, up and down. He had his left hand on her breast and was massaging it with alternating squeezes. Her nipples were jutting out in her bra, and were hard. She was aroused. He fingered them until they stood out firmly. He wanted to put them in his mouth,

Darla pulled her sweater over her head and was braless. Her breasts were firm and full. They bounced in the moonlight, while she tugged on her pants, struggling to get them off. Her long slender legs were now spread before him. She took her panties off.

Nothing like this had ever happened to him before. She made the first move and he had to try to keep up. He had his pants half undressed and was finding it awkward to get in a position where he could penetrate her. He slowed down and got naked. It was cramped and he struggled.

"Let's move to the back." There was not enough room in the front seat but Darla was in a hurry and she was irritated. She did not want to stop, not even for a moment.

"Okay, hurry." She climbed over the seat and brushed him in the mouth with her foot as her legs and ass disappeared into the back seat. Luke scurried over, and landed on top of her in the process. His full weight pressed on her, pinning her.

"Ouch." She was annoyed. The seat was not long enough. Their legs were too long and Luke was still finding it hard to get into a position where he could maintain his balance. He reached down and found her clitoris and began to rub it in a circle. She moaned and changed motion. He started to rub up and down and back and forth.

She responded and lifted her pelvis onto his finger forcing it into her opening. She began pumping, forcing his fingers deeper into her vagina. She wrapped herself around his hand until she was forcing herself on him. He rubbed the inside wall of her vagina. She moaned.

"Sit in the seat and I'll get it in you." She knew what she wanted and since he was struggling she took command. He sat back, penis erect and let her take over. She climbed on top and with one hand inserted him into her wet and warm cunt. Even though it was dark, her full breasts were visible hanging in his face with both nipples erect as she began to bounce up and down on him.

"Those are beautiful, beautiful." Luke was overwhelmed with admiration.

She was increasing the force and speed of her bouncing motion. Her breathing increased and soon she was making groaning noises. He was pumping backhard. He got her left breast in his mouth for a few moments but the speed with which she was moving made it hard to keep it there.

He wrapped both hands around her buns and squeezed them pinching them. He started helping her to move up and down in a smooth piston like dance. A light went on in his brain and he felt his penis exploding in rapid bursts and contractions. She reacted and rammed her body downward, tightening her vagina squeezing him in quick fluid contractions.

His penis kept expanding while she was tightening and contracting. They pounded against each other. Their automatic convulsions repeated until they found themselves gasping and struggling for more air in their lungs. Their hot wet fluids melded and mixed until they reached a moment where all they could do was hold each other and the storm of young love.

Luke drifted in the calm peaceful joy of their having had a mutual orgasmic climax. Darla lay quivering for a long time, making little noises that he took to be satisfaction.

After a bit, his mind settled back into the moment and it occurred to him he was naked, with a naked woman laying beside him, alone, in an unlocked car, in the dark, in a deserted isolated spot.

"What if it is not deserted?" "What if someone is out there?" He thought of Jarvis and Jake and then whoever else there might be living in this place. The thought came pounding in on him without mercy. "I am defenseless." He did not want her to go to sleep. He shook her, bringing her back to life.

"We should get dressed."

A feeling they were being watched slipped like a shadow into his awareness and became prevalent and unshakable, he locked the car doors.

"Let's go home," he said.

She was annoyed that he wanted to get away from her right after the climax. But the truth was he was feeling vulnerable. He was naked in a strange place. He had the strange feeling they were being watched. Getting away from her was the farthest thing from his mind. But he couldn't shake the feeling they were being watched and so he wanted to leave.

As they drove home Luke pondered what had happened. He never had an experience like this one. Most women were shy, or at least pretended to be. Most avoided having sex and played difficult to get. He often was the aggressor and found his attempts to move things into sexual realms had been rebuffed or slowed down to a near freeze. Kissing, hand holding and petting were the usual limits of affection young women allowed. For a brief second he wondered how old she was.

He had never had a woman be so aggressive and so interested in being with him. He thought she was at least ten years older than he was. The fact sunk in. The age difference intensified things, and was becoming more obvious.

He studied her profile and thought she has far more experience than anyone I have ever been with before. He liked it, he liked it a lot. He thought "hell this is our first time alone together, what is the second going to be like?" He wondered why he had avoided older women in the past.


Chapter Twenty One-

Luke awoke to the sound of a fist pounding on his door. Darla, and the delightful night he spent with her, was still fresh on his mind. He put it aside and faced the new day. Al was at his door and in his face. Al had Peg and Dean and Charlie in tow. Charlie was saddled up and ready to ride. Al was holding out Luke's shotgun.

"You were in such a hurry last night you forgot your gun." At the sight of the gun, memories of the hole Al had blown in the wall came flooding back to him.

"Darla ain't coming. Said she didn't have much sleep last night." Al gave Luke a wink that said I know what you have been up to ol'buddy.

"Too bad, the show would be better with her in it." Luke avoided eye contact with Al. Let him guess and wonder, he thought.

"Peg is gonna stand in and be the damsel in distress." Peg nuzzled up next to Al, and for a moment reminded Luke of Olive Oil in a popeye cartoon.

"Nothin much to your walls. Shame what happened." Luke commented. "How you gonna tell Don?"

"I'll tell him you had one too many drinks. He'll understand." Al had settled on making Luke the guilty party.

Luke supported Peg, she had dug her heels in and would not take the blame. At that moment Al decided it had to be Luke's problem.

"Excuse me? How do you figure that?" Luke took the rifle and glared at Al.

"You were drunk, you slipped and blew a hole plum through the whole house. It was right careless of you." All tried hard to command him to accept his fate.

"I see." Luke began considering his options "Is the gun loaded now?"

"It's got blanks now! Loaded it myself to be sure." Al twitched looking for resignation in Luke's voice, and not defiance.

"That was quite a hole you blew in Al's wall last night." Dean joined in repeating Al's theme. "You should be more careful."

"Hole I blew? I blew? I had nothin to do with it." It was all much too! Peg wouldn't be an obedient wife and take the blame, so Al had turned on him. He was expected to be the fall guy.

"Now, now, it's okay, Don will forgive you. You are just a kid. Kids are allowed to make mistakes." Al was firm, but fair. If Luke stepped up and admitted to his carelessness, he would be forgiven. Al could have nothing to do with it. He was the senior man. The man everyone counted on. Al paused and waited for Luke to do the right thing and accept accountability.

"Did you find the script?" Luke sighed, changed the subject and decided to move on.

"Naw, I tossed it out. I member it how it went." Al was relieved. His ploy had worked, Luke was resigned to his fate.

"I'll try and repair the damage to the wall. Don don't come over to the house much so if we're lucky you won't have to face him, or Sue either for that matter." Al offered up his hope as consolation.

Luke pondered what he would say to Don if confronted. He decided he would just leave it to Al. After all, Al was the head stuntman and was responsible for the movie set.

"As I see it, you and ol' Charlie are hiding at the end of the street. We'll bust out of the store wearing masks dragging Peg behind us. She'll scream for help and we'll be shootin' up the store. Dean will have a bag of money in his hand."

"You put blanks in both your guns, right?" Luke asked.

"Of course otherwise we'd shoot up the town and Don would be furious." Al was annoyed with Luke, first the kid blows a hole in my house, and now he doubts my integrity. This is my damn show. How dare he question me like that?"

"Just checking, wouldn't want something bad to happen. You know, like when I tripped and the gun went off in your living room." Luke grimaced. "I wouldn't want to make the same mistake twice." Getting along with Al was not easy.

"You're forgiven, young'un. The show must go on." Dean butted in.

"It's only a hole, no one died. Hell on a bad day, Al could have done it hisself."

"Dean's right, forget about the accident. The show is what counts. After we come out with guns blazing, you'll ride up as fast as you can firing. Jump off Charlie and shout for us to drop our gun." Al was excited.

"How fast do I have to ride?" Luke asked worriedly.

"Full speed! Dean will fire at you. He'll miss. When you shoot, he'll jump backwards actin like you shot him dead." Al ignored Luke's question.

"How do you make a horse gallop at full speed?" Luke asked again.

"You'll turn on me and I'll rush you and we'll fight. When you'll knock me out and win. That'll be the end." Al was anxious to move forward.

"If I'm going to fire this gun at Dean I want to be dead certain it has blanks." Luke said afraid.

"Shit test it out then." Al was wary, once they start to doubt you, you've lost control.

Luke spun on the nearest building and fired. Sure enough, it was a blank. The wall was unharmed and there was no recoil.

"Glad to see it. I feel better, knowing for sure." Luke let up a sigh of relief.

"Course, Nothin but packed powder in them casings, no pellets, nothin but powder" He handed Luke a replacement shell. "Now mount up and ride Charlie down to the end of the street."

"You gotta have a little faith, boy. " Dean echoed Al's enthusiasm and anxiety.

Luke took up Charlie's reins and pulled. Charlie did not budge. Luke tugged harder but Charlie still refused to step forward. Luke persisted but Charlie just kept trotting ignoring Luke. It was evident that Charlie had not yet read the script. He was unaware of his role in the drama.

Luke tried to act confident and in command. Charlie was unimpressed and did not acknowledge Luke's efforts. It was at that moment that Luke realized that Charlie was a lot taller than the mule he rode at the national park. "A lot taller."

Luke approached the challenge of mounting Charlie with caution. It felt awkward trying to sneak up on the calm unassuming animal. Charlie was imposing.

"He's so tall. Grab my rifle and hand it up to me. I'll try to mount." Luke needs help.

"Just put your foot in the stirrup and put a hand on the knob and swing up. You only need one hand." Al directed him. "Geese you're green. Ain't you never mounted a horse?"

With his shotgun in hand, Luke grabbed Charlie's saddle horn and tried to mount him. He swung his body upward with as much gusto as he could muster, and kicked his leg skyward. As he swung forward, the barrel of the shotgun caught and wedged under the saddle and stuck. It stopped Luke's momentum dead.

"Crap, I'm stuck." He tried to push forward using even more force but the gun was wedged in and dug ever deeper under the saddle.

"Careful boy, you'll fire again." Al tried to help Luke who was hanging half on and half off Charlie.

"You gotta put more arch and more swing in your leg. Try it again and try to kick the toe of your boot skyward." Dean offered some advice.

Luke took Dean's advice and kicked skyward with all his might. His toe landed dead center in Charlie's anus. Luke felt it penetrate and push several inches deep into the horse's rear.

The startled nag let out a loud screech and rose up on his hind legs. He bounced up and down several times on his back legs and kicked hard trying to fend off his attacker. Luke was thrown and landed hard, jamming his elbow into the ground,knocking the wind out of his lungs.

Bam! He fired the gun into Charlie's belly, and all hell broke loose! The would-be stuntmen rushed to calm Charlie who was certain that life as he knew it had come to an end.

"Not much of a horseman are you?" Al stood over Luke who was gasping for air.

Luke sucked and gasped and recovered.

"Never said I was." He answered.

"Never said you wasn't either. You gotta try again. Getting on the horse is the easiest part." Al helped Luke to his feet.

"Don't know." Luke felt shaky and weak. He realized at this critical point truthfulness might be an ally. "I'm not sure I'm up to it."

"Now is the time to try." Al was exasperated. "Ain't much to gettin on a horse."

Embarrassed, Luke tried again.

"Okay, but I need to have my hands free. I need you to take the shotgun for now." Once he had his hands free Luke swung up on Charlie's back. "See, not so bad. Gimme the gun and let's get on with it."

Luke yanked on the reins turning Charlie's head toward the end of the street and gave him a nudge. Charlie responded by beginning to walk towards the end of the street. After a few steps, he lost interest and stopped cold.

"Shit boy, give him a command, kick him a bit in the ribs and let him know what you want. Be the boss. He'll do it if you command him to do it." Al pushed Luke to act.

"Right." Luke kicked Charlie hard. Charlie was not interested. Nothing happened. He smacked him with the reins. Charlie remained oblivious.

"Get down from there. I have had enough. I'm changing the plan. I'll be the damn sheriff, you and Dean can be the robbers."

Luke could not dismount with the shotgun in his hand. He held out the gun and motioned that he needed help.

"Never seen anyone so green. Some stunt man you're gonna make. Can't dismount on a horse and can't get off one." Disgusted Al sent a stream of spit flying out in Luke's direction.

Mercifully, Dean took the shotgun and let Luke dismount. The smell of alcohol surrounded Dean like a fog bank. Luke inhaled, and was overwhelmed. Dean was having trouble keeping his balance and was leaning on Charlie for support. Luke guessed correctly that Dean was having trouble staying upright.

"I came here to learn. Never pretended to know everything." Luke responded. "At least I can stand up straight. Not like some people I know."

"Knock it off, No more bickering. We got a show to do. We gotta be perfect!" Al jumped up on Charlie and kicked him hard and they headed down the street. The old nag mustered a slow unsteady trot. They stationed themselves at the end of the street, Al called for them to begin. Dean and Luke went into the store, and then came out dragging Peg!

"Help! Help me!" she called out in her high scratchy voice.

"I'm commin!" Al shouted and kicked Charlie in the ribs expecting a gallop. Charlie stood frozen in his tracks. Al hit with his whip and swore at him. Charlie responded with a cautious step forward. Al swore at him and kicked him again, Charlie sauntered down the street. Nothing that Al did mattered to him. Al could not force him to move a step and lost patience. He pulled up way short of the band of robbers and jumped off, standing out in the middle of the street.

"Drop your guns". He yelled to the mob that was waiting halfway down the block.

There was a quick exchange of fire! Dean, stuck to the script, and fell face first to the ground pretending to be dead. Luke pretended to fire.

"You are out of bullets son, drop the gun." Al pointed the pistol at Luke's head. Peg pulled off to one side and got out of the way.

"Listen up, " Al broke character. He was no longer Al the actor, instead he had become Al the "director."

"At this point, you drop the gun and unsuspecting I'll let you rush me."

"From way down here? I think we're too far apart."

"Never you mind that part, You need to close in on me. I'll keep looking the other way and you can jump me and try to take my gun away."

"Okay, I got it." Luke dropped the gun and when Al let his guard down he rushed him. They met and Al whispered in Luke's ear.

"I am going to teach you how to fake a fight."

"Okay," Luke whispered back, holding onto Al like he was a dance partner. Then it hit Luke for the first time. Like Dean, Al reeked of beer and body order. It was overwhelming.

"I will clench my fist and swing at you. You keep your jaw jutted on my fist. I will pull back and my hand open will slap you while you roll your face away. It needs to appear and sound like you got hit.

Al whispered the plan to Luke who was in his arms and getting nauseous from the stench. Luke struggled to maintain his hug as they rolled on the street.

"Got it" Luke answered "I move toward your fist, then I pull back, then you slap at me and I roll my head, right?"

Luke repeated it. They stood, frozen, like statues. Luke's stomach knotted up. He tried to calm the urge to vomit.

"Right" Al answered.

Luke moved forward and tried to pull back in the same motion. It didn't work. Wham! Bam! Al hit him hard flush in the mouth. Spit flew, and snot ran down Luke's nose. He winced in pain.

"Got to roll back a little quicker Luke. Let's do it again. You gotta be quicker." Al insisted.

"Right" Luke said with eyes blinking, and a blinding pain shooting through his jaw. He was drowning in alcohol and body order. In the next instant, Al's fist was descending again at his exposed jaw. The scene repeated itself.

Bam! Al hit him again, harder this time. The rolling out of the way maneuver was not going well.

"Al you hit like a girl." Luke mocked Al and tried to shake the cobwebs out of his eyes. His jaw was exploding with pain.

"Not bad. It was better, You're getting quicker. You'll get this down soon enough." Al winced and shook his hand in the air trying to relieve the sting.

The combination of body odor and stale beer caught up to Luke. He vomited on Al's boots. Al was shocked and tried to shake the vomit off his boots.

"You're hitting me too hard, I need a break." Luke's jaw was throbbing and getting sore.

"You're a natural." Al rubbed his injured hand. "Never hit anything so firm before."

"I think some of my teeth are loose." Luke ran his tongue over a raw spot and spit out a little stream of blood. He sensed a lump was forming on the side of his face.

"Don't be a sissy, no place for a sissy in the stunt business. Sides, think about my hand, you ain't the only one hurtin." Al 's knuckles were raw and red.

"Yah, Your knuckles are red. Must hurt like hell." Luke rubbed his expanding jaw and leaned his head back. The beer and the stinking bodies of his fellow stuntmen had taken a toll.

"I think we got it down enough to show Don and his investors tomorrow." Al shook his sore hand and called it a day. "It's quitting time. We'll be fine. Woman, I need a beer."

Peg came running with her basket of beer. She was prepared to meet any emergency.

"I put some ice in the bucket this morning but it melted.You should put your hand in the bucket, It'd help reduce the swelling."

"Hard work deserves a reward." Al downed a beer. "Damn, I wish it was colder. It is a little warm. Soaking that hand is just what the Doctor ordered."

"You think our show will impress the banker?" Luke was worried! How would his face be by show time?

"You were great! Took a lickin and kept on kickin" Dean got up from watching Luke accept his beating.

"Yeah. Luke's a natural, leads with the jaw like he's done it his whole life." Al confirmed that with admiration he had never landed a punch on a harder jaw.

"It's good to know we're all set and ready to go." Dean slapped Al on the back for a job well done.

Chapter Twenty Two

Sue got word that Don was bringing an analyst from the bank, and an old construction partner, to survey all the properties and assess their values. She called another meeting.

"The man from the bank is going to inspect our houses and the movie set to determine what kind of "equity" we might have in them."

Sue stumbled as she said the word "equity" making it sound like it might be a swear word in ancient Greek. Whatever it meant, Don understood it, or at least seemed to and had made it clear it was the most important factor in determining their futures.

"Don said if you were all paying regular rent it would increase our "equity value." That's what we need. It is mighty important. We need a "fair market estimate" and you got to start carrying your weight! With that Sue hoped they understood and would cooperate. She was dead sure the days of rent free housing were about to end.

Peg and Liz sat and stared blankly back. "Equity" "Fair Market value". had made their heads spin. What in the world was she talking about? They had no idea.

"The loan officer thinks it is important to our getting approved for a future "line of credit." If you pull your weight and pay your share the bank will give us better terms. It sounded like she was reading gibberish and Like wondered if she had understood any of it.

"Damn" was all Al could think of to say.

To relax he went to the cabinet where he kept his whisky, pulled out a bottle and took a long gulp.

That was when Sue noticed the hole in the wall for the first time. She was so intent on explaining "equity" she had not yet focused on anything else. It startled her and she let out a huge gasp of air. Then her eyes popped out.

She walked over and stuck her head in the hole and followed the path to the back of the house where the hole expanded out into the yard and the street beyond.

"There is a hole in the wall. It goes plumb through the house and out to the backyard." Her mouth hung open for a second as she sounded the alarm. "We could almost climb through it."

"Yeah well Luke had a little accident. He was fooling around with the shotgun." Al named Luke as the culprit and took another swig from the bottle.

"I had nothin to do with it." Luke objected, even though he knew he was destined to be the fall guy.

"Fool was a bit greased, tripped on the rug and the gun went off as he fell. Thank God no one was in his line of sight." Al growled and glared at Luke.

"I did no such thing." Luke resisted again.

"Don't matter much how it happened. The bank officer is commin tomorrow. What is he gonna think?" Sue walked over to Al, took his bottle and downed a slug herself. She paused, peering at the hole and took another slug.

"It's right inconvenient, that's what it is. We need to fix it, or hide it, we can't let him find it. What would he think? I'll tell you what. He'll think we are all nuts. Can you do something before he comes?" She asked.

"Don't have nothin to fix it with. No wallboard, no plaster, no paint. Have to go to Bakersfield to buy that stuff. We got no time to do that".

Al knew what he could fix and what he couldn't. The hole was going to remain a problem  when the assessor came to visit. That much was certain.

"Can't be avoided, he'll be here by noon." Sue was worried. "He's for sure gonna examine this house."

"We could hang some stuff over it and he won't notice." Peg suggested.

"What do you got in mind?" Sue was desperate.

"It is an Indian rug or somethin. I got one in the garage. It's filthy but if we cleaned it up, it might work." Peg jumped in.

"Got to try sumthin, anything! The way the wind is howling, it's like we got a wind tunnel running through the house." Sue was frantic.

"It's an old Navajo rug I inherited. It's stained, so I gave up on it. It don't fit right with these floors no more."

Peg retrieved the relic and they unrolled it in the living room. The odor of mildew filled the room.

"Been in storage for years. Don't know why I been keeping it." Peg explained knowing  the rug was worthless.

"Don't know what's worse, the stench or the hole in the wall." Sue thought about it and said, " It's the hole, we can clean the rug!"

They hung the filthy old carpet out on a closeline and Al began to beat it senseless. His knuckles were still swollen and raw from the plastering he had given Luke's jaw.

"Damn that is painful," Al was angry withLuke "This is your doin'.My hands are bleeding again cause you"

Luke's jaw was hurt worse than Al's hand but he stepped forward intent on hammering the defenseless rug into final submission. Each time he swung he took a moment to pause and block out the pain. Once pain free he wound up and clubbed the carpet causing dust to fly in the wind. This ritual was repeated again and again.

"I think that about does it." Luke said, delivering a last violent thumping that got no dust. "I believe it is dust and dirt free."

"Still smells like rotten eggs," Al lamented.

Peg poured some sweet honey oil on it and they let it hang in the hot sun. It dried and soon was stiff and hard.

"That'll do the trick. Like a giant band aid for the wall." Peg jokes.

"Looks like art." Sue stood back and admired it.

It took over a half dozen long, thick nails to hang it. It was an awkward fit and to a trained eye it might have been out of place. The living room smelled like someone was washing their hair in the shower.

"It is as if it belongs there." Peg marked trying to stay on the bright side.

It served the purpose. The hole was hidden, and the wind tunnel effect was plugged.

Peg sprayed it one last time with vigor. It was badly stained and the spots were getting darker.

"Let it dry, when it dries it'll be better." But there was no denying it, the cleaning fluid had made the spots stand out even more.

"The odor will go away if we leave the doors and windows open." Peg opened every window in the house.

"If he is making an evaluation of the place he is sure to walk around the entire property. He is likely to find the hole in the wall outside." Al spoke up, making the obvious point that only one hole was covered.

Lights went off in every mind all at once! Sure enough there was an exit hole on the back wall and it was even more jagged.

"I don't got another rug." Peg had to answer the problem.

Sue walked up to the hole and pulled a few splintered pieces of wood out of the aperture. "Anybody got any ideas on what we can put in front of this to hide it?"

"A wheelbarrow! I got a wheelbarrow and an old canvas paint rag I used to cover the floor when I painted last. I'll nail the canvas on the wall, and use the wheelbarrow to pin it up. It'll cover it, and look like I have been doing a painting project of some kind." Al was amazed at how brilliant it all sounded. Damn, I'm a damned genius, he thought.

"Might work." Sue nodded "Got to try somethin. I think it's our best shot."

Al scurried off to gather the items needed to arrange the camouflage.

He pinned the canvas to the wall and propped up the wheelbarrow with its nose down and handles up, securing the rag to the wall and covering the hole.

"It fits like it has been there for years." Al admired his handiwork."I'll put a can of paint and some brushes out here. It'll camouflage and hide it."

"Perfect! He'll never suspect." Sue was relieved. "Remember now, tomorrow at noon. Be ready. Be in costume, and put on a good show. Don is depending on you. All of us are depending on all of you. Our fate is in your hands. You are the Professional Stunt Crew representing Silver City. Break a leg!"


Chapter Twenty Three

Luke was worried, the rehearsal had been difficult and not gone well. He was plagued with anxiety about the set and its future. To make matters worse his jaw was swollen and sore, and his teeth were loose. He questioned if luck was on his side, or was it just an illusion? Was it all about to crash and burn?

Anxious, he drifted off to sleep and had another dream. In it he and Darla were waltzing together under a starry sky. His conscious mind knew there was no dance floor anywhere in Bodfish, but it did not matter. He was having too much fun to care. There were other people dancing and having a wonderful time as well. They are all celebrating and it was real.

What was his dream about? He didn't know, but he started to believe his dreams were portents of important things to come. He decided his dream might be a message alerting him to a future task or event. It brought him a feeling of peace.

Luke opened his eyes at sunrise wanting to spring into action, but the rest of the world was still asleep. He was ready to explode. As soon as the hour was decent he went up to Al's place to get breakfast. Dean was sitting at the table. He and Al were deep in conversation and beer.

"Peg won't let me leave." Al said while having a beer with his eggs. "I could try to get the cab driving gig back. The problem is I don't want it back. Been thinkin I about looking for the gold mine again." He shot a meaningful glance Luke's way.

"We ain't failed yet, and I don't think we will." Dean scolded Al for being negative. Today was the day they had been waiting for.

"We have a plan and all we need to do is stick to it. But it's a good thing to have a backup plan in life." Al responded.

"I'm thinkin the banker will be impressed when he sees our show. We just need a break to get started. Once we get rolling nothing can stop us. What do you think Luke?" Dean asked.

"I came here hoping to be in the movies and I still hope that happens. I still want that to happen." Luke answered.

"Mornin Luke, Darla is takin my place today. She is younger and prettier. I think it'll be a lot better. Do you agree?" Peg hovered over Luke.``

Yeah she's pretty." Luke's jaw hurt so much he had to chew gingerly.

"We need investors, you gotta give em a good show and convince them. Anything else is a failure." Peg addressed her plea to everyone in the room.

"It won't be easy. The place rattles and shakes at night. I know, I sleep in it." Luke grimaced.

"What are you talking about?" The stuntmen were flabbergasted at how negative Luke sounded.

Luke concentrated on his eggs. He worked to keep up his strength for the day ahead. The future depended on them making a successful presentation.

"What about the slide?" Dean was agitated. " What do you think Don will say when he sees it for the first time?"

"I have no idea." Luke became defensive.

"There's nothin to do for miles around. If we give 'em something to do. It's a certainty they'll come in. It's a natural." Dean slammed his hand on the table. "You gotta see that's true!"

"I don't know. How should I know?" Luke wanted to dodge them, all of them.

"Don will be so happy once he understands how hard we worked to get that slide for him. It is going to make him a fortune. I can't wait to spring the surprise on him. He will be so grateful he has us here." As far as Dean could see it was inevitable.

Luke's whole summer in Bodfish was beginning to feel like madness. He knew that all the buildings creaked at night and seemed like they were about to fall over, the slide was even worse. It tilted ten degrees. The only good news was the moss on it was drying in the hot sun and had turned from green to brown causing the moss to fall off in chunks. None of this filled him with confidence.

"Well if'n we can't make money out making movies real soon we have a problem. We all need to be looking for answers." Al mumbled in between bites.

"I agree, but right now we have a show to do. After the rehearsal we did yesterday, it would be best if you two tried to do it sober." Luke was agitated and worried.

Luke had watched the whole group of them drinking beer and fumbling around out of control. It was all coming down to a stunt show and the judgment of some money men from the Bank of California. What if they hated it? The idea made him choke.

"Al will do just fine." Peg stood behind her man. "After all we all know it was you who drank too much and blew that hole in our wall. Fine thing, and now you are saying my boys can't carry their weight."

"I'm just saying that we need to dazzle the loan officer with a professional presentation. It will help if we are all clear headed and on the same page."

Dean was angry with Luke for having challenged him. The slide was his "ace" in the hole. His plan was to bring it into play if all else failed. His "slide" would come to the rescue and save the day!

Al went to the fridge door and grabbed his third beer of the morning.

"Good mornin!" Darla entered in costume. She was ready to go. When she saw Luke and came over and gave him a firm kiss on the lips.

"Well I'll be damned!" Dean was floored at Darla's show of public affection. It crushed him. It was like a bucket of cold water had been poured on his head.

"Anyone heard from Don or Sue?" Darla had her red hair tied up in a bow.

"You look great." Luke squeezed her hand.

Al had vanished into the back bedroom and came back carrying a large box of ammunition.

"All blanks, made em myself last night." He dumped them on the kitchen table. "Load your weapons boys."

Luke put two in his shotgun, "You're sure these are all blanks?"

"Course I am!" Al nodded.

"Okay," Luke pointed the gun at the empty wall and fired. Bang it exploded but there were no holes.

"I just wanted to be sure before I shot Dean today."

Chapter Twenty Four

"It's mighty hot and dry today," Sue had sweat pouring from her armpits staining her blouse.

"Yeah the wind's blowin' from the desert and that always dries things out. Hope they get here soon!" Peg fanned her bright red face.

Everyone was gathered at the gate as Don requested. They were all in costume, and ready to entertain Don's entourage of investors.

Don pulled up in his red pickup truck. He was followed by a black Lincoln. They parked and baked in the hot sun. A graying, middle aged man, sharply dressed in a three piece suit sat behind the wheel of the Lincoln. Luke strained to get a glimpse of the man who was destined to decide their future.

"He's gotta be the main loan officer. Bet he's suffering in that suit."

Dean nodded in agreement and made a circular motion around his ear indicating the man was crazy to be dressed like that in the noonday sun.

The banker had short, neat cropped hair. His ramrod stiffness gave off the impression he had once been a military man, but he was much too frail and fragile for that to have ever been true. His suit pants were pressed matching a crisp white shirt and a skinny red tie.

Don was dressed in overalls, suspenders, and a cowboy hat. There was an unidentified stranger sitting in the back..

"This is Silver City, this is what it is all about! Every building here is original!" Don's face was glowing and twitching as he blew Sue a kiss! He was so proud of her, she had assembled his entire crew of "stunt persons" for the occasion. Don's chest swelled with pride. "His" people were there right on cue. Everything was ready to go. All was well!

"This here is Alfred Jones, Loan Officer from the Bank of California." Don tried to put his arm around Jones who recoiled and pulled back as if he feared contamination.

Jones surveyed the band of actors, with a critical eye, and opened a black notepad and recorded his first impressions.

Luke felt Jones' cold stare from across the road, and wondered what he was writing down. He decided that Jones had a thin neck and a large Adam's apple.

"Good day, I am looking forward to seeing your show. I hear it is a recreation of the old west." As Jones spoke Luke marveled at his oversized Adam's apple. It seemed to be bobbing up and down punctuating his every word. "I am told it is genuine and authentic, just like this old town."

Jones swallowed a ball of spit as he talked, and Luke watched the liquid travel down his throat. It seemed like he gulped, bobbed and swallowed all in one breath.

"Well, howdy! Ain't this place a peach!" a high pitched voice interrupted. It was Jinbo, the unidentified passenger, who had climbed down out of Don's truck and was surveying the town for the first time.

He was short, fat and balding. He was also drowning, lost in a huge sport coat with sleeves so long they suggested that his coat was borrowed from a much larger man. Jumbo's baggy pants were held up by an oversized belt and pulled up way past his waistline.

"I like it! I like it a lot! The place feels authentic."

Jimbos' beady eyes narrowed to slits. His face sat perched on his two hundred and fifty pound body as if it was about to pop like a water balloon.

"You betcha Jimbo! Welcome to the Silver City movie set, where the magic of the movies is going to happen." Don put his arm around his old friend. "Folks, this here is my oldest friend in the world and former partner, Jimbo John Collins."

"Pleased to meet you Jimbo." Sue welcomed him with a wave.

"These are the stunt men and women I told you all about." Don introduced his crew.

"Howdy!" The two stuntmen spoke in unison. "Pleased I'm sure."

"So this is it. This is where we put the bank's money to work."

Jones peered down one side of the narrow street to the end and then back again. He let his eyes absorb and to trace the details of each building. He shook his head and whispered inaudibly. He jotted down notes in his black book. He swallowed and his Adam's apple and bobbed.

"Yes sir, they are all originals almost as they were when they were first built over a hunert years ago. Cept, they are much older now than they once were." Don's voice swelled with pride once again.

"When it's all finished we plan to give tours and rent it out to movie companies to make westerns." Sue chimed in with the company line.

"Well they are at least that old. Somehow, I thought you had restored them a bit." Jones' eyes narrowed in disbelief. He swallowed a long stream of spit causing his apple to bob as the spit passed by.

"It's true they were shaky when I first found them. But I reinforced them when I moved them here. It was a chore, but we got em here all here in one piece." To Don's mind, authenticity was the key and these were authentic. He thought by God's grace these are all originals and that means everything. It had to count for something!

Luke looked once more at the little street where he had passed the summer. Every building was tilting or leaning. Some leaned right, others left, and some were angling forward.

For the first time Luke appreciated the fragility of the place. He imagined he heard a flute and a drum core. Followed by the image of old wounded soldiers, struggling on crutches, bandaged and damaged, limping home flashed in his mind's eye.

"They seem worn and weathered. They must be a hundred years old. They must be uninhabitable." Jones said, swallowing hard as he scribbled in his notebook.

"I live in the sheriff's office." Luke pointed to the dustbin where he had slept for most of the summer.

"Seems impossible?" Jones seemed amazed. "Conditions seem primitive. You are an intrepid young fellow!"

Luke was engrossed watching Jone's furious note writing, spit swallowing, and wild Adam's apple waving.

"There's an outhouse out back. I don't use it much." Luke pointed at a little wood shack at the back of the jail. He pinched his nose with his fingers to indicate what the problem was.

"I wonder what this place would work on film? Have you ever filmed it?" Jones asked Don. Once again jotting notes, swallowing and bobbing.

Luke pondered the thought, "filming it to see how it looks," it made sense. What a good suggestion he thought.

"Don't know. Never thought bout it." Don shrugged his shoulders.

"It seems to me a movie set must appear life-like. The buildings must seem to be ready to be lived in. They cannot appear to be run down as if they are actually from the year 1860. That will not happen if they look as if they are actually a hundred years old." The obvious truth of Jones's statement hit everyone at the same time.

"It will take a lot of work to bring this place up to code." Jimbo broke in with his thoughts. "Having lots of visitors would put real stress on the place. What if something fell on someone?"

"Don't think it matters bout code here in Bodfish." Don stared down at his feet and shrugged. Living in Bodfish he had gotten used to overlooking things like building codes. No one cared much about such niceties.

"Say how bout we put on the show for y'all?" Al spoke up. " We worked on it all day yesterday. Everyone that is cept Darla. So please cut her a little slack. Once you see the show, you'll see for yourself just how much fun this place is gonna be."

Darla sparkled, Luke thought the last thing Al needs to do is make excuses for Darla, she ain't a problem.

"Well I guess since I came all the way out here, the least I can do is see the show." Jones said, jotting and swallowing and bobbing away.

Mr. Jones found himself downwind from the stuntmen. The smell of beer and cigarettes and whisky hit him like a shock wave making it difficult for him to catch his breath. Nausea grabbed him with a vice-like grip! His sensitive nose began twitching with repulsion! He stepped back and put distance between them. He had to fight to keep from passing out.

"You boys are right on top of me. Give me space! Let's start the show, and hurry, please hurry!" Jones directed them upwind. Unable to breathe, Adam's apple went still and stopped.

The crew all scurried to obey, sensing Jones' urgent need to get started they got going as possible!

"Yes sir! Enjoy the show!" Al kicked Charlie in the ribs and the horse trotted to the end of the street.

"Just try to imagine there is a crowd of people, arms full of trinkets an' souvenirs and they don't expect a thing." Al laid out the scene so that Jones and Jimbo could appreciate the "magic" that was about to engulf them. At his signal, the show got off the ground.

"Give me all your money or I'll shoot!" Dean's voice boomed out from the general store. A series of gun shots followed. Dean staggered out dragging Darla behind.

Darla lay limp and passive in his arms, she was forcing Dean to support her full weight. Her dead weight was more than he could handle; he faltered and fell. They slammed against the doorway frame! The rotting wood of the ancient door splintered and cracked apart. The door swung dangling loose on its hinges in the wind.

Darla bounced off the door frame and her feet came out from under her. She grabbed Dean and they fell hard. He landed on top pinning her to the floor. It was a moment he had long hoped for and dreamed of, but instead of the unbridled lust he craved it was a drunken mess.

They had become an inert heap of flesh floundering and helpless. He was far too inebriated to push himself up off the ground. She squirmed and jiggled and bit her lip, angry and resentful that he had found a way to jump on her. She suspected he had fallen on her on purpose.

In desperation she shoved him to relieve the pressure he was exerting on her breasts. Dean's face was inches from hers and his breath was full of tobacco, beer and cheese. It was awful. She tried not to breathe.

"Help! I'm being kidnapped!" She had delivered her line late in spite of the hardship. Al heard it.

"You delivered the line late." Dean mumbled criticizing her to her face.

Damn right, she thought, hell, of course it's late, you're crushing me and your breath is horrendous. "Get off me!" she pushed again, harder this time.

Dean rolled over on his side and propped himself up on his elbows. Tears filled his eyes and pain shot through his shoulder. He was unable to focus, he stared in pain out at the street.

Jones was an indistinct blur, writing and swallowing, while his bobbing Adam's apple kept time to his pen strokes.

Luke panicked and put his hands around Darla's firm waist and lifted her out from under Dean.

"God that hurts, I think I broke a bone." Dean's face was contorted in a macabre grimace.

"Take your hands off her, you varmints." Al shouted from the end of the street ready to charge. He whipped Charlie until he bled.. But instead of the desired gallop, Charlie responded by trotting and prancing down the street!

"Move you mangy beast." Al gave Charlie a violent swat and Charlie reared up on his hind legs, causing Al to fall backward in the saddle. In panic, Al grabbed at the saddle horn with both hands. As he did so his pistol fell to the ground. Charlie bolted with Al bouncing and dangling a foot off the ground!

Al lowered himself to safety. He shook his trapped leg until it came free. He fell to the ground free of the erratic horse. Al was prone in the dirt minus the pistol than he needed for the gunfight. He was a hundred feet short of the porch where Darla was waiting to be rescued.

"Drop your guns." Al yelled trying to recover from the fall, and regain his place back in the script.

Dean ignored his painful state, got to his feet and fired at Al.

Al, with his gun lost and lying abandoned back the street, decided to fire his finger in the air. Charlie let out a snort of disgust and bolted off to the barn to hide. Al fired his finger at Dean. "Bang! Bang Bang" Al mouthed the words. "Bang, bang, bang!" his finger jerked back imitating a recoil.

Dean took the cue and yelled out, "You got me!" He grabbed his chest and fell forward once again landing on the unforgiving pavement below. His teeth rattled as he came crashing down on the rotten old porch. The floorboard split open at the point where Dean's shoulder and head made contact. He had fallen like a man whose body was all dead weight.

He was in such agony that he was unable to lay down and play dead. His shoulder was twitching and he grabbed it in a convulsive reaction. Instead of performing the "dead" act as required, he was writhing in intense pain.

"Drop your gun, you dirty varmint." Al had drawn a bead on Luke with his finger gun. Darla turned away from Luke and Al and their impending gun and finger fight. She grabbed hold of Luke's shotgun hand. Bang! The gun fired into her exposed belly..

Don and Jimbo gasped in unison at all the unexpected turns and twists in the plot. Jones kept trying to record the show for posterity, by scribbling in his notebook. Darla was horrified, wondering how to bring the show back on script.

Luke stuck his hands in the air "I surrender sheriff!"

Al realized Luke was back on script! On cue, Al took his eyes off Luke who jumped him. They wrestled and the fight scene began in earnest.

Luke approached moving his face and jaw forward offering it as a target for Al's bunched up fist. Al seeing Luke's face was once again being offered up for punishment delivered a killing blow on Luke sore and aching chin.

"Shit" Luke moaned as his head snapped back as a cut opened in his mouth. Blood splattered into the air and fell out on the street.

"God Damn it." Al shook his hand in the air in pain. "Damn that hurt."

"Al, this is a bad cut, we need to stop!" Darla had her shawl in hand and was pressing down trying to stop the flow of blood from Luke's mouth.

"Cut!" They all yelled in unison. The show came to a halt. There was a long silence. No one knew what to say. Jones wrote one final note and closed his book.

"I have the general idea. I must say it did seem realistic at times. A little violent as well,"

"We still got a few bugs to fix. But I think it was a good first effort." Sue stepped in and tried to bridge the silence on the set.

"Well I have to ask, are you guys planning on doing this every time?" Jones' voice made them all shiver.

"We can do better." Al pleaded.

"Parts of it were realistic, I must say. All the blood seems real from here." Jones turned another page in his notebook, swallowed some spit and shook his hand. " Your show made me do a lot more writing than I am used to doing. My fingers feel worn out."

Jones was not impressed. They feared all might be lost.

"Here, you're still bleeding bad." Peg gave Luke a cloth napkin from her basket.

"Woman, is there cold beer in that basket?" Al stuck out his hand. "I could use one about now."

"I'll grant you it needs some smoothing out, but you can see the potential?" Don pleaded his case.

Jones was silent. Everything and everyone went silent. What could be said? The show had not gone well. The silence was awkward and it stayed that way for what seemed like an eternity.

"I have a surprise! It will make yer day!." Dean's head had cleared and he was on his feet. It had all come down to him and his slide. It was just as he had envisioned it and he strode forth determined to save the day.The glory would be his!

It was time to reveal the magnificent slide and waterpark plan. Dean marveled at how the giant edifice had gone unnoticed. It was in clear view and towering above all of the buildings of the town the entire time. How did they all miss seeing it?

Sporting his best toothy Tennessee grin, Dean radiated enthusiasm, goodwill and cheer. Certainty flowed from his being. He had transcended the pain from his cracked ribs and rose up to save the day. He was a true professional, the show must go on, and he was determined to make it happen. This was his moment.

"What are you talking bout?" Don was aghast, what could come next? The wild west show had shaken him to his core. He had no idea what was coming next. But he knew Dean.

"Didn't you notice it when you all came in? It was standing right there. Dean shrugged his shoulders in disbelief.

"I didn't notice anything." Don shook his head.

"Well come on then. Prepare for a surprise." Dean led them to"his" shrine.

It was, out back, waiting, tilting to the left, towering above the long rows of junk autos. Jones let out a gasp of disbelief. He saw for the first time the legacy of the junkyard. The back half of the lot was stacked with junk.

A ground squirrel poked its head out of a car door and galloped off in fear, surprised by the horde of humans tramping through its home.

"Ain't she a beaut?" Dean presented the "grand old slide" standing in its blue plastic magnificence towering above the sea of junk by a full two stories.

"Ain't she a beaut?" Dean repeated his question and flashed his smile again. He waited for gasps of awe and approval but none came.

Jones sat surveying the line of old rusted cars and shook his head in wonderment. He couldn't stop shaking his head, what a mess! Don searched for words, he was dumbfounded. What did this mean? What had his boys been up to?

"If II didn't know better I would swear it is the slide from Jake and Jarvis's place. I helped them move it there from the county park then they bought it at auction twenty years ago. How did it get here?" Don knew the history of the slide well.

"We won it in a trade and moved it here." Dean was excited. The full reality of the moment had begun to settle on Don. "I spect it'll make us a fortune."

"A fortune? How? It's old and spider infested." Jones noted several nests, " I think I saw a black widow. How do you figure this old slide is going to make a fortune?"

"We'll buy a swimming pool and put 'em both out in the hot sun. Kids'll love a slide. We'll put up billboards on the highway. On super hot days people will rush to let their kids cool off in the refreshing cold water. It'll be like Frontier Village waterpark back home. We will make a fortune."

Dean could hear the cash register ringing up one sale one after another. Ka-ching, Ka-ching. All was going to be well. He was met once again with silence.

"Don't you see it? It is a natural, It can't miss!" Dean pleaded.

"What did you pay for this?" Jones interrupted.

"It was a steal, we got it for a case of Jack Daniels." Al chimed in, he was not about to let Dean take all the credit for the initiative being shown. "Well two cases to be truthful."

"We drunk the old coot and his crazy brother under they couldn't stand up and they gave it to us." Dean gloried in his victory.

"It was my plan, old Jarvis did not want to let go of it. He or maybe it was Jake, can't say for sure. But I convinced em." Al stepped up and cut Dean off in mid sentence.

"You dismantled this and moved it here and all it cost was a case of whiskey? Damn that Jarvis is a lot smarter than I thought." Don shook his head in disbelief. "You know how much it costs to build a swimming pool?"

Al had not considered the issue of buying a pool. He kicked the dust a bit and chewed on his lip.

"Well I was thinking on buying one of them cheap plastic jobs bout three feet high." Dean had considered it. "Ya have to have a pool". He was certain a water park would only work if it had a pool. No use for them kids sliding down into hard dirt or hot sand. Not out in a broiling sun over one hunert degrees."I seen em priced pretty low, it'd be a start."

"You think families with kids will come here if you put up some road signs with pictures of this old slide and a plastic pool?" Jones's Adam's apple was jumping like a salmon jumping upstream against a waterfall.

"Course I do! I can smell the dogs and the cotton candy. We'll have lemonade on scorching hot days" Dean was waving his arms in the air now. "There'll be no stopping us."

Dean searched from face to face, where was the joy? Where was the excitement? Al came to the rescue.

"Well I understand we will have some work to do to spruce things up. Luke figures in three more months we will have this old mess of cars out of here." Al saw that Jones was anything but convinced.

"What do you think Don? A little clean up and it will work sure as shootin." Al asked.

"Tell the truth! Everyone got slobber faced drunk when you did this deal!" Don knew them all too well.

Al kicked up a little dirt once more and leaned left. just like the slide. He had been working on a twelve pack since he woke up. It was not what he had hoped for. Not at all.

"Was Jake there too?" Don knew the brothers wouldn't do this without consulting with each other.

"Did you guys sign any papers or anything like that?" Jones asked, breaking his momentary silence. It occurred to him that the bank held the papers on this property and if the slide or anything else fell and landed on anyone there might be some liability. "Your slide is antique. Is it stable? What's keeping it upright?"

"Right now one of the legs is bent a little which makes it look a bit wobbly. It got bent when I tore it down." Luke spoke up, he had been silent a long time. "It looks worse than it is."

Jones was at a loss. He took a deep breath. He had adjusted to the smell of beer and whisky. He had overcome the need to vomit but he was still a bit unsteady. He jotted a couple more notes in his little record book.

"Well your loan was based on two income properties with a regular cash flow. Now it turns out these two characters are living in them rent free. The bottom line is you're running behind in your payments so I have to decide whether we should extend the bank's investment or take another course."

"What can I do?" Don pleaded.

"Nothing here gives me much hope. Do you have anything in writing? A business plan? Anything I could put in the file to indicate this is all about to change and will start making money in the foreseeable future?" Jones opened the door, and offered a way out.

"Well I think we told you the story and now you have seen it for yourself, what more do you want?" Don had never heard of making a business plan. He was into moving buildings. Picking them up, moving them and saving them from ruin was his idea of productive work and besides it was a lot of fun.

"What makes you think anyone would pay good money to come here for this? this?" Jones waived at the two lines of old buildings as they creaked and shook in the warm wind. "I cannot  even  describe this place."

"Well awhile back some fellers came through and Luke gave em a tour and charged em five bucks." Don was grasping at straws. Anything to make it look like this thing would pay off and come around.

"Is that right?" Jones nodded at Luke for confirmation.

"Yep. Four fellas from the Hells Angels come through and I charged em a dollar a head, so I got four bucks. I already spent the money though." Luke felt a little guilty but dinner with Darla had been worth it.

"Four dollars? After two years you have a gross sales of four dollars? And zero rent?" Do I have it right?" To Jones it sounded grim.

"Well Luke kept the four dollars. But I was there, I helped finish up the tour right after Jake dusted their skirts and Luke ran up the hill chasing after the shooter. Right nice fellas" Don said recalling Sonny's visit.

"Dusted their skirts?" Jones tried to visualize how Jake, the previous owner of the slide, had dusted Sonny and his fellow bikers "skirts". He was unable to picture it. He just stared at Don.

"Dusted their skirts? What does that mean?" Jones wanted to find out.

"Yeah well old Jake ain't all that friendly to strangers and took a dislike to them boys because they showed up in the middle of the night and had their loud all night parties. So when they came down here for a tour, he opened fire at their feet to scare them off. Later he said he was just "dusting their skirts to see em dance. It was Jake's words, not mine."

"I understand now." Jones was taken aghast. "So one of your neighbors shot at your customers?"

Jones' was overwhelmed trying to calculate the potential damages if someone was shot during a paid tour on a bank property. His mind spun and he got dizzy from the possibilities.

"I doubt Jake was tryin to hit anyone. Jake is a cracker jack shot. He had a heat on and was a bit drunk for sure. I think he got a bit carried away." Al offered his opinion.

"Even if it was Old Jake, he was only playin. Luke ran up there after him but he didn't catch no one. Could have been anyone firing them shots." Dean jumped in, it was all normal enough. It was the kind of thing that might happen anytime Jake had a heat on. Why try to predict or control that?

"I think you have all been out in the heat too long." Jones turned to Don. "In regards to the loans, if the two rental properties can start generating some income and you get caught up to date on your payments. It will work. I have a man coming to make an inspection. He will check them over top to bottom and give me an idea of what they should be making. If these boys can't pay that amount, then I think you will have to find some new tenants who can."

"That ain't fair". The stuntmen spoke up in shock.

"My real estate adjuster will be calling you later this afternoon. Be prepared to show him around. I have evaluated this movie ranch, tourist site, whatever you want to call it myself. I have to tell you this old place ain't got much of a future in my opinion," with that he turned and headed for his car, leaving Don and the boys cursing under their breath. As Jones drove off he left the group to contemplate and fear for their futures.

"That man don't know nothin bout bizness." Dean spit it out as Jones vanished down the road.

"Don't know nothin at all. He ain't got no vision."


Chapter Twenty Five

The property assessor was scheduled to arrive in the late afternoon. Don and his worried crew decided to meet early in the day to prepare for the dreaded event.

"We best have a plan. We'll have one shot, and if it don't go right, we are in for a world of hurt." Don advised them.

"What can we do? He'll be here and there's not much we can change now." Al wondered if Don knew that there was a hole in his wall.

"You're right, it is out of our hands. We'll just have to be as friendly as possible and show him we have nothin to hide." Don replied.

With that response Al knew Don was unaware of recent developments, because they had a lot to hide.

"Don't reckon I met an "assessor" before. It sounds real important. We should make him a nice lunch" Dean said. "Ain't nothin works better influencing a workin man than helping him to tie on a free feed bag. "

"We got nothin but beans and franks. Being cuttin' down and tryin' to go cheap. What you got over at your place?" Al wondered.

"Cupboard is close to bare." Dean shrugged it off.

They were all in awe of the assessor and the power he possessed. His opinion that would determine their future and that of the entire movie set project. With a few strokes of his pen he could evict them and put them in the streets.

As usual, Al and Dean responded to the crisis by getting up early and drinking beer all morning. They had plenty of beer so they worked at it all day.

"Let's do him like we did with Jarvis, make him so drunk he can't think straight." Dean suggested.

"We could try that. it would work with Jake and Jarvis, but the accessor is a mystery." Al was reluctant to go down that road. "It might not be the right approach for a man from a big, important bank."

"It worked before, what have we got to lose?" Dean was relentless."I say when in doubt, get 'em drunk."

They spent the morning imbibing and pondering the probable drinking habits of the assessor. They were unable to decide what the best plan was to win over the mysterious stranger.

For Don and Peg, the day of reckoning was at hand. If the evaluations were not favorable they would have some tough decisions to make.

"No use deciding what to do until we have the final word." Don advocated taking a conservative wait and see attitude.

"I never agreed to let your boys stay for free. I never thought it was a good idea." Sue was preparing herself for the inevitable. If an eviction was called for she was ready to step up and do the deed.

"Well, there must be a better way, we just haven't found it yet." Don was not ready to throw his crew out on the street.

"Well you're just too nice, if it has to be, I'll do it myself." Sue steeled herself, she was ready to drop the hammer on Al and Dean and their families.

By noon, the mighty assessor had still not arrived. Sue called the women to meet and discuss the options.

"You all know I like the lot of you and am hoping for the best." Sue began by attempting to reassure the wives.

"We have worked hard to transform the junk yard into a movie set and now that the job is almost done, it's like the rug is being pulled out from under us." Peg complained using her whiny nasal voice. It was a voice she reserved for occasions like this.

"Yeah, and everyone knows it was my Dean who came up with the idea of securing the slide. He deserves all the credit. Without him it would still be in that old man's back yard growing moss." Liz backed her man and his "vision" to the hilt.

"That's true, I reckon we have Dean to thank for getting that old slide.

But I believe Luke did most of the real work." Sue replied.

"Yeah, but it was Dean's vision that made it happen." Liz doubled down on her ace in the hole.

"I'll tell you what, after we have a pool and the first child slides down it and we bank our first buck I'll remember to thank your husband. Right now we need to try our best to make the properties stand out and shine. They are what is being assessed."

They discussed the fine points of each of their residences and what made them unique. It was a short discussion. They had to cut it short when they ran out of things to say. The houses were old and nothing had been done to maintain them for years.

"I reckon he will just come and see for himself. Ya can't make a silk butt out of a pig's ear." Sue said, calling an end to it."We are as prepared now as we can be."

The desert wind was blowing hard, and the harder it blew, the hotter it got. Dust was everywhere making it difficult to breathe. Don had made his way to Al's place and they all chugged beer, waiting, and worrying.

"What bad luck, the air is so full of dust. Nothing looks good when it gets like this. Last time this happened it blew for three days and covered the whole house with dirt and sand" Al moaned as he tossed back a warm one. "Damn beer is almost as warm as the wind."

"It plays hell with my lungs, I cannot breathe." Dean added.

Al's worried mind turned to the hole in the wall. Would it stay hidden? So far the deception had worked, Don had not caught on. The winds were whipping up the debris and the sand was filtering into the kitchen and living room. It had just started, how bad would it get?

"I got a little problem." Dean broke in, distracting Al from his gloom.

"What's up?" Al asked, wondering what could be worse than trying to hide a shotgun hole that ran the length of your house?

"Well, Liz wasn't keeping a close enough eye on Bubba and he got into my shed and got the paintbrush and went to work." Dean spilled the beans on Bubba.

"Went to work?" Al asked.

"Yeah he painted  green cows, horses and pigs all over the walls. They're not good likenesses. Can't pretend they are art. He messed up the doors and floors too. I haven't had time to fix it. I was so busy stuntman acting and getting the slide ready." Dean's toothy grin returned.

"Green cows and horses on the walls?" Al grimaced. "That is bad. First impressions are always important."

"The walls and the floors are all green animals. The pigs are the best, they are lifelike, except of course they're green." Dean gave them a whistle " I have been too busy to fix it."

"Won't matter." Jimbo, Don's oldest friend and close buddy, picked this moment to speak up.

"How do you figure?" Dean wanted forgiveness for his wayward friend."

"All the bank cares about is how much money can be made. A little paint won't make a difference. You boys will have to start paying rent, the real question is how much will it be and can you pay it?" Jimbo had hit the nail right on the head.

Jimbo continued on, "Money! That's what's gonna save the situation. If you can't pay they will foreclose on Don's loans." Jimbo said it with ruthless authority.

"We all been working at it for two years and where we are." Don was sullen and gloomy.

What Don worked at was finding old buildings, moving them and getting them set up again. That was Don's idea of a good day's work. To him his old town was perfect! He liked it the way it was."

"To tell the truth, myself, I fell in love with the idea of a swimming hole. Sounded like a natural." Jimbo nodded in approval and slapped Dean on the back.

That's what I'm talkin bout." Dean's country grin rolled back on his face stretching from ear to ear. He had found an ally.

At that instant a shiny Blue Packard pulled up in the driveway. Sue was in the passenger seat. The accessor was driving. It stopped and she hopped out.

"This here is Karl. He surveyed our house first, and then we done Dean's place. Al's is the last in line." Sue had been "escorting" the accessor from house to house.

In reality, she was dogging his every step, determined to influence his decision making. Karl kept his head down and ground on with objective determination. He was a man with a mission. Karl ignored every word she said. He was brusk and cold.

No matter how she tried to coax him into seeing the humanity of their situation, he could not side with three little families trying to live the American dream. Karl could not be inspired to dream the dream with her, and instead only grunted under his breath, nodded dismissively and plowed on.

"We're down to the last property. Hope you saved the best for last." Karl's voice was an inaudible whisper.

Sue's long face told everyone she had failed and was desperate.

"Karl has evaluated everything else. This is the last stop." She sounded tired and resigned.

The little man's face was ghost-like, bloodless without color. Luke thought Karl was so frail that his spindly body might get swept up in the wind. When he slumped, it was like watching an accordion collapse. From his vantage point Luke could see that Karl had been sitting on a stack of phone books. Luke guessed that he could not see over the steering wheel without them.

The tiny little man climbed out of the car. He coughed and wheezed in the hot dirty wind. Like his boss, Karl was impeccably dressed in a three piece suite and was wearing a bowler hat. He bowed to the assembled crowd and held out a card hoping whoever was in charge would take it.

Don took the card and Dean tried to slip a beer into the assessor's hand.

"These are my properties, all of them." Don accepted Karl's card and read the title, "Property Assessor". "Glad my wife showed you around and splained things a bit."

Karl handed the beer back to Dean with a slight growl, "Don't have time to drink, too much work to do. Don't like beer and I never drink on the job. No one does at the bank. Alcohol and work never mix at the bank. We have standards!"

Karl sauntered up to the front door and let himself in. The crowd followed, surrounding him inside. Luke, with his shotgun in hand, found himself looking down at Karl's bowler hat.

"Step back, and let me work. You're crowding me!" Karl pushed Luke and made his way to the back wall. "Let me work!"

Karl got down on his hands and knees and pulled out a tape measure. He mapped out the length of the room recording it inch by inch.

"Need to know the total square footage. It's not in our records, the original loans were made on sketchy information. I'll fix that." He mumbled to no one in particular. "Damn dusty in here, it's like the wind is blowing straight through the walls." He shot Peg a disapproving look. "Damn dusty."

He continued crawling on his hands and knees until he had surveyed the entire living room floor. Karl marked down the dimensions of the room in his little black book.His quest brought him to the exact spot where Al had hung the Navajo rug on the wall to cover the bullet hole. It was flapping and fluttering, reacting to the gusts of wind that were pummeling the house. The carpet slapped against the wall making it seem alive.

"That is very strange." Karl became cautious, at that moment a huge gust of wind slammed into the side of the building. It shook the frame making the walls moan and tremble. The rug moved and fluttered in the harsh wind.

"I think there is an animal trapped under the rug trying to get out." Karl said in fear.

The air in the room was thick with dust and sand. Karl wheezed, and choked. A fresh layer of filth had come streaming in from the desert.

"It's almost as if the wind is blowing straight through your walls." Karl spoke out loud to no one in particular. "Damn strange. Damn strange."

Al and his accomplices stared out into space.

"You got snakes out here don't you?" Karl's pasty white face had turned green. With trepidation, he started to lift the rug. "Are they poisonous?"

"Yea," Peg said, "Rattlesnakes, a lot of them."

Karl dropped the rug in fear. What was it? Was it a snake, or worse yet a giant lizard? What? Could it be a rat or a bat! Karl lost his nerve.

"We ain't got no snakes in the walls!" Don brushed Karl aside and lifted up the rug.

Dumbfounded, Don unveiled the giant hole. He gasped in surprise."Well I'll be," Don asked for an explanation. "There's a gunshot hole in the wall. It goes straight through the house."

"It ain't nothing dangerous." Luke chimed up.

"Strange. Very, very Strange." Karl repeated himself looking at Al and Peg. "You got a jagged hole in the wall. It appears to be from a gunshot. What do you say to that?"

"Peg should never have given Luke the shotgun. He is too young and inexperienced to carry it everywhere and have it loaded all the time." Al called out Luke's failure.

"I didn't do a thing." Luke curled up in a defensive stance.

"Hush up. I am sure you both meant well." Don waved off their frantic explanations

With the cunning of a master detective Karl strode into the back yard and yanked down the canvas. It was now clear the tunnel and the bullet path cut across the length of the house. The mystery was solved! Ventilation was the force moving the rug and flooding the rooms with dust.

"Never seen anything like it. The hole gets bigger as it travels along. It keeps expanding outwards until it gets enormous right over your bed. Must be hard to sleep under it when the weather is bad. I am told it rains buckets on a stormy night.

The back exit hole over the headboard was three feet in diameter. Karl wrote it all down in meticulous detail in his little black book. He made a note about how the holes became more jagged as the tunnel grew.

"What should I tell Mr. Jones?" He muttered to himself. "For one thing, who could live with a hole like that right over their bed? Gotta be drafty, it's just awful."

"How do you sleep with that hole over your bed?" he asked her.

"You learn to accept things." Peg glanced away as she spoke, unable to look Karl in the eye.

"You are a patient woman. You have your hands full. Your husband is blessed."

"Al means well and tries hard. Sometimes I just find myself looking at the bright side and hoping the next thing that comes up will be better."

"Anyone could blow a hole in the wall at any time. It is a little thing, nothing I needed to report to Mr. Jones. But you are all due a discount for the inconvenience." Karl nodded affirming his conclusion.

"That's great, I swear to you the boy meant no harm and it'll never happen again." Al slapped Karl on the back in joy.

"I estimate a hundred a month for rent, at least $20.00 to cover the discomfort for the hole. Maybe it should be more. Can't say as I would want to live in a place with a hole right through the middle of it."

"You can get used to anything." Al couldn't believe it.

"Got to be hard having it hanging over your head at night. What do you think? What kind of a discount is fair?" Karl stopped and stood waiting for Al to provide an estimate on what the appropriate discount should be.

"Discount? You're asking how much discount should I get?" Al thought it might be a trick question and he had better not answer it.

"The other place needs a paint job in the worst way, and so I am going to recommend a discount on it too. That boy is a menace, grabbed my leg and rubbed his snot all over my pants ."

With that Karl packed up and headed for his car. He left them all to ponder how they were going to come up with enough rent money to cover $140.00 per month. In Bodfish cash it was a fortune, a princely sum!

Chapter Twenty Six-

"Our luck has run out! I don't know where the money for the rent is gonna come from." Peg lamented.

"Dean ain't never been much of a provider. Ain't likely he's gonna change." Liz said wistfully.

"The blood washed out! The stain is gone."Peg held up Al's plaid shirt.

"I'm surprised the shirt came clean. That was a big cut. I hated seeing Luke's pretty face busted up like that." Liz chimed in.

"Ya, I thought he was gonna need stitches." Peg said, she held the shirt to give Liz a closer look. "But it looks like he'll heal up fine."

"I wish we could help with the loans!" Liz lamented. "I don't see a way out. The end is near."

"We don't got enough money to keep food on the table. Somethin' has got to change soon." Peg's shaky voice could not hide her worry.

"We got to do something to help ourselves." Liz lamented.

The financial pressure created by the bank's decision to review Don's properties and business dealings constituted an emergency for Peg and Liz. They knew neither of their husbands was likely to find any kind of work in Bodfish. There wasn't any work to find.

"I don't know what we can do if Don has to close down the movie set. We been banking on it being a success for a long time." Peg finished folding the clothes. "I'm afraid he might go back to Los Angeles and try cab driving again. "

"I can't stand the idea of Dean going back to playing honky tonks." Liz said was despondent.

"I'll worry if Al tries to drive a cab, but I'll worry more if he starts backin the hills looking for that stupid gold mine." Peg was distraught, it was a lose lose situation.

"I used to think it was terrible that Dean was always hiding what he was doing from me." Liz continued, "but then it came to me that the only thing worse is to be aware of what he has been doing."

They wanted to preserve the illusion that the "Movie Ranch" was going to become a financial success. If that happened, all would be well and the last two years of sacrifice would make sense. Could they do something to make it happen?

They decided to turn to Sue for help. Everyone knew Sue was a hard headed woman. But both Liz and Peg believed that Sue in her heart of hearts wanted the same thing they did, for her man to be happy.

There was no avoiding the fact that Sue's "plan" had always included getting rental income from her two houses. From time to time she would rant and rave about it but the rants died down and faded away. They all knew she had come to accept them as family. It was also clear that Sue loved Don and if his dream was to make a tourist attraction out of the row of antique buildings she would help him.

Sue knew that not many people lived and survived in the high desert because real work was almost non-existent. She also knew that If Dean and Al and their families were evicted and put out on the streets, the line of qualified tenants with money would not stretch around the block. In fact there wouldn't be a line at all.

Long before Peg and Liz and their families had shown up in Bodfish the two houses were empty. Sue knew that finding paying tenants was an unlikely dream. The ideal solution for everyone was for the movie set to become a success.

Every load of salvage that they cleared away reminded Sue that the junk yard had been a failure long before Don settled on making it a movie set. It had not produced much income and now that it was being cleared away it never would. They couldn't go backward.

"You can't give up now," Peg pleaded with Sue. "The backlot is almost clear of rubbish and every day it seems more and more like a movie set and less like a junkyard."

"Al and Dean have been committed to the success of the movie set from the beginning." The two wives complained, begging in unison.

"Without them, it wouldn't be the place it is today." Sue had to agree.

"Yeah, the banker never saw it like it was before. What does he know about the progress we made?" Liz and Peg argued their case.

"Yes, yes, progress has been made, but the cold hard facts are still the cold hard facts. We need to start making money!" Sue knew there was no denying it.

She also knew that It was Al's arrival in Bodfish that had transformed Don's hobby of restoring old buildings into a plan to enter the movie business. Al's tales about his adventures had paved the way!

Don went from being a man with an obsession for accumulating antique buildings to the owner of a prospective movie set waiting for Hollywood to discover it. Don had taken a ride on the coattails of Al's promises of movie glory.

For that reason alone, Sue was sure it was all Al's doing. She held Al responsible for the imminent foreclosure of all their properties. But to be fair, she could not imagine a better road they could have taken. There had never been a clear road to riches running through Bodfish.

Sue meditated on the dilema long and hard and decided the answer to it all was a "Chili" party. She would make a huge pot of her beloved Chili. Don would supply a keg of beer. She planned to gather the entire clan and lead them in a "Brainstorming" to save the movie set.

It was not an "original" idea. Sue had come across the concept of "brainstorming" in a woman's magazine. She figured if anyone ever needed a "brainstorm" it was her little group and they needed it now.

"Each person would be required to think of a way to make Silver City pay off and start making money!"

Sue's own idea on how to solve the problem was to throw the Chili party and gather together the "Brain Trust of Bodfish." Her sponsorship was her contribution.

Liz and Peg felt their job was to support their men and help them to complete their endeavor. It was their baby and they knew it best. The date for the party was set for the following Saturday evening. Financial solvency was the goal. None of them could use the word "solvency" in a sentence.

In her secret heart of hearts Sue knew Don had been the happiest finding, moving and "restoring" the old buildings now sitting in the transitioning former junk yard. They were a monument, a remembrance of the forgotten days of the old west. All three women were in agreement with the basics. They all wanted Silver City to succeed. When Sue announced the brainstorming party it was with a hopeful eye to an abundant future.

Saturday afternoon came and a light breeze blew in from the desert. It was warm, and comfortable. The braintrust of Don, Jimbo, Al, Dean and Luke sat on folding chairs drinking cold beer from Don's keg. They were listening to country music.

"Don, how'd you get the jukebox?" Al already knew. He had heard the story many times. It didn't matter, the story had been retold every time they got together. They all listened in rapture as Don recited all the familiar details of how the beloved jukebox had found its way to Bodfish.

"I took it in trade. I was doing some contracting for a bar in Bakersfield and they offered to pay with that jukebox. They had just got a new one, so they offered it in trade. Best thing I ever did. I got a couple dollars to cover materials, but we did the job straight up for the box. I love havin' my own jukebox."

"Best trade off ever!" Dean nodded with approval!

Having his own jukebox with the best country songs was something Don was proud of. He played it whenever anyone came over and drank beer with him.

"The darn thing works like it is brand new. I never get tired of it." Jimbo chimed joining the circle of jukebox worshiping savants.

"I refinished it myself. That glossy shine took a lot of elbow grease." Don reminded them all about the effort it had taken to get it in such pristine condition.

"It's a real beauty," Luke added his stamp of approval. "What kind of wood is it made of?"

"Mahogany! It feels rich don't it?" Don responded.

Country western music was pouring out of the box in stereo, Don had placed a speaker in every corner of the yard. The "box" was stocked with all of Don's favorite country tunes.

"I got all the greats! It don't get no better than this." For the entire day they listened surrounded by Hank Williams and Patsy Cline with a little Ernest Tubbs and Marty Robbins sprinkled in for a change of pace.

"Chili will be ready in a half hour, Cornbread is baking and is almost done." Sue's called happily from the kitchen window.

Don heard the voice of the young woman he had married years earlier calling to him. It seemed like having a chili party was bringing out the best in Sue.

The Sheriff, with his wife, arrived and were followed by Jarvis and Jake. They had come to join the "meeting of the brain trust".

Luke doubted the "brainstorming" potential of the twins.The image of Jake drunk and helpless, stuck halfway down the slide, was embedded in his memory. It could not be forgotten or ignored. To Luke the brothers were almost always shit faced and flying six sheets to the wind.

To Luke, Jake was a wild card who could hug you in bliss or fly off the handle in a blind rage. He had invented the phrase "dust your skirt" to describe the time when he opened fire on a band of hell's angels. Today they were not yet drunk but Luke figured it was only a matter of time.both able to walk a straight line.

"There's folding chairs up against the wall." Sue greeted them, proving once again that she was a good hostess.

"I ain't never been to a brainstorming afore" Jake said pulling up a chair and squinting at Don. "I hear that's what we are gonna do. Am I right?"

"What in hell is a brainstorm?" asked Jarvis. "I can gets a might worked up in my head when I drink my Jack. It's more like a drownin' than a stormin though. Trouble is we ran out of Jack. Heard you got some beer. Is that right?"

The two brothers were ready to tie into the keg and if need be experience a brainstorming party. Today it was all about being social and being accepted.

"According to Sue, brainstormin' is like when you help put up a barn but instead of four walls and a roof, you put up an idea. You see we need to start making some money, and get Silver City to start paying off somehow." Don echoed Sue's lecture. He always did what Sue told him to do.

"Help yourself to the keg, it would be best if you boys have a beer or two afore we start to storming." .

"I brung the last of our cousin Jack." Jake pulled out a full bottle whiskey and took a swig. "I jus cum for the Chili and Cornbread."

"You been holding out on me? I thought you said we were out of Jack." Jarvis was annoyed but delighted.

"It was my slide, it's my Jack." Jake held out the bottle and offered his brother a sip.

For the first time Luke was able to see them and study them. The afternoon sunlight showed their age and how much they looked alike. "They are identical twins," he said out loud.

"Course we're twins." It was Jarvis. He was staring at Luke. "Are you being a smart ass?"

"I was talking to myself." Luke answered.

"Yell you should talk less. I'm the good lookin one." Jarvis let out a loud laugh. "I am the young good lookin one. What do you make of this brainstormin' business?"

"Sue read something bout it in a book. It's a way to solve problems. Y'all know we have a problem right?" Luke looked from face to face trying to see if they all knew there was a problem.

"You all drink too much and don't work at all. That's the problem." The sheriff's wife chimed in, her statement drew a round of hearty laughs.

"We work as hard as the next man in Bodfish. Half the beer I drank, I drank with your husband." Don countered, confirming there was never much for the sheriff to do in Bodfish.

"She don't mean nothin bad." The sheriff defended his wife. "Your set is sitting there gatherin dust! I thought you said your stuntmen had some connections, ain't they supposed to get someone to make a movie someday. Ain't that the plan?"

"I'm a drummer. Never been no stuntman." Dean confirmed he was relying on Al to come through with the movie money. "Never been to Hollywood!"

The pressure was on Al, he was the Hollywood connection and he had to come through. Al knew it and had been thinkin on it.

"I got the answer! I think we need to make a portfolio." There was a stunned silence when Al made the announcement.

"Never heard of it." Don spoke up. "What is it?"

Al had never had one in his hand before. He had heard of them and thought they were important. Besides, he had movie experience. He had been an extra in a John Wayne movie, which made him an authority. It was also a fact that the producers had cut his big scene! He had been hiding that secret for years! No one in the brainstorming group had ever been in a John Wayne movie. He intended to make sure it stayed that way.

"A port-holeee-oo? How come you never told me I needed that afore?" Don was surprised to learn there might be some steps to success that had been skipped.

"Chili's Ready" Sue, the two women burst through the kitchen door carrying corn bread, and a pot of steaming Chili.

"Serve yourselves. There's onions, cheese on the table. This batch will curl your toes!" Peg warned the unwary.

Al's hand was still swollen and sore. His knuckles had not recovered from the damage done to them from his encounter with Luke's rock hard jaw bone. He struggled to manage the chili, the cornbread and holding the silverware at the same time.

"Yawee that's hot!" Al rolled his eyes. In desperation he lunged for his beer. Chili and bread crumbs went flying in all directions.

"Your hand must be painful." Luke remarked, his loose teeth had tightened and his fat lip was almost healed. He was getting better every day.

"You should put the beer down and concentrate on the chili. It's hard to eat and drink at the same time" Sue said, feeling pity for Al and his useless hand.

"Way too hot for that. I'm gonna have to put the chili down and concentrate on the beer." Al responded.

"Shouldn't have hit the boy so hard." Jimbo chided Al.

"His teeth did a number on your knuckles."

"Chili is hot! Just take little bites till you get used to it."Peg warned them all.

"God almighty that is hot" Dean cried out. "My mouth is burning."

"You got no reason to doubt Al. He's been in lots of movies." Peg came to her husband's rescue. "If he says we need a portfolio then we need one."

"Okay, okay, How do we build a Porthole?" Don was feeling agreable. He loved Sue's Chili. It always made him feel better. Years and years of eating it and he was still unfazed. "I love hot Chili dear!"

"Well a Portofolio is a book with pictures of Silver City and tells the story about what we got here. We give it out and when they need a set, they will think of us and call us up." He made it up and was bluffing but he saw from their faces that his explanation had sounded plausible.

"How many do we need?" Sue joined the conversation. "At this point I'm willing to try anything. If the chili is a bit hot, just combine it with the cornbread and beer. That will cool it down."

"Don't know, a few, I guess we need to leave one with each studio and producer." In a flash Al wondered just how many studio's there were. He had only been to one.

"Chili was perfect!" Jimbo shouted out his approval. "Five alarm fire requiring a beer to hose it down." His reddened face grinned as he spoke.

Al tilted back in his chair and tried to gain authority. He had been to one studio and that was more than anyone else had done. He didn't know a single movie producer, but what the hell, how hard could it be to fool 'em to consider this wonderful opportunity?

"I never made a book." Don tried to envision the process. It was intimidating.

"It is just a lot of writing with some pictures. Once we get one done, I'll head down to Hollywood and present it to the studio chiefs." Al kept pushing the idea forward. I can believe I can convince them. "I can do it for sure."

"I still like Dean's idea of a slide and water hole best." Jimbo said, shoving down spoonfuls of chili with gusto.

"What did you like best about it?" Dean skipped the rest of the chili and went all in on the beer.

"I can just picture them little kids coming down face first, happy and laughing. I can taste the cotton candy. It is perfect!" Jimbo slapped his knee and rubbed his belly.

"You are a man after my heart!" Dean was ecstatic.

Sue glanced around the table and took the score. Her chili had knocked most of them on their butts, and to her that was a sign of success. Her motto was Chili is always best when it is hot. She figured about half of them were happy campers and the rest were in need of more beer.

"It will be super hot here in a month. We are a long way from getting the slide ready for use. A pool, even a plastic one will cost money we don't have. It costs money to put up billboards on the roads. We need some money fast." Sue jumped in and took over, she was desperate and willing to try anything.

"If we got the pool and slide running how much you think we'd make?" Don asked.

"I figure a minimum of fifty cents a head. All the money is in the cotton candy. It always is." Dean was energized by Jimbo's allegiance.

"So for fifty kids we'd make a grand total of $25.00?" Sue did the math. "Do you figure we'd ever get fifty visitors? Fifty in a day?" Sue knew it was impossible. They were just in love with the idea and could not let it go.

"So far the Portholio seems like the best idea. Does anyone want to make one?" Sue asked the brainstormers for a volunteer.

"I'll give it a try?" Peg raised her hand. "Al's been in movie westerns. If anyone can do it he can". She stood by her man and declared "He was once shot off his horse by John Wayne hisself."

"That's right, I was." Al was puffed up with pride recalling his finest hour.

Al's and Peg's speeches were followed by a long silence. Everyone knew that things were desperate. Luke looked from desperate face to desperate face.

"I had a dream, and I think a dance party might work. We got the jukebox and all we need is a dance floor." Luke was trying to follow the guidance of his dream vision. If ever there was a time to trust his dreams, this was it. It was the hour of need.

"What?" All of them thought he was nuts.

"Well you need money quick right? I say we lay down a slab of cement, set up the Jukebox. He would string up some outdoor lights, sell beer and hot dogs and have a dance party. There is nothing to do around here at night." What he wanted to do was dance the night away with redheaded Darla. After all, he had seen it in his dreams.

"Well we do have the jukebox." Don looked at the blank faces. "What do you all think?"

"A lot of junk has been cleared out and I think there is a big spot ready right now." Luke pointed to where the future parking lot was going to be.

"I could spring for a truck load of cement." Jimbo jumped on board.

"You got the jukebox for music. Darla and I will make fliers and post them all over the county. We can charge an entrance fee and sell beer. We can hold it every Friday night. If it works we can do it Friday and Saturday night." Luke was feeling inspired. "The way I see it there's nothin to do in this town and this might catch on fast."

"That ain't a half bad idea." Don was feeling giddy from the euphoric effect of the chili, corn bread and beer. "I got some lights in my shed and a generator. I could hook up the jukebox. Once we pour a dance floor we'll be all set."

"I don't care what Jones says. We will do it all! Make the Porthole, and put up a billboard on the highway and get a plastic pool. We can use the money from the dance to get this thing rolling! We'll catch on and soon we'll be makin movies and we'll all be rich." Dean jumped up and raised his beer in salute.

"Wait just a minute.." It was Sue. She was pleased that her five alarm bowls of chili woke up their brain cells. The 'brainstorming' party was working!

"Sheriff we won't have problems with the law will we?" Sue asked.

"Are you kidding this will put Bodfish on the map!" The Sheriff had been draining the keg and was in an agreeable mood.

Sue turned to Jake and Jarvis. "Jake, you won't be shootin at any of our guests now will you? I know you don't like strangers coming to town but how else are we going to make a living?"

The brothers had finished up the last of the Jack. Jarvis had started on the keg of beer. "What's that?" They both managed to ask.

"You will not shoot at our guests? Right?" Sue spoke firmly with Jake to get his attention.

"Well how loud will they be?" Jake squinted at her. "How early and how late?"

"It's a dance, a dance party you moron." Jarvis was exasperated with his brother. "People will be having fun, there'll be music, food and beer."

"Can I come?" Jake asked.

"Of course." Sue replied.

"Then I won't shoot at anyone." Jake responded.

Chapter Twenty Seven-

The Bodfish braintrust dedicated themselves to solving an unsolvable problem. That problem was their cash flow. They didn't have one.

If Luke's suggestion of holding a dance was to become the permanent solution it required a permanent location.

"Got to have the dance floor away from the movie set. Can't have a dance floor in the middle of a gun fight!"

Al's thumbs formed a square box shape and he pretended it was an old fashioned camera. He pivoted as if he were filming and surveying the breadth of the town.

"I thought we'd put it out back next to the slide." Dean chimed in.

"Hell! It'll be months before we finish clearing the junk out. I understand that some day that space will be for parked cars. But we need a dance floor right now. Can't have no delays! We got to have the cash coming in." Don's shaky voice reflected his fears. The clock was ticking!

"Yeah, that's what I figured too. The entire south side is clear of debris. I think it has to be on the southside!" Al focused his make believe camera on the southern end of the lot and kept turning the imaginary handle on the reel.

"Is it gonna be big enough?" Jimbo asked, trying to follow the line of sight created by the imaginary camera in Al's hands. "That depends on how big you want to be." Don was deep in thought.

"How big do you think it needs to be?" Jimbo asked again.

"We need places for guests to sit when they're not dancin'. Ain't no point in doin' it if we don't do it right." Dean joined in the debate.

"Too much room and they'll all be spread out. I hate it when all the girls are on one side of the room and all the guys are on the other. We gotta make sure they mingle." Luke chimed in.

"Hot damn, we should just throw a net over them and rope 'em in a pen." Luke chuckled. "Next thing you'll be suggesting we spike the punch."

"If we create enough crowd space. The dancing and mingling problem will take care of itself." Jimbo continued.

Don could not remember when he had last danced with Sue. Did he still know how? Would she dance with him? It was a worry.

It was decided by unanimous agreement that the south side of the Silver City lot was the only and best spot to pour the slab for the dance floor.

"It's perfect, so long as they can see the slide while they're dancing. Just imagine the impression the slide will make while they're dancing cheek to cheek!" Dean clapped his hands to celebrate.

"Just try and imagine the romance of it all." Luke said knowing in his plan would block from view. He wanted it hidden behind the line of musty old buildings and Charlie's odorous stall and pen.

"Boy from the tone of your voice, I get the idea you may have lost faith." Dean prodded Luke. "Let me remind you, this dance thing is all you're doing. It was your dream!"

"I've gone this far and I am ready to see this whole thing through all the way to the end!" Luke replied, annoyed at the suggestion he might want to quit.

"My slide and the swimming hole are like cream corn." Dean was cocksure his vision would prevail. "Once people accept that their kids can slide down into refreshing cool clear water on a boiling hot day, it'll be a done deal."

"I hope you're right." Don needed a dream to come true. Any dream!

A dance, a slide, a movie set, it didn't matter anymore. They were all in process and all had a chance.

"We'll have posters announcing the grand opening of the slide and pool surrounding the dance floor! It is never too early to let people know what is coming. It will be good marketing."

"Marketing?" Jimbo's eyebrow raised at Dean's use of the fancy idea.

"It just means letting people know what ya got. No good keeping it a secret." Dean grinned his happy grin.

The wives chatted up the impending project with the neighbors trying to help build anticipation that something special was about to happen in Bodfish.

Word went from house to house that Don had hired a cement truck to come from Bakersfield and pour slabs of concrete. He was going to make an outdoor dance floor and sell tickets to a party. The rumor was met with skepticism.

"Ain't never been a dance in Bodfish. Don't think anyone dances"

The town residents all liked Don, but in recent years there were some who questioned his sanity. He had always operated a junkyard and sold used auto parts. You always knew where to go to buy hub caps cheap. Most people were satisfied with that.

Then without warning Don had begun moving decaying old buildings and collecting them from remote corners of the valley. They were collecting dust in his junk yard. As the collection grew so did the talk around town. Most people wondered if he had gone mad. Now after two years of work he had assembled thirteen old relics in his yard. The rumor was he intended to make movies in Bodfish!

"Don't make no sense." One neighbor commented only to to hear another retort, "Ain't doin no harm!" followed by, "Ain't doin no good either".

One neighbor who had digested the whole process would sum it all up with: "Do you ever wonder where they are taking all the junk? I mean the place was full of junk, Where'd it all go?"

That was always met with a brief silence, until wisdom prevailed and the conversation was always closed with: "Whatever makes him happy."

Then they would shrug, shake their heads, laugh and move onto sharing some other bit of gossip that was making the rounds.

"I am pretty sure I member when that slide was in Jake's backyard. I saw it up there twenty years ago. I liked it a lot better then." Most were amazed it was still around and useful.

"Wonder why they put it in the junkyard lot".

"Damn thing is tilting to the left something fierce." Another commented.

None of the critics of the Bodfish brainstrust knew how to reconcile the addition of a forty year old slide with any sane commercial idea. A rumor went around that a plastic pool was the next item to be obtained and tickets would be sold on hot days. There were whispers that it was a plot orchestrated by the stuntmen to fleece Al and his wife.

Seeing the slide standing next to the thirteen ancient wooden structures and the pile of old rusting autos was hard to explain. Luke had survived the patchwork wooden fence when he first arrived in Bodfish. The drunken encounter with Al in the moon night was hard to block out.

"It's those boys he hired, it's their fault." One woman said.

"Nah, he's gone loco." Another chimed in.

"Not likely to pay for that" or "I'd rather jump in the lake" were some of the other standard reactions and it was almost always followed by cascades of laughter.

Despite the skepticism, excitement built around the idea of watching the cement truck that was coming to town to pour its contents all over Don's south lot. The much anticipated event came to be known as the "pouring" and all the townsfolk began marking the day on their calendars.

Everyone in town was planning on going. Many were determined to get there early and to get a good seat. No one dared to miss it. It was turning into one of the biggest social events to happen in years.

Only the "Bodfish braintrust" was privy to how much careful consideration had gone into the planning of the "pouring". They had engaged in a loud and contentious debate on how large the new dance "slab" must be.

If it was too small the future crowds would be jammed together, perhaps even colliding and bouncing off each other while twirling around the floor. Jimbo and Dean had both envisioned a scene where dancers went out of control like bumper cars! That would be a disaster!

"It is delicate!" Jimbo allowed there were many things to be considered.

"You need room to kick up a fuss but not too much room. I don't want guests feeling lost and alone under the spotlights." Dean grabbed on to Jimbo's train of thought.

Don argued for "large", he was optimistic and it was part of his nature to lean towards the optimistic view of life.

Jimbo took charge as he was, in his own words, "Born to be a concrete pouring man." This claim was followed by, "I been pouring concrete before most of you was spoiling your diapers."

"I think we need a consistent floor depth of five inches. The slab will have to be a rectangle forty by eighty feet. No one could dispute it."

The Bodfish braintrust was convinced that Jimbo knew his stuff and since he was writing the check for the job it was decided, a slab 40' by 80' was right.

The "pouring" became the number one item on the Bodfish to do list. Urgency was in the air! The boys worked feverishly to clear a spot on the southside of the lot. They patched together a wood frame to hold the cement by raiding some planks from the old fence that surrounded the town.

"Don't like tearing down the fence. Leaves the town wide open to vandals." Don lamented as he watched his stuntmen dismantle the far south wall.

"We don't got a choice. It's the only wood we got. Besides we got Luke to guard the town at night." Al said as he pulled down a ten foot section of fence. "We need a mold more than we need a fence."

The boys, minus Dean who was busy, cleared a suitable patch on the south side. next to the main entrance. They hammered and grounded the frame to hold the cement.

"You were right Al, this was the easiest spot by far." Don was ecstatic that his boys had gotten the job done in two days. They were going to bring the project in on time!

"Yeah, I only wish we had more time to level the ground." Al gestured at a slope in the lot.

Anticipation in the town reached a crescendo! No one could afford to miss Jimbo and the pouring, and they were all gathered in mass when his mixer arrived, churning and circling full of fresh wet cement. The day was here and the time was now and the crowd was feverish.

Don blessed the event by hooking up the half empty keg of beer that was left over from Sue's chili party. It was free to all who had come to help celebrate the wonderful days that were right around the corner.

"The beer is for future good will." Don confided in Sue. "Help bring em all out to the dance."

"I hope you are right." Sue watched as the many devoted followers of "The pouring" helped themselves.

"The lot looks fine to me." Dean gave the job two thumbs up! "We are ready to pour the floor!"

Jimbo had versed his crew on the intricacies of spreading cement when it rushed out. Everything was in place and he began the "pour".

"You need to fill it to the far edges of the rectangle, and be careful to keep the thickness even. It's got to be five inches deep in all spots."

Al and Luke began shifting and pushing the cement trying to level it out evenly.

"It's too far from the edge, you go to make it level." Jimbo yelled out at his crew. They attempted to level the flow.

Some of the old boards taken from the fence for the frame and used to build the frame were split and cracked. Others were too long or too short and left tiny gaps where the cement was oozing out. The cement was seeping out and patchy.

The wooden frame had corner holes where poles were to be "set in the cement for the dance lights".

"Them poles ought to be straight across from each other." Don admonished his crew. At the last second they realized the poles were not aligned.

"Poles not lining up gives the floor character. They are not so boxy " Jimbo dismissed the problem,"There's no good use being too critical."

"Land slopes too much." Jimbo screamed as the cement flowed down the slope.

"Too late to change now." Don cried out.

The mixer kept turning relentlessly, it was a very hot day and it had to be poured. The cement kept rushing out of the mixer and was running down the grade to the bottom of the rectangle frame. It was then that Don noticed a half buried metal pipe jutting up in the air.

"Get that pipe up outta the ground. Couples got to be able to glide and slide." Don yelled at the boys " we can't leave a pipe sticking up like that."

Luke and Al grabbed the pipe and rocked it back and forth in a frantic effort to free it.

"Pull left when I pull left." Al yelled at Luke. The cement was flowing down the hill towards them!

"Okay, pull harder!" Luke put his back into it and yanked until the pipe broke free. When it did, Luke fell to the ground in the path of the oncoming cement.

"Get the hell out of the way, you fool!" Dean yelled at Luke who hustled to his feet.

"Frame is crooked." Jimbo noticed that the frame was way off angle. "It's not gonna be a rectangle. Sides are caving in! It's gonna be lopsided!"

"It's only an inch or two off." Al yelled back!

"No one will be able to tell," Dean agreed,

"Hell I hope so!." Jimbo had no choice! He kept the funnel down and let it rip.

It was midday and well over one hundred degrees. It was arid and dry. The available stuntmen moved the cement around trying to even up all sides. It was no use, it was futile, the cement was drying too fast.

"It's dryin too fast." Al shouted at Jimbo. "Gettin harder and harder." Vapor and steam was rising off the wet cement as it sat in the boiling sun.

"Most places we got bout three, maybe four inch thickness, other spots less." Al shouted at Jimbo who had no choice but to pray for the best. It was turning out that the five inch depth was not to be.

"Damn, we're gonna be thin."

The drum had emptied out. They had some thick spots and some very thin ones. The cement had dried too much and could no longer be moved. It was no use to try and level out the load.

"It's just too damn hot. The cement set super quick." Don knew now that they had made the frame way too large. "We'll have to wait and see how this dries. "

"Thin spots might crack open real bad if someone stepped on em." Jimbo pointed out the problem. None of these frustrating doubts mattered, They set the "Grand Opening" for the coming Saturday. There was no turning back!


Chapter Twenty Eight-

The "pouring" was both a disaster and a huge success! There were frustrating doubts about the quality of the dance floor but the good news was that they had a dance floor and it was ready to go! The brain trust announced the "Grand Opening" would take place on the upcoming Saturday night. The plan to rescue Bodfish's future had been set in motion and there was no turning back!

All the parties shared an unspoken understanding that the dance was only the "first step" in the larger project to rescue Don from financial ruin. It had to work so that the rest of the plan could follow.

"We just need one fantastic night!" Don proclaimed.

"We'll invite the whole town." Al agreed. They were all dreaming of a better, more stable future.

The letter from Jones at the bank arrived and was intercepted by Sue who set it aside. She figured they would open it after the dance had made a pile of cash. She believed the cash flow had to start soon if the movie set was going to survive.

Luke and Darla stood over the kitchen table looking at a map detailing the area surrounding Bodfish. There were no other towns within five miles. It was farmland and wilderness. "Not much of an area to draw on." Luke bemoaned the lack of prospects. "Without any large towns, there can't be many people."

"I think it may surprise you. There's Squirrel Hollow and Shirley's Meadows. They're each less than an hour's drive from here. There's more people in this part of the county than you think." Darla tried to be positive. She was committed to the rescue project. She had designed, and crafted a stack of finely lettered posters promoting the upcoming dance.

"These are great! We'll hang them everywhere." Luke said, holding one up and admiring it.

"Let's hope they get the job done." She had stayed up late into the night drafting the announcements.

"First thing is to hang them in strategic points around town. " Luke said.

"Of course, I plan to hang some in Shirley and then swing up to Squirrel." Darla was a step ahead.

"It's lucky you know the area so well." Luke rubbed her hand affectionately.

"There are clusters of farms and people living all along the drive. We will contact more people than you think." Darla told Luke.

The town was abuzz in anticipation. The original gathering at "the pouring" had been small. The fortunate few who had witnessed it had become royalty. In the aftermath the number of claimants to the honor of attendance had risen to fifty. The dance party to raise money to save the movie set was the talk of the town!

"First things first!" Luke left nothing to chance. He headed straight for the bar and liquor store and nailed Darla's poster to the wall. Bodfish was tiny and that nothing was ever a secret for long!

"The best part of the "pouring" was watching that young stuntman hustle and sweat in the hot sun with his shirt off. He looked real good." The comment came from a middle aged woman drinking at the bar. Luke turned to find her staring at him.

His name's Luke, he showed up a couple of months back, and has been busting his butt ever since." A young blond chipped in.

"Have you been keeping track of him?" The matron asked, surprised.

"I can see the set from my back porch. He sleeps in that old jail house." The blond answered.

"You think he'll be at the dance?" They both had their eyes riveted on Luke. They spoke about him as if he were not in the room.

"I bet he comes with the redhead from the motel. They've been together for a while now."

Luke could sense their disappointment. He left the bar with his ears on fire.

"How'd it go?" Darla asked as he edged himself into the front seat of her Nash.

"We are getting a good reaction. Everyone seems to be looking forward to the party." Luke answered. Darla's dazzling blue eyes helped him to block out the flirty banter in the bar . He focused on her as she pointed the car north in the direction of the town of Shirley Meadows.

"Keep your eyes open for clusters of mailboxes. There's a lot of farm houses on the way. We'll stop when we see them." Darla advised Luke.

"You have a real knack for lettering." Luke admired Darla's work.

"I love drafting. I took a class once. I wanted to pursue it, but then everything changed." Her voice trailed off.

"It's never too late to try again." Luke was sure there was a lot more to her than changing motel bed sheets.

"I worked as a waitress and went to school while my husband was away in the war."

"You had to drop out?" Luke sensed the frustration in her voice.

"He made me. He was jealous. My job made him crazy too. He made me quit them both." Luke saw the pain in her face as she told her story.

"So you left him?" Luke was having trouble concentrating. All he could think about was getting her naked again.

"It kept getting worse. He got mean when he drank."

She pulled into a side road next to a cluster of farm homes and Luke left fliers in the mailboxes. Luke wondered when the owners would pick up the mail. Would it be in time for the party on Saturday night?

"Sounds like he made things dangerous for you." Luke picked up the thread of the conversation.

"I filed papers and got a restraining order but he ignored it. They locked him up for a couple of weeks but when he got out he was meaner than ever. I had to leave town."

"So you came to Bodfish?" Luke wondered just how bad it was. "Did he ever beat you?"

"Yeah when he did I left and came here." Her face froze in a knot.

"I bet you can't wait for it to be final?" Luke said.

"My papers are pending. I have to stay close to Bakersfield until it's done. For now this is a safe place."

Another hamlet consisting of three houses appeared and Darla stopped and motioned he should put out and put fliers in their mailboxes.

"There are a lot of clusters like this, we will be stopping all afternoon." Her eyes sparkled. Luke wondered who lived in these places? What did they do?

"You must be bored here, living alone." Luke brought the focus back on Darla.

"Sometimes, but I know this will pass. What about you? You like it here?" Her smile said she could look out for herself.

"I was looking for something different. I thought maybe I could get in the movies." Luke answered.

Darla broke into laughter. "You think Al and Dean are ever going to own a movie company. I thought you were smarter than that."

Her directness was a shock.

"I just got tired of school and working so hard. I had to do something." Luke was starting to wonder if he had been reaching out for a dream when there was nothing there to be had.

"You have time to figure things out. No one can see the future. But when the bank forecloses there will be no place for you here." Darla's words seemed harsh, even ominous.

"We're comin up to Shirley's Hollow." Darla slowed down and pulled into a gas station. It had a convenience store selling groceries.

"There's about fifty or so homes here in town." The downtown consisted of the gas station and store.

"Should we go house to house?" The houses were far apart and it would be time consuming.

"Nah, we just need to put up the sign in the store. Leave it to me. I know the owner." Darla took several fliers with her and headed for the entrance.

"Darla, good to see you again sweet thing." The man's voice was so loud Luke could hear him from the street.

"Lester, I need a favor." Darla asked.

The tone of her voice made Luke nervous. He decided he better check in on her.

"Sure doll you name it, you know old Lester. I'll do anything for you." He grabbed her and threw his arms around her. She struggled and could not get loose.

"Lester, my boyfriend is out in the car."

Luke got to the front door and his stomach churned at the sight of Lester and Darla struggling.

"Well, invite him in. I'd like to meet the lucky fella." Lester glared at Luke as he came up to the door.

"Lester, I have these posters and I need you to hang one in your store. We're havin a dance and we want people to come." Darla pushed him away and handed him a poster.

"How bout that? A dance? You don't say. In Bodfish?" Lester looked it over. "Bet this will be fun. Maybe I'll come. Will you dance with me if I come."

"Will you hang it for me or not?" Darla edged towards the door.

"Sure thing, anything for you." He moved toward Darla as if he expected a reward. She backed out of his reach.

"Hey you out there, why don't you come in and buy your girl a nice popsicle? I got grape and cherry. I bet she'd like to suck on a cherry pop."

Darla edged out of the store and pushed Luke back into the car.

"Sorry. I forgot what a creep he is." She started up the car and sped out of town. "I should have remembered what he was like."

"I thought you said you knew him?" Luke asked.

"I have stopped here a couple of times on my way to Bakersfield. That's all." Darla looked out the window. "He's a pig. I just forgot how much of a pig. It's thirty minutes to Squirrell Mountain. Things will be better there."

Everything went silent. Luke began to ponder how vulnerable everything in his world was. Was the movie set doomed? His current future was riding on it. Did it have a chance to succeed?

"Maybe I should head up into the mountains to look for that gold mine." Luke waited for Darla to react.

"There's gold up there for sure." She looked straight ahead. "Sorry about Lester and what happened back there." Darla apologized.

"You didn't do anything wrong. He did." Luke protested.

"I knew he was a pig and should have expected it. I never should have gone in there or dragged you into it." She was upset.

"We need to find customers for the dance. So we went there to try. I have changed my mind about the mine since you told me about Edward."

"I don't blame you, the story of the mine is real. I cashed those ounces and they were worth a lot. " Darla kept her eyes on the road.

"When Al told me I thought the whole thing was bullshit. You changed my mind. " Luke said. "How did you get to know Edward so well?"

"I checked him in on the day he arrived. That same day the two of them got drunk at the bar. Edward started coughing and spitting up blood. Al got him back to the motel. Edward couldn't get in because he locked his keys in the room. They called me to let em in."

"So did you hear what Edward said when he gave Al the map?" Luke asked.

"Edward never gave Al the map. He just showed it to him and then he passed out cold and Al took it "

"Al stole it?" It was a different twist to the story.

"Not exactly, he told me he was going to take it and copy it. I figured he intended to bring it back in the morning." Darla's voice got a little timid. "I am hiding here, I don't want to make a fuss and draw attention to myself."

"Did he ever try to bring it back?" Luke asked, thinking he already had an answer.

"Edward woke up for a while later that night. That's when he told me his secret." Darla glanced over to see if Luke was paying attention.

"What secret?" Luke could feel that Darla had something important to say.

"There are a lot of abandoned mines, but the right one, the one with the gold, has a huge cross marking its entrance. If it doesn't have a cross at the entrance it's the wrong mine". Darla paused and waited.

"A giant cross, wow! And Al doesn't know?" Luke asked.

"Edward told me and then he closed his eyes and drifted off. He never woke up. You and I are the only ones who know. I hope you can find it. Did I judge you right? There is a lot of gold ready to be found. Let's escape out of here together."

Darla pulled off the road. She threw her arms around him and kissed him until his toes curled. She reached inside his pants and grabbed his penis. He was aroused. and jolted to attention. She shed her clothes and was naked in an instant and mounted him by the side of the road.

It was explosive and wild. When he came back to his senses, Luke felt alive, more alive than he had ever felt before. She was powerful and sensual in a way he had never known before. She was the most confident woman he had ever met.

"More than ever I gotta find that mine." The secret of the cross had convinced him to go treasure hunting.

Squirrel Mountain was about the same size as Bodfish. Luke hung up all of his remaining flyers and talked up the virtues of the dance to everyone who would listen.

Darla drove them home in silence.He wanted to spend the night with her. He didn't want to let her out of his sight. He could taste her and smell her. He was on fire.

The one thing he couldn't do was invite her back to the jail house. She had never seen the dusty, dirty bed he called home. What would she think if she saw the squalor he slept in all of this time?

"See you tomorrow" She indicated he should get out. He did as she asked.


Chapter Twenty Nine

The Bodfish brainstrust spent the better part of two years moving old buildings from all over Kern County and relocating them in Bodfish. Everyday the boys labored to turn the old junk yard into a movie set. Gradually an old western town was taking shape where once rusting old autos had been stacked out in the hot desert sun.

The project was running out of time. It was in jeopardy and financial failure was imminent. In desperation, they had chosen a plan based on Luke's dream of a dance party and had set about trying to put it into action. Everything was riding on it working and the matter was coming to a head.

Sue worked up the nerve to give Don the letter she intercepted from the bank.

"I thought you should see it first hand." Sue said, handing him the letter. "We ain't got much time."

She was relieved to have shared it with him. He read it over and over again, and now had it sitting on his night stand within easy reach. They were many months behind on all three house payments. The letter demanded that they be caught up in full. If not, the next step was foreclosure.

The letter went on to day that Jones and the board had reviewed its discoveries about the old town and determined it must start showing a profit. In addition there was a long list of "Required Improvements" that needed to be done. It made Don's head spin.

They were no longer considered the  place to be an asset, instead it was now considered a liability. To complete the grim picture their savings account was empty and they had nothing to fall back on.

"I'll show em who's liable for what!" Don was defiant

"The dance will be a success. I have faith" Sue nodded, trying to be as supportive as possible. "It's got to be, there's no turning back now. It's the best plan we got."

"I'm sorry I let you down." Don tried to apologize for the desperate situation he had put them in.

"Don't worry! I made your favorite breakfast." Sue put a plate on the table in an effort to try and comfort her husband.

"Biscuits and gravy! I love biscuits and gravy!" He said and dug in.

"I think this dance thing will catch on just like Luke said. It has to," Sue did her best to sound optimistic.

"I never been any good at makin' money." Don smiled, thankful that Sue's gravy was lifting his spirits.

"It's all in the past. If there was ever a time for a big change, the time is now." Sue didn't care much for biscuits and gravy herself.

"You make the best gravy in the world." He said. I feel better already. "I think we're goin about this all wrong. It don't feel right, I don't think we should charge an entrance fee to the dance." Don winked, giving Sue a sheepish grin.

"Not charge? This is all about getting up the cash to save the old west town. How are we gonna do that, if we don't charge?" Sue felt a panic rising up in her gut. Was Don about to throw it all away?

"Well, in the past the entrance has always been free. People walk on the set anytime they want and we never charge for it." Don had thought it out.

"Yeah well this is different, we have a dance floor and music and food." Sue countered.

"We need the whole town to come, we gotta let em in for free. We will still charge for the beer and food." Don insisted. "We'll call it a "benefit." We need to pack the place."

"If no one comes, it's over and we are through." Sue agreed.

"I'm right. I can feel it." Don insisted. He was sure no one would pay for something they had already done for free.

"We need a lot of money and we need it fast." Sue reminded Don.

"If we ask for help, I think we'll get it." Don voiced what he thought was their only real hope.

They decided to put out a donation box so each neighbor could make a contribution to the cause.

Don made a sign that read:

"Donations for the Survival of the Silver City movie set gratefully accepted!"

They would put the sign and cash box next to the keg of beer.

"They can't miss it." Don was sure his town could be counted on to help when it was most needed.

"I hope you're right." Sue said.

Don's crew received the news with panic and disbelief.

"Got to charge." Jimbo asserted as soon as he heard the change in plan.

"Beer and food. They are always the money makers!" Dean rebutted Jimbo's fears. "Take my word for it. We'll make money."

"Darla and I put flyers up all over. We expect lots of out of towners." Luke argued. "They'll all pay! None of them will have ever seen anything like it before. It's a once in a lifetime event!"

"How many out of towners do you figure we'll draw?" Jimbo rubbed his hands together in anticipation.

"We covered a lot of ground. I think it'll be big." Luke's voice swelled with pride. He imagined them all pushing and shoving to get in the door. It would save the town and it would all be because of him.

"Sounds real good. All we have to do is sit back and reap the profits." Jimbo slapped his hands together like they were two sticks making fire. "You wouldn't have no dance floor if I hadn't sprung for the cement." He reminded everyone again.

"Reckon we all owe you." Dean raised his mug in recognition of Jimbo's all around goodness. The whole crew rose in unison and raised a glass to salute Jimbo.

"To Jumbo" They all praised him.

The biggest question now occupying Jimbo's attention was how they should recognize him and give him credit as a co-founder.

"What sounds better to you? "Managing General Partner? Or Director of Operations?" He asked. "Which title fits me the best?"

"Can't say I know, it's a tough one." Dean and Don both dodged the question.

"Maybe I'll have two cards printed. One with each title. That way I can switch back and forth depending on what works best at the time." The moment he shared the idea, he fell in love with it.

"I can be the Managing General Partner when I am busy managing things. Or if need be, I can become the Director of Operations, when I am busy directing,"

"Best you buy card holders and mark em. It would never due to mix em up." Dean offered his advice. "You best keep apart from each other."

"Damn you are brilliant. I'll do just that." Jimbo made a note of it. His next important investment would be two sets of cards with matching card holders.

The whole crew prepared for the benefit dance. The stuntmen strung and tested the outdoor lights, while Don hooked up the sound system. He turned the sound all the way up and Hank Williams' nasal voice went booming into every house in Bodfish.

"That'll get em all ready!" Don shouted gleefully above the music.

"Turn that down!" Sue came rushing out. "You got teeth rattling all over town."

"Just offering up a little advance notice! Letting 'em all know what to expect."

When Saturday morning arrived, it looked to be a beautiful day ahead. The sheriff appeared at Don's door with his hands full of red, white and blue cloth.

"Whatcha got?" Don was surprised to see the sheriff was up and about so early. It was only nine o'clock. He was never out on the streets before noon.

"Bunting. Town uses it on the 4th of July and on election days to spruce up the ballot box site." The sheriff offered Don the cloth bunting. "I thought maybe you might cover the entrance Silver City it. It'll be real fancy and make it more like an official grand opening."

"Bunting? From the 4th of July?" Don was overwhelmed by the thoughtfulness of the act.

"It belongs to the city but I doubt anyone will care." The sheriff's wife had suggested it to him the night before. Now as far as he was concerned it was his idea, and a damn good one.

"You and the missus is comin? Right?" Don asked. He had assumed they would be there.

"Of course, word is the whole town will be there." The sheriff promised.

The sheriff's wife knew everyone and if she did not know them, she knew someone who did. She and Sue were the queen bees of Bodfish. Together they had alerted the whole town. Excitement was building and Don was thankful for the women who had made it happen.

The outdoor lighting and generator were in place. The bunting was swinging on the entrance gate. It all gave the place a special touch. The grill was ready to be fired up. Sue all set to serve some burgers and dogs.

There were two full kegs of beer chilling and ready to go. One was already running while the other was in reserve as a backup if sales were brisk. Sue had trays of potato salad and a big pot of chili out for the taking.

The dance was scheduled for seven, a full hour before sundown. It had been over a hundred all day. But it was cooling down in the shade as the exact moment approached. Conditions were ideal and luck was on their side.

The whole group gathered one last time to review the plan. Don was gonna serve the beer, Sue was cooking. Luke was to guard the entrance.

"I was gonna charge at the door. But I changed my mind. Entrance will be free." Don explained to Luke. "I need you to guard the door and make sure we don't let in no trouble makers."

"How will I know if they are gonna make trouble?" Luke was still determined to charge any out of towners that came. He got no answer about troublemakers. He figured he was on his own.

"Everyone must look like they're having fun all the time. Everyone needs to dance all the time!" Jumbo kept repeating his mantra. The crew were expected to keep up appearances and it was crucial that they appear to be having a grand old time no matter how desperate things might become.

"Laugh and the world laughs with you." he said, flailing his hands in the air. "If you are havin fun it will encourage everyone else to have fun. If no one dances, everyone will sit around and act dead."

"If there is women just sittin round then Luke needs to dance with em. Darla should do the same with any men who are left alone."

As twilight approached folk began to drift in from all parts of town. They came in little groups of three or four people. As soon as the women were situated the men headed straight for the beer.

"Fifty cents a mug tonight, proceeds are going to the future Silver City and our crew." Don was anxious and ready to pour.

Fifty cents? I can buy a six pack for a buck. It's always free at your parties! Why did you decide to charge? I left my wallet at home." The attendees were offended and shocked.

"Well, sir, this is a benefit, we made that clear to everyone right from the start." Sue stepped in when Don stumbled.

"Maybe so, but I left my money at home." One customer, with his mug in hand, offered to give back his half empty glass.

"Your credit is good with me, Sam, Just remember to make it up to us as soon as you can." Don agreed on making new credit arrangements for his many friends.

"Got to offer credit or shut it down." He confided in Sue.

The sheriff and his wife were among the last notables to arrive. Right behind them came Jake and Jarvis. The brothers stumbled in with their rifles in tow for company. It was obvious they had been drinking all day long.

"You planning on dancing with your guns in your hand?" Luke asked. He wanted to make them leave the guns outside. But Don had given instructions and let em carry.

"Don't "poke the bear" was Don's suggestion to Luke on how to handle the twins. Luke's biggest problem was he couldn't decide which of the two was the bear.

"I don't go nowhere without my rifle." Jake squinted out at Luke. "Don't feel dressed."

The two brothers headed straight for the keg. The sun went down and everyone had a burger and beer. An hour passed, Luke saw there were fifty or more people spinning in a circle on the hard dried concrete.

Luke and Darla forgot Jimbo's edict that they should keep the crowd engaged. They spent the entire night dancing with each other. Neither of them bothered to see if there were any customers who needed their attention. As it turned out, none did.

Neither Al nor Dean did any dancing with their wives. Neither had ever danced before and for them the keg was a far more interesting companion. Jimbo took turns spinning Liz and Peg around the concrete floor. He turned out to be a dancing fool, he was born to cut a path on the concrete slab. The women accommodated Jimbo's wild side. It was the first time either had danced since they were girls. They turned back the clock by dancing and laughing the night away.

Don turned the Jukebox up as high as it would go and the party heated up. Everyone was having the time of their life except for Don.

He was trapped pouring beer and watching. He was missing the party. And true to his nature, he could not bring himself to charge a single neighbor.

"That one's on credit." He agreed.

In his mind he was still "creating goodwill" with all the familiar faces. He thought: You can't charge your neighbors for drinks at a party you are giving. It ain't right.

After all, he had the donation box in place and if they had a good time, they would all take care of him. Maybe the future of the movie project was hanging in the balance but he had realized this party was a one time event. He should enjoy himself. Life is short. Money be damned!

He grabbed his wife and headed out onto the dance slab. The floor was anything but smooth, it was hard to glide, but they were soon twirling and bobbing along with glee. He figured, hell you are never too old to dance and laugh with your wife.

"Let our guests make their own burgers. " He said as he spun her to the center of the revolving circle floating and gliding beneath the stars.

Two young "outsiders" came late and didn't know anyone. They bought a few beers and paid Luke for them. They left early disappointed. They had come expecting some "action."

Don and Sue forgot they had a problem. They stayed glued to each other the rest of the night.

"Help Yourself! Just be sure to remember us at the Donation Box." They called out when anyone asked for another beer.

Jake and Jarvis got so drunk they were bear hugging and singing along to "Your Cheatin Heart" at the top of their lungs. They sang through their noses and were badly out of tune. Jake kept tripping over his own feet and each time he did he nearly dragged Jarvis to the ground. They were scrapped and raw but Jarvis managed to keep Jake from falling hard.

"I got ya, baby brother." he called out every time Jake tripped.

Luke loved it, the whole town had turned out for the "dance". He had the comforting feeling that it was a success. He spent most of the night squeezing Darla, who looked prettier and prettier as the night wore on. They snuck off every few minutes to a dark corner behind the jail house. Darla's fire lit up and she tried to replay the night at the lake. Luke was too shy and afraid to risk it. There were too many eyes about.

When Don pulled the plug on the jukebox, Luke had a warm feeling of satisfaction that all was well. He had been so entranced in dancing and holding Darla he had failed to notice that all of the guests had gone home. It seemed the whole thing had happened in the blink of an eye.

"Time to count the money. We can clean up latter" Jimbo's voice was thick from the beer. "Let's see how we did. How much from the food and beer sales?"

There was no answer, only the noises of the desert night. Sue had her head down and was trying to look busy cleaning up. Don was scurrying around picking up trash.

"Well how much did we clear? There was a lot of beer drunk tonight. What was the total?" Jimbo asked the question and focused directly on Don.

"They was all our neighbors and friends." Don looked sheepishly at his feet. "I invited them all to come."

"That's right, so how much was the total?" Jimbo was beginning to understand. At first he didn't want to believe it but as he stared at Don it became clear.

"I couldn't charge our neighbors. They came as friends and guests." It dawned on Jimbo that Don had not charged anyone for anything Sue had done the same with the food.

"I made the kids from out of town pay. They had one beer apiece so I collected a dollar." Luke spoke, they had made a dollar for sure.

"You mean to tell me that you only got a dollar for the whole night?" Jimbo himself was busy finishing his seventh beer. "Sue what did you charge for the food?"

"The two boys from out of town paid for the hamburgers, thirty five cents each. The rest, well I let em have them for free. Like Don said, they were our neighbors, came here because we invited them. Don't see how we could charge them."

"You mean to tell me that for all of this we made a $1.70 total?"

Luke remembered he had charged the two visiting boys a dollar each when they arrived at the gate.

"I charged the two outsiders a dollar each." That means $3.70 for the night. "I let the rest in free. Like Don said they were neighbors.

Jimbo had to sit down and let the truth wash over him. The party had been a success but they were further in debt than they had been before it had started. Three dollars and seventy cents would not come close to covering the costs involved in the "party." The beer and food had cost far more than that. Not to mention the cost of the concrete.

"Jones was right." Jimbo hung his head.

"Wait a minute, there is the "Donation Box." We have not counted the cash from it.e

Don made his way to a small rusted box. He had been eyeing it all night. It seemed to him very few people had approached it. He knew his neighbors were all as poor as he was and the likelihood was that it was empty. He picked it up and shook it.

He listened for the sound of loose change jangling. When it was poured it they had made just over seven dollars. Some generous soul had left a five. By Bodfish standards they had made out with a haul.

"You have to admit, it was a fine party. Without question the best party ever held in Bodfish." Don always tried to look on the bright side after all he had never thought that he would make a living building the old town or give dance parties in it.

"Hell, $10.70 cents! It was a nice party." Jimbo wanted to cry but a man in his "executive position" needed to show leadership at a time like this.

They went home sure that the night had been a success after all they each had a grand old time. Money be damned! Of course, the future was more cloudy than ever and it was unlikely that Silver City was going to survive. It would never be the money making machine that they had once dreamed it would become.

Luke had spent the night in a blissful union of red hot dancing and holding Darla close. His night was a success. However his plan to rescue the Town from financial ruin had failed.

He wasn't sure what he wanted from his blossoming relationship with Darla. He was certain he did not want it to end. Luke went to sleep fearing that he had reached the end of the road in Bodfish. Perhaps he would be forced to let Darla go and walk away. Finding the mine had become the last chance and the only way out. It was a terrible and lonely thought. He did not sleep well that night.

Chapter Thirty

At his core, Luke believed that all that was needed to succeed in life was to persevere, stick to the path, and fight the good fight. If you did so everything would be made good. He had come to Bodfish looking for a more interesting and exciting life, and maybe break into the movies. All of these hopes and aspirations had faded and become less real everyday.

In the struggle, he had grown close to Al, Don and the small group fighting to make Bodfish a success story. He cared for them. He felt driven to help them if he could.

Landing in Bodfish had brought Darla into his life. She had lit a fire in him. She was exciting in ways he had never thought possible. She was beautiful and sensual and confident. She was also ten years older and married. He believed that unless the town became a success he was without a future. How could he ask her to commit her life to him?

"That gold mine is out there, I know it is, and you can find it." He imagined Darla's sexy voice, she was clear and direct. She always seemed sure of herself and of what she said.

"I believe you, but it is a big country. It could be anywhere out there." Luke lay next to Darla in her bed. She folded herself up against him and rubbed her breasts against his shoulder and chest.

"Al wants you to look for it. He'll help you get started. You're going to find it." She licked his neck and kissed him.

"Yeah, but Al tried and failed." Luke kissed her on the lips and she parted them and put her tongue in his mouth.

"You are the one that's going to find it. It's your destiny, not his." She opened her legs and helped him. He slid into her for the second time that morning. She locked her legs around his waist and pulled him into her. They screwed until they were both dripping wet with sweat. Sex kept lasting longer and getting more satisfying every time they did it.

"When you find the mine, we can go anywhere, live anywhere we want." Her bright green eyes lit up when she said "go anywhere".

"Yeah and we could stay here and make this place a success." He was spent, and felt himself drifting off into sleep.

"Talk to Al about it," she whispered encouragement.

"Okay, I will." he answered and closed his eyes. He slept for a little under an hour. When he woke she was naked lying face down fast asleep. He got out of bed and dressed without waking her. He pulled the bed spread over her and left.

He considered everything that had brought him to this point. His plan had failed and they were running out of time. Darla was certain he was the one destined to find the gold mine.

She envisioned them striking it rich and leaving Bodfish to begin a new life together. It was the kind of commitment he had never considered before and he was not sure he was ready for it. He wondered, was he rushing into it? He was attracted to her but what kind of a commitment could he make? What should he do?

If he threw in the towel and quit now, the whole adventure would be a failure. The more he thought about it, the more he wanted to accept Al's challenge and go out and find the lost gold mine. Darla had provided him with the key information on how to recognise the mine when he found it. It proved beyond a doubt that she believed in him. Maybe it was a matter of persistence and all would turn out fine.

It was boiling hot when Luke arrived at Al's kitchen door. Al was even more hungover than usual. He was sipping coffee and staring off into space. He looked lost.

"Morning." Luke felt like grabbing Al and shaking him from his stupor. He wanted to yell in his ear! "Cheer up, help is on the way!"

"Damn, you're up early…" Luke could tell Al was not in the mood for company. Everything important in his life was slipping away.

"Well there is no tryin to ignore it. We failed last night." Luke started right in. There was no use sugar coating it, the future of the town was in serious doubt.

"Easy for you to say, you don't got two years of work and your entire future riding on it." Al was in a dark mood. "If you want, you can go to do something else. No one is depending on you."

'Yeah, well last night did narrow down our options. We are down but not out." Luke was ready to move on.

"What you getting at?" Al heard the hopefulness in Luke's voice. "Why are you so chipper this morning?"

"I am ready to go. I want to do it." Luke said it with confidence.

"You are? What changed?" Al was surprised. Something was different. What happened?

"Darla told me all about how you got the map from Edward. I know it's real. It's out there, I gotta go find it!" Luke was excited.

"She told you?" he had forgotten about Darla being in the room with them that night. "What did she say? What did she tell you?"

"She told me you listened to his story. The old man had no reason to lie. She believed you, so now I believe." Luke made it clear he had come around.

"So you believe her, not me." Al leaned back and shook his head a bit.

"I believe you both." Luke did not want Al to back out now. He had to bankroll the project.

"Okay, I still have all of the gear from last year. But understand, this is a hard thing to do. You have to walk off into the wilderness. You will have to survive alone." Al assessed Luke and liked what we saw.

"I have done a lot of wilderness stuff. I rafted down the Colorado with my cousins. It took us a week to do that. Done a lot of camping alone in the mountains. I feel good sleeping out under the stars." Luke loved doing all things outdoors.

"Well, I can purchase a mule! It can carry all your food and gear. That'll help you stay out on the trail for at least ten days." Al desperately wanted to send Luke out.

"I'm ready! Let's do it," Luke leapt at the idea.

"I can have everything ready in two days." Al gave him a hug. "We need to go over a few things. I can teach you."

"Fire away, I'm ready."

Al fetched the old miner's map from its hiding place. He spread it gingerly on the table making sure Luke could see every detail. Then he unfolded a second map. Luke had never seen the new map before.

"This here is a topographical map covering the same area Edward drew. It shows all the hills, creeks and canyons." Al unfolded the new map.

"Edward didn't mark his map North or South, so I played around with it and completed the puzzle. See? I traced the boundaries of Edwards's map onto this one. I think it is in the backcountry about forty miles up river." Al encouraged Luke to check his work.

Luke studied the two maps and saw how Al had pieced it together. He couldn't be sure but he realized that Al had one thing right, the mine could be found.

"It is a large chunk of real estate to cover." Luke calculated that it might be 30 square miles or more.

"I searched for a week. Covered the territory west of the river. I shaded out the part already I did. You need to go east and explore those directions.." Al pointed out some light gray lines on the map.

"Okay, that will make it a little easier. It's still a lot of land." Luke was intent on doing whatever needed to be done to succeed.

"Good. I gotta warn you, don't be out in the afternoon sun. Only work or travel in the mornings or late afternoon. I got a half tent, it sets up quick. Just quit and stay out of the noon sun."

Luke was sure that this was his last shot. He could stay or leave but he needed money if he wanted Darla with him.

"I got no problem! I can handle it!" Luke was confident.

"We'll take Charlie's trailer and drop you and the mule right here." Al pointed to a spot where he wanted to drop Luke off to start the search.

"There's a lot of big hills on this map " Luke was still studying Al's new map.

."Yeah they're rugged and will be hard to climb. But somewhere in there you'll find my lost mine." Al's feelings of depression had lifted.

"Great, I wish I could today!." They shook hands.

"We're partners now!" Al had succeeded.

Al got busy and pulled everything together. There were shovels, picks, pans, nightlights, ropes, a canteen, several large water jugs and a half tent to sleep in to stay out of the sun. It was late July and it was well over a hundred every day. It was a brutal time to undertake hiking in the hills. But this was the time it had to be done.

"I bought at least ten days of food." Al and Luke went over the inventory of supplies together making sure Luke had everything he would need. "They are bringing the mule tonight. We'll leave for the drop off point as soon as we got him."

The next day the mule arrived, the gear was packed and everything was ready to go. The entire town prayed for Luke's safety and success. They all believed Al had failed in his attempt to find the mine. As a result most of them had written the idea off. Now Luke was heading out into the wilderness all alone. Darla smiled and said nothing. She was happy. She hoped it meant that the two of them had a future together.

"There are a lot of side roads and back trails. The mine has got to be somewhere off one of the main trails." Al traced a path on his topographical map.

"Yeah there's choices to make. There is no sure way to plan a route." Luke had been pondering a way to cover the most ground he could. He studied the creeks, and streams coming down from the mountains feeding into the Kern. Were they full of water or were they dry? It would make a difference.

"I will start here and follow this creek to the first large hill. I'll camp at the base." Luke laid out his plan.

"Yeah I think you'll find a lot of mountains and even more canyons. You need to climb to the mountain tops. Always look for trails that seem to go nowhere. The truth is they must lead to something." Al's eyes bore into the back of Luke's skull. He wondered if Luke was listening and making note of his instructions.

"Don't worry. The final call is my decision. I'll make the right choices,"Luke wanted to make Al back off.

"I trust you, but keep your eyes open for blackish dark spots. They could be mine entrances or cave openings. You need to always keep moving and searching. I think we will get lucky. God always helps the man who helps himself." Al delivered his last pep talk with authority.

Luke nodded and thought. "Yeah and when I see a cave with a cross in the front I am gonna head for it like a bee to honey." He was armed with secret information.

"Be sure to keep a record of everything you do." Al handed him a thin black book.

"Yes, I got it. I got to walk the land, eliminate territory and keep a good record of where I have been." One more time Luke reassured Al that he was on the right page and was prepared to follow directions.

Luke couldn't sleep. They were up at three in the morning and left in the dark of night.

"We got to make sure you are on the trail as early as possible. That way you can get in half a day's search before it gets too hot."

The dirt road leading to the drop point was narrow and hard to see in the dark. The moon was a quarter full, and the stars didn't provide much light. Al had to go slow to stay on the road. Luke must be fresh when they arrive at the trailhead. Al woke him to offer some last minute advice. to offer.

"When you stop to rest, find a place with a lot of vegetation. Tie up the mule and let him water and graze. Every canyon has a little creek running down to the Kern so if you pick a good spot to camp, you can keep the mule fresh."

"Sounds easy enough."

He had to be free to roam the area without having to return to the river to make camp. He hoped the creeks were full of running water. That would make it easier.

"Mules can go three days without water but you need to limit it to two. Else it'll get sick. Don't go no more than two days without water and you won't have a problem. Mule knows what to eat. You can trust him on that score. But don't try to stretch the time without water or you'll lose the mule." Al pounded Luke with details on how to care for a mule.

"Okay." Luke had heard it now a dozen times.

The winding dirt road came to an abrupt end. Al pulled up and stopped. They had reached the drop off point. The sun was rising and the day was on its way. One trail headed off into the west. The same trail stretched back into the mountains and headed east. Al unloaded the mule. It was time for them to part ways.

Chapter Thirty One

It was early morning and the majestic Sierra Nevada's were taking shape and becoming visible. The night was giving way to the new day. Luke opened the horse trailer door and found Al's mule was asleep on his feet. Most of the camping gear was stacked in the front of the trailer.

"Lucky thing you don't have to hike the Sierra's. It'd take forever if you had to search all those tall mountains on foot."

Al climbed in and tried to wake the sleeping mule. It was a light sleeper. It woke up startled.

"Easy, easy boy." Al backed the animal out and down to the ground.

"Lucky for me, the tallest peak I have to climb is only thirty five hundred feet" Luke unpacked the camping gear and stacked it by the side of the road.

"You will have six hours to search today before it gets too hot to be outside." Al strapped all of his canned goods on the mules' back. "You should head east. I figure it is somewhere in the eastern quarter." He pointed to a wide range of hills stretching for miles.

Luke finished loading all the gear on the mule who was waiting by the side of the trailer.

"This mule is a good old boy, I'm gonna call him Andy." Luke lashed the last piece of gear in place.

"I like that name, it's nice and friendly." Al smiled to let Luke know he approved.

"He's gonna be my only company for the next ten days". Luke tugged hard on the pack.

"It's secure, you know how to tie a knot." Al approved.

"I'll be lucky to cover a third of the area in ten days. It's a lot of territory." Luke was overwhelmed by the imposing task he had ahead.

"You can't hope to cover it all, we just gotta get lucky." Al was encouraging. "I'm just glad it's you doin this and not me, it's a young man's job."

"Darla said she thinks destiny is on my side. She says I am the one that's going to find it. I hope she's right." The mention of Darla made Luke tingle with excitement.

"I got you pointed in the right direction. Now it's all up to you." Al made a silent prayer. "See you back here in ten days, partner!"

"I better be going while it's still cool." Luke put his backpack on and tugged on Andy's rope. Luke took off towards the hills with Andy's rope in one hand and rifle in the other. The journey began on the same one lane gravel road that Al had taken a year earlier when he tried to find the mine. Al's attempt had ended in frustration. Back then when the road forked, Al went left to the west. On this trip Luke went right instead. He and Andy were going to explore and map the opposite quarter.

The gravel road turned to dirt and Luke found himself following a dried up creek bed. Following Al's instructions Luke followed it until it came to a dead end.

"One dead end checked and marked off the list. The first one went nowhere."

For fun, Luke informed Andy of their progress as he crossed the dead end off his map. He decided to treat Andy like he was a partner in the search. It was a process he would repeat in the days to come as they narrowed down the list.

"Wonder how many of these dead ends are in our future?" He asked Andy who stood by waiting for a signal to move on.

"Can't know until we follow 'em to the end." Luke had begun to think and act as if Andy was an interested participant in his search. Andy never responded but he helped by always dutifully following Luke's lead.

"This stream is way different than what I was expecting." Luke confided in Andy, "On the map it seems to be a trickle but it is large and fast moving. Must have been a lot of rain this spring."

The plan was to follow the mainstream back. It led to the base of one of the many mountains that had to be explored. After several hours of hiking they reached the first mountain on the map. It was listed as 3658 feet in elevation. There was no clear path to the top. Luke tied Andy up and began the ascent alone.

At first it was easy, the path was clear and without growth. About half way up the "trail" vanished and Luke had to fight his way through patches of thick tangled brush. At that point his shotgun became cumbersome. It required both hands to pull and tear at the brush. He slung his shotgun over his shoulder to get his hands free. It bounced awkwardly on his back.

The climb got difficult and his breathing became heavy and labored. Progress was slow. The soil and rocks beneath his boots came loose and his footing was treacherous. He slipped and fell, scraping his hands. They bled and turned red.

"Ain't' supposed to be easy. If it was easy, anyone could do it." He redoubled his efforts. An hour later, he found himself on the peak staring out at the expanse below.

He focused his binoculars and did a 180 degree survey. His view moved from hill to hill until he found a black spot nestled in the green and brown vegetation. Was it a cave opening? Perhaps an abandoned mine? His heart skipped a beat, it was an important lead.

He kept up the search and was rewarded with still another dark spot. It was miles away and off to the left. His heart raced. Maybe one of them had the "sign of the cross" and was waiting to be discovered. Would he get lucky on his first day? The anticipation of instant gratification made him rush forward.

He found the climb down was easier than the climb up. It was high noon when he reached the bottom and the sun was blazing overhead. He had to set up camp, take shelter and get out of the heat. He put Andy out to graze, and tried to read a book.

It was too hot and he couldn't concentrate enough to read. His eyes raced over several pages and then he realized he had no recollection of what he had just read. He took an uncomfortable cat nap, and dozed off.

"I'm glad I spent the summer working in the sun. I can handle it." Andy was out of the sun, grazing with his head down. "Damn Andy looks like you like the sun."

Andy did not react and kept on grazing with his head down ignoring Luke.

"I saw a couple of black spots a few miles away, they might be mine entrances, or perhaps caves. We got to go check em out."

Luke got Andy packed up and they headed for the first of the prospective dark spots. Were they caves or mines? Would he find the cross?

"What do you think the odds are that I will find the lost mine on my first try?" Luke asked Andy for his opinion, but Andy was busy hauling a hundred and fifty pounds of gear and paid no attention.

"There it is, right there. Can you see it now?" Luke pointed out the dark patch to Andy.

The first dark spot was visible so Luke pulled out his binoculars and focused on the dark opening. Now that he was close he could see it clearly. It was triangular in shape and had a jagged mouth. It was the opening to a cave, not a mine. There was no cross in sight. He decided not to bother with the difficult climb.

"No use climbing this one. I ain't gonna bother going up there." Andy did not argue.

The second black spot turned out to be further away than Luke had estimated. The trail leading up to it disappeared back up into the mountains.

"It is the remnants of a flash flood along this part of the path," Luke commented as he picked his way up the canyon. At that moment Andy stalled, objecting to the climb. Luke pulled hard but Andy was turning out to be stubborn. He refused to budge.

"Imagine that a stubborn mule." Luke complained out loud. "Of course the damn mule is stubborn! All mules are stubborn!" " He pulled and prodded, but Andy, who was under duress, refused to cooperate.

"If you don't get moving I am going to stick my foot up your ass!"

Luke cajoled the difficult beast, pushing and pulling without success. Suddenly and without warning Andy's whole body seemed to relax.Whatever had caused Andy to resist had passed. The mule had been straining and was tense, almost fearful and now he was willing and compliant. Luke was baffled, why was Andy so determined to resist one moment only to change and become amazingly cooperative the next? In a matter of a few moments his mood had transformed and he was a different animal.

"I guess mules are moody. Are you moody Andy?" Luke knew there had to be a reason Andy was so uneasy. He just couldn't put his finger on it.

Luke guided Andy up the path in the direction where he had seen the mine opening. There it was! Right before him! A quarter of a mile away and it looked to be accessible. It was a favorable sign.

The trail was easy to follow and in minutes they were standing at the mine opening. Luke searched for a cross. There was nothing, no cross was visible or apparent. He could tell  right away this wasn't Edwards mine. He decided to explore it anyway. He tied Andy up, and put on his gloves and entered, shining a flashlight as he went.

The entrance was a narrow tunnel that led back into a bigger mine. He crouched and inched his way along. It was dark and dry inside. He shined the light on the walls and checked to see how deep it might be. He could not see to the back wall. Beer cans and coke bottles were left in a scattered pile.

He shined his light on a rock formation on the north wall. Someonehad been digging and chipping away. They had left a lot of debris. Nothing Luke saw resembled the mother loads depicted in Al's library book. The search was turning out to be futile.

"Can't afford a snake bite out here." He reminded himself as he inched along in the darkness.

The tunnel was hundreds of feet deep. He wondered how many years of hard labor had been invested in this mine by the former owners? What had they gotten for their efforts? Anything? There must have been something here or why dig this deep? But another part of his mind answered back, "they deserted it, there is nothing here".

Since it was not "the" lost mine and he knew it was a waste of time to continue. It was after seven o'clock. The sun would be down soon. He made the walk back to the creek and settled in for the night.

Luke allowed Andy to wander loose on a hundred foot rope. He was free to water and feed. In the distance, there was another mountain waiting to be climbed. He would head for it in the morning. If he was lucky there would be another set of mines and he could begin the search all over again.

Luke made a little pit for a campfire. As he dug he cut through several layers of leafy foliage buried in the pit. He started a campfire, and let it burn for a while. He waited until the red embers of the fire were crackling hot, then he wedged a potato wrapped in aluminum foil deep in the coals. The potato was smothered in butter and wrapped in bacon. He let it cook for an hour. When he pulled it out it was steaming hot and ready to eat. It made a satisfying supper.

A band of coyotes began howling in the distance. Were they howling for him? Did they know he was listening?

He had not seen a single person since saying goodbye to All that morning. Andy had become his only companion. His imagination turned to his love affair with Darla. The thought of her made him feverish. The attraction was strong and it was physical. He knew that for sure. It was intense and overwhelming. What would happen with Darla?

"I gotta find that damn mine. This day's been a dud, I hope tomorrow will be different." It was certain that finding the mine was the key to keeping her by his side.

His first day of looking had turned up nothing. Doubt gnawed at him. Was he on a fool's quest? What if he never found the mine? If he didn't find it his chances with Darla were minimal. What did he have to offer her? Nothing! He had no money and no plan for the future! He fought off the fear of failure and went to sleep. It was a dreamless night.

Luke woke at dawn. He had kept Andy tied up in a grove with plenty of low hanging foliage. He was well fed and watered when they started for the next mountain.

It was several hours away and the trail was overgrown and hard to follow. Andy continued to be stubborn and progress on the trail was a battle won with difficulty. Even so, by mid morning they reached the base of the mountain. Luke decided to make the climb up alone. It was much too difficult for Andy to undertake. Once again the view from the top was magnificent and rewarded Luke with the discovery of several new dark spots. Were they mines or caves? He sketched a route and formed a plan to survey them by the end of the day.

He retrieved Andy and they started for the nearest of the spots. The journey was taking them deeper and deeper into the countryside. Both dark spots turned out to be deserted mines and they explored them. It was clear that no one had worked in them for a long time. There were no giant crosses and no evidence of ore or gold. Day two of his treasure hunt turned out to be a total bust! They were dead ends.

He made camp by the side of a new stream that led even further back into the hills. Luke was relieved because at least water was not a problem.The second day had come and gone and he was without results. He had accomplished little and had nothing to show for the day. His note in the black ledger book recorded the amount of ground covered and marked the search as futile.

He was becoming frustrated. The idea of saving town seemed unlikely. He was unsure of himself. It was intimidating to think he had only been out for two days. He had a growing respect for the amount of ground that had to be covered. It was immense. What if this day turned out to be the result he got every day? What a waste of time and energy that would be. It had to get better!

There were still eight days left to explore but he started thinking about following a loop. It was crucial that he arrive back at the pick up point on time to meet Al. He began to plan the rest of his trip so that when he was making his way back he would cover fresh ground. It would be stupid to come back the same way he came!

Luke plotted out an ellipse and tried to tie the path together in a way that made sense. He drew an elliptical circle going north east for three more days. He marked a point at which he should turn and start to head back to the south. The ellipse swung out connecting hills and mountains and canyons as best it could be done. In reality he had laid a zigzag course that circled back to the starting point. It was achievable and realistic.

Luke felt his "adventure" was beginning to feel like hard work. He had learned a lot in a short time. He had gotten a feel for how long things take. He knew how many miles he could expect to hike in a day. It was far less than he had originally thought.

For the next three days he stuck to following his ellipse. He and Andy climbed mountains and discovered caves and abandoned mines. Everyone of them turned out to be a bust. Luke decided they had gone as far out as they could and had to turn around and loop back. He began to take a course to arrive back at the rendezvous point. He was becoming discouraged and losing faith.

There was a huge area "out there" still to be covered and to his dismay he could not be sure that the ground he had covered had been fully explored. It was possible he had missed something and overlooked a key spot. It had become clear that this project could require many, many trips and they might never fully account for all the territory He had to get lucky if he was to succeed. The thought was discouraging.

He and Andy had been hiking for five days and it felt like much more. Luke was getting numb from it all. At least he always had fresh water and plenty of food. Hiking, climbing, and examining old abandoned mines was no longer exciting, It had become dull and repetitive, It was tiring, tedious hard work.

Andy had become a close and trusted companion of sorts. Luke talked to him and pretended Andy understood what was being discussed. It never mattered to Luke that Andy did not understand a word of it ever. He kept on talking to Andy anyway. It was reassuring.

Often as they hiked, Luke played his harmonica and sang. When he did Andy perked up and there was a little extra bounce in his step. Luke thought he was less contentious and more co-operative under the influence of music. Every day Luke grew more and more fond of Andy.

On day six Luke found himself unexpectedly locked in another ferocious battle with Andy. Andy objected to the path they were taking. Luke had to tug and drag him along. Once again he shouted at Andy, and threatened him. He even played music for him. None of it worked. Andy rudely dug his hooves in making it clear he had no desire to follow. For some unknown reason Andy was spooked.

Luke was in no mood for a battle with Andy. He looked for and found another route to the top. Changing direction seemed to sooth Andy, who calmed down and took to the new trail with a bounce in his step. They circled around the mountain base and came to a clearing that was being served by a well used walkway. This path led them to the mouth of a prominent but deserted mine.

"We must have come up to it on the back side." There were obvious signs of recent activity around this site. "Someone has been here recently." Luke wondered if that someone was Edward.

The mouth of the mine was an opening at least ten feet across and more than eight feet high. A stout beam cut right across the upper third of the opening. The beam cut the opening into uneven quarters and was propping it open.

Luke gasped, it hit him like a lightning bolt! The cross beam was connecting both sides of the mine. He was staring at a huge 10 ft by 8 ft cross! It served to reinforce and prop up the opening to the mine! This had to be it! All doubt and anxiety flowed out of this body. Waves of joy washed over his being when he realized he was standing at the mouth of a mine marked by a huge cross! He had found it!

Luke relaxed inside for the first time since he and Andy had begun the search. It occurred to him that he had taken the failure of the dance party as a personal failure. It had been his idea and it had failed! He had let everyone down! Now hoped he would be the one to rectify the situation! In his imagination he could feel Darla wrapping her arms around him. It lit the burning flames of lust and desire for her that was always burning in him and was never far away.

Luke entered and found evidence of recent activity everywhere. He shone his light around the cave and it rested on a vein of quartz wrapped in granite. It was surrounded by chunks that had been chipped out. He rushed to inspect his find.

This was it. Edward's lost mine! He ran his fingers down the face of the vein. It was just like the long thick streaks of yellow metallic rock in Al's book. It had to be gold. He decided he would dig for a couple of days and mine as much of the yellow as he could. Then he would head back to the pick up point!

"God Damn It Andy we found it!" He bellowed in triumph.

It was a huge relief. He imagined all of his friends' reactions when he delivered the news. He would toss gold dust on the table right before their eyes.

Luke set up camp and went to work. He calculated it was about a three day hike back to the rendezvous spot where he was to meet Al. That gave him at least two days to do nothing but mine and accumulate gold!

He tied up Andy, allowing him enough rope to wander and threw himself into the work. He began digging, and collecting gold with the energy of ten men. Burning the lantern he worked until midnight stopping only to heat and eat a can of chili. He would return with enough of the precious metal to make an immediate difference.

"I'll already have enough to even up the ledger by myself." His chest swelled and he envisioned the Bodfish braintrust handing over ounce and ounce of the precious metal.

He could not wait to see Darla again. He imagined the look on her face when he showed her the gold and described how he had found the treasure.

His little voice had been silent. Now it reminded him she was ten years older than he was. It told him to remember that she had a husband. It told him she had far more experience than he did and that it had become a problem. It was annoying. He told the voice to go away.

When he stopped work, he could not fall asleep, even though he was exhausted! His little voice kept asking himself question after question, what do I want from her? Would we be together if I hadn't found the gold? How well do I know her? What is her favorite color? The realization hit him hard. He could not answer.

He had no idea of how to answer any of these questions. The more the voice asked its questions the more he was not sure of anything. It stunned him. Only a few moments before he had been sure of everything. When he finally fell asleep he was full of doubts, wondering if he knew what he wanted. The cold reality swept over him, and it was that he did not know.

Luke was startled out of his sleep by a terrible braying sound that sent chills into his body. It was Andy's voice! It seemed to have become almost human. He was crying for help in panic and fear. The screech was pure pain and terror and anguish. The call went out into the night and came echoing back amplified by the hills until it sounded like there were a dozen mules crying out simultaneously. Luke heard a hissing noise and the sounds of a struggle.

He grabbed his gun, and ran to the spot where he had left Andy tied up. The mule was writhing on the ground, kicking wildly in the air trying to get to his feet. Andy's neck was in the mouth of a full grown mountain lion who had him pinned to the ground. Andy kept trying to push himself up but the beast had leverage and kept him down. Its jaws were exerting a vice-like pressure on Andy's throat.

The lion shook Andy's head violently trying to rip him apart. It made loud choking noises and Andy cried out for help! The mule brayed and cried in pain. The lion banged Andy's head repeatedly on the ground. It pulled away briefly revealing a huge mouthful of flesh it had torn from Andy's neck. The lion spit out the fresh flesh and dove in for the kill.

Luke pointed the gun in the direction of the lion and fired. A loud explosion filled the night and echoed back from the hills. The echo came reverberating from the hills as if the gun had been fired a dozen times. The cougar spun its head and hissed at Luke. It planted its feet in the ground for a brief second and then shot off like a bolt of lighting vanishing into the night.

In a flash the lion was gone and Andy lay on the ground whimpering and crying and shaking. Luke felt a wave of nausea sweep over his body. He rushed to Andy to see what damage had been done. Andy's voice was broken and cracked. It sounded like he was crying. His whole body shook in terror.

Blood was spilling from his neck and even in the dark Luke could see a jagged tear near the front of the neck. Andy was struggling to stand on his feet but each time he tried to rise, his left knee buckled and he could not stand. Luke took off his shirt and wrapped it around his hand. He located the gash in the mule's neck in the dark and tried to cover it with the shirt. He put pressure on the wound and attempted to stop the bleeding.

The shirt was soaked and useless. The wound had cut an artery or a vein! Luke kneeled above him and placed both hands on the gash and tried to apply even more pressure. His hands were warm and wet with blood. It was no use, too much damage had been done. Andy wanted to get up but could not do so. Luke gave up trying to keep his hands on the wounded animal's neck.

Andy jerked spasmodically and gave up trying to stand. Luke examined the left knee and saw it was also badly ripped. The lion had grabbed Andy by the leg to bring him down and had shattered the knee. Once he had Andy down he had locked onto his neck and gone for the kill.

Luke stepped back and surveyed the damage. He himself was covered with Andy's blood. He felt an overwhelming sense of helplessness and loss. With every drop of blood that spilled out he was watching the life drain out of the mule and there was nothing he could do about it. The noises from Andy's throat got worse, and his breathing became more and more labored. He was suffering terribly. He stopped braying and was gurgling. His chest heaved as he whimpered.

"I have to put him out of his misery. He is going to bleed out no matter what. I got to help him."

Luke reloaded his shotgun. He had never killed anything before. The idea was frightening, and sickening. He stood over the suffering animal and put the barrel to its head. Luke stood there frozen unable to bring himself to pull the trigger and then it hit him.

Andy was already dead, he could not be saved. Too much damage had been done. It was either going to happen now or as soon as his blood supply ran out. Making him wait for death was cruel. He had no choice. He had to act. He pulled the trigger.

Andy's head bounced with the impact of the blast and he went silent. His body tightened up for a second and then went limp. In an instant everything had changed. Andy was gone.

Luke was many days walk away from his rendezvous point and now had way more gear than he could carry. He sat down by his tiny fire and tried to collect his thoughts. What do I do now he asked himself. He had found the gold mine and that was the good news. He would mine the open strip of rock collecting as much ore as he could and then head back to the pick up point. He would have to leave a lot of Al's gear behind.

He couldn't possibly carry it all without Andy. It could be collected on a return trip which was certain to happen now that he knew where the mine was. He would just have to leave Andy's carcass to the mercies of nature.

He tried to go back to sleep but it did not come. A regret, a sorrow at having been forced to take a life was eating at him. Andy was only a mule, but he had spent over a week with him and he felt like he had lost a friend. Andy had been a fine companion.

Luke understood full well that he had to pull the trigger, he reminded himself of the facts and kept repeating the thought that it was the lion that killed Andy. Shooting him had been an act of mercy. The actual killing was the lions doing, and was what lions are born to do, so it had to be accepted. However the fact mattered very little, he still had a terrible feeling of loss.

Chapter Thirty Two

When sunrise came Luke was shaken and starving. He gave in to his hunger and ate some beef jerky. The night's adventures had left him drained and worn. He was both exhilarated and depressed. He was certain that lady luck had smiled on him and that the exposed vein he was working was just the tip of a rich deposit.

"This is the opportunity of a lifetime. There's not a second to waste! It's right out in plain sight begging me to take it." Luke was flooded with an overwhelming desire for gold. He hammered away at the open vein, chipping away bits of the colored rock. Everytime he swung his pick he broke away chunks of ore loaded with the precious yellow metal. Gleefully he collected his new found treasure.

"This is easier than I ever thought it could be." He addressed his comments to Andy. Then he remembered that Andy was lying dead rotting in the morning sun a couple of hundred yards away, "This is your victory just as much as it is mine!"

Luke avoided thinking about Andy's confrontation with the mountain lion. He could not bring himself to go down to the spot where it had all happened. 'I'll do it later' he told himself. "There's nothing I can do? He is too heavy to carry and would be hard to bury." It was certain that the crows, owls, and coyotes would all take a turn at picking Andy's body clean. All he had to do was let nature take its course and it would dispose of Andy's remains for him. It did not seem fair, Andy deserved a better fate.

"It was out of my hands. It happened so fast there was nothing I could do." Luke said it out loud as if he was apologizing to the dead mule.

Luke was on fire with gold "fever". It drove him to work diligently, gathering up every bit of yellow the vein provided. As he chipped away the thought, "this vein reaches far down into the mountain" echoed in his mind. He grew giddy imagining the vast amount of gold that had to be buried there. His sack got heavier and larger as he worked. He guessed it held five pounds, he hoped for more!" He held the bulging sack skyward imagining the joy it was going to bring everyone in Bodfish.

He could almost hear their happy voices, filled with delight, thanking him and listening in awe as he told and retold the tale of finding the mine. He rejoiced in the bright future it would bring them all.

"There is a lot buried here, enough to provide everyone a place on easy street. Even little Bubba." The rock formation was huge and the promise of abundance enlivened everything he did. He kept his concentration on the work.

"Stop that right now! I have had about enough of that." Luke froze in his tracks. It was a loud, powerful, angry male voice and it was right behind him. Luke dropped his pick and froze as commanded. After a moment, he slowly turned his head around to see two men standing in the entrance to the mine with guns pointed right at him. "We caught you red handed in the act."

"What the hell." Luke turned and faced them."You guys are crazy. I ain't doing nothing."

"Looks to me like you've jumped our claim. I think you are stealing our gold!" The threatening voice belonged to a burly man with a flowing black beard whose rifle was aimed right at Luke's head. His jaw was set firm, and his eyes were flashing with anger and rage.

"Who are you people? I ain't stealing nothing." Luke took a deep breath and managed to speak in a low slow calm voice.

"We're the owners of this mine and you're trespassing. You are digging our gold. We can see it from here. It's plain as day. Johnny, what do you think we should do bout this boy?" The big man in the plaid shirt spit out the words.

"Don't rightly know." Little Johnny waved the barrel of his rifle and shook his head. "We could tie him up and let the law deal with him I guess."

"There ain't no law in these hills." The big man in the plaid shirt kept the gun pointed and ready to fire. "Tying him up and keeping an eye on him sounds like a lot of trouble. I bet he is here all alone. I'll bet no one knows anything about him."

"No one would miss him." Little Johnny agreed.

"You alone boy? You sure look all alone, I'll bet no one would miss you." The big man was talking to Luke again.

"You saying you own this mine? I doubt that. I got a map here from the man who once owned it. He gave it to my partner just before he died. I can show it to you."

"Let's hear him out." It was a woman's voice. "Let's hear his story. I don't want you doing anything rash." She came out of the shadows, and stepped into sight.

"We should tie him up and let the county sheriff sort it out." Johnny piped up.

"That would be a can of worms and you know both know it." The woman didn't back down. "Let's hear his story."

"I say we tie him up." The big man chipped in.

"If we tie him up and hold him we will spend a lot of time dealing with him. We'd have to take him to town, and file charges. We'd end up in court for a long time. Put the gun down, can't you see he is just a kid? He ain't gonna do nothin. There's three of us."

"Maybe so, but he's stealing our gold." Larry did not drop the rifle and kept it pointed at Luke. "I don't want to kill nobody, but he is causing trouble and we caught him."

"This ain't the old west, you can't kill a claim jumper." The woman's voice was harsh.

"I ain't stealin nothing and anyways I am a deputy sheriff in the town of Bodfish. I got my badge somewhere in my pack." Luke blurted it, grasping at straws.

"It's dark in there, come on out where I can see you. Come out and show us what you look like." Big Larry waved his rifle in the air and dropped the barrel so it pointed at the ground. Luke walked slowly out into the light.

"What's this you're saying about a badge? Where is it? Let's see it." The woman asked.

"It's in my pack. I'll get it and show you if you'll let me." Luke nodded to the mound of stuff he had piled in the mouth of the cave.

"Damn, he is all covered in blood. What you been up to, boy? He's got blood all over his shirt and face." Larry asked in amazement. "You've been in a fight? You kill somebody?"

Luke hadn't been able to clean up from the night before when he had attempted to stop the bleeding from Andy's neck and knee. After the panic ended he had done nothing to clean up. He was still wearing the same clothes he had on when he had chased off the cougar.

"It's nothin, it's just blood from my mule, Andy. His body is lying in the trail. A mountain lion attacked us last night. I tried to save him, but he was torn up real bad. I ended up putting him to sleep."Luke motioned to the spot where Andy's body was lying. "Can I show you my badge?"

"Johnny, go check what he's saying. See if there is a dead mule down the trail. I'll check for his badge." Little Johnny went off looking for Andy's body. Larry started rummaging through Luke's gear.

"You say you're from Bodfish?" It was the woman's voice once again. This time she sounded calm and no longer angry. Luke decided to try and talk to her.

"Yeah that's right. I am a deputy sheriff in Bodfish. I work at the movie set ranch." It wasn't a lie. Hell's bells! He had the badge to prove it. They had sworn him in but no one ever swore him out.

"I found this old badge in his bag. It looks official." Larry held up the badge confirming Luke's claim.

"Ain't Bodfish the town on Edward's death certificate? The place where he died? You picked up his body at the morgue in Bakersfield but it was shipped there from Bodfish. Ain't that right?" The woman was connecting the dots.

"That's Right," Big Larry answered. "Maybe there's something to the boy's story."

"Why don't you let him tell it." It was the woman again.

Luke told them the tale of his misbegotten summer at the movie ranch. He focused on Al and the map and Edwards' death. He highlighted their desperate need for cash and the last minute search to locate the lost mine. He deliberately skipped over the part where he suspected Al might have stolen Edward's map. He emphasized how Darla had been with Edward at the end and he had given her the clue of the cross. He made sure that they understood how she had provided comfort to Edward during his last hours of life.

The woman relaxed and introduced herself as Sally Joseph, the niece of Edward Joseph the old miner who had died in Bodfish and had given Al the map.

"Somehow it don't feel quite right. I don't believe Edward would give the map or the mine to a total stranger. In fact a few weeks before he died he sent us a letter with all the details. He told us he had struck it rich and asked us to help him come work it." Sally looked at the blood drenched figure before her and tried to absorb the tale he had told. It made some sense, she thought.

"I got my details second hand. It all happened before I came to Bodfish. Who knows about Edward's state of mind at the end? Darla thought he had valley fever."

Luke now knew it was a lost cause. These three weren't about to let Al or anyone else file a claim on a mine they clearly owned. He came to grips with the fact that the movie ranch would not be saved by a lost gold mine. All he wanted now was to slip away without any further trouble.

"Larry here is my husband, and Johnny is his little brother. My Uncle Edward walked these mountains for years and nothing ever came of it." Sally angled up close to Luke and shook her head at the sight. "You're covered in dried blood. I'll get you a wet towel. You should wash off."

"Well it looks like Edward's effort finally paid off. I must look awful. In all the excitement I never thought about cleaning up."

"First, we thought he was a sick old man dreamin' crazy dreams." She put her hand on Luke's face and scratched a lump of blood off his cheek.

"I must look scary, I tried to save Andy. I tried to stop him from bleeding but..... I couldn't do it." He rubbed his face harder. "The blood is dried and caked on."

"When Larry claimed Edward's body we got his journal. I read it, and got the whole story. It told how he staked it out. All about how he hit a mother lode. Where to find it exactly " Sally finished her tale and waited for Luke to react.

"Well I can see that you're the rightful owners. I was not trying to jump your claim. We knew nothin about you." It was settled, Luke accepted that Al had no claim. He wondered what had really happened on the night Edward died. Luke decided he would never know the full truth. It didn't matter either, he decided Al had no claim and he would not try to prove otherwise.

"We got a base camp about five miles down in the valley below. We can drive right out jeeps up to the base camp but we got to pack here. Why didn't you notice this was an active site?" Sally wanted to believe Luke's story but he should have seen it was being worked and it belonged to someone else. All the signs were there showing someone was working it.

"There's a dead mule down the road apiece, looks like someone blew its head off." It was Johnny reporting back about Andy's fate.

"I had to put him asleep. Hell I have been out here for a week looking for this mine. The map was not very good. I got lucky and found it. Now I wish I had never bothered."

"Looks like you dug out about a pound of gold." Big Larry had Luke's sack in his hands and was shaking it in the air. "Is this it? Is there any more? Are you hiding some?"

"Naw that's it. I found your mine yesterday. That's all I had time to work it. Search if you want but that's it." Luke waved his hand indicating they could search all they wanted.

"Make a search in all his gear Johnny." Big Larry ordered his brother.

"I was at the end of my trip and was getting ready to go back to Bodfish and bring the others out here. I got to be at a rendezvous site I got to be at soon. If I don't show, they'll come looking for me."

Sally had decided Luke wasn't a thief or a claim jumper, just a kid with good intentions and bad information.

"You lost your mule, and you got a mess of gear with you. I'll help you bring your stuff down to our base camp. You can clean up there, but you ain't welcome here no more. I want you out of here." Sally was firm.

"Al ain't due to come out and rendezvous with me for three more days. I got nothing to do until then. Can I help you work the mine? I need something to do to pass the time."

"I'm going down to Bakersfield tonight to purchase supplies. You can ride with me and I'll swing by Bodfish. I'll drop you and your gear tonight."

Luke felt like the world of Bodfish was collapsing all around him. He had done everything it was in his power to do and it felt like a lost cause.

It was after two in the morning and all the stars were quietly out when Sally dropped Luke off in front of the entrance. He opened the gate as quietly as he could. He didn't want Al waking up in fright and have him come charging down the street waving his pistol. Luke thought, "the third time might be the charm. He might finally shoot me."

Luke went to sleep in the old bunk and his sleep was dreamless. He woke at sunrise, and all of a sudden Bodfish seemed like a very odd place. He had spent the whole summer sleeping in a hundred year old jail and had never once been motivated to clean it or put the room in any kind of order. It was exactly as it had been when he first walked in the door. The dust and cobwebs were a little thicker and he had worn a path from the door to the bed each night, but those were the only real changes.

"Not much of a stuntman school." He shook his head and laughed at himself.

"What a fool I have been." He said it out loud, knowing it was time to move on. He pulled his boots on and packed up the few things he had lying around. In ten minutes he was "packed" and ready to go. All of Al's mining gear was piled up on the jailhouse porch where Al would be sure to find them.

He wrote a brief letter explaining what had happened with Sally and big Larry. He described Andy's tragic fate explaining how he had left Andy's carcass to the coyotes and the crows.

When he finished the letter he took out the badges they had given him, and placed them on the table along with the shotgun. "Won't be needing these anymore." He realized he still had the two dollars he had charged the two boys who came from out of town to attend the party. He placed them under the gun barrel along with the keys to the locks of the various doors of the town. He signed the note offering his sincere thanks for all they had done for him.

"Pretty sure they will understand." He said it out loud to the empty cell. "They can't afford to keep me around no more. Never really could."

It was sunrise and no one was up as he walked alone down the main street of Bodfish. It was fifteen miles to the highway. He was determined to walk all the way if he had to. The town felt deserted.

He had come to Bodfish in pursuit of an entry into the movies. Looking back it now seemed unbelievable that he ever took the project seriously. Still he felt absolutely no regrets about it. Why regret what you cannot change?

After walking several blocks Darla pulled up next to him. She appeared out of nowhere. She reached across the seat and opened the door to her Nash. She did not say a word as she motioned for him to get in. As soon as he did, she took off in the direction of the highway. Her timing was perfect. He wondered how she knew?

Luke wanted to say something to her, to explain why he had to leave. Her eyes told the story. It was clear she understood he was leaving and had not intended to say goodbye. Her silence told him that she wanted to leave herself if she couldn't. He had no idea where he was going or what he was going to do. So how could he ask her to come along? It was impossible.

What could he say? She was not a leaf floating away in the wind like he was about to become again. "You wanna go nowhere?" It sounded crazy.

She pulled up the hill that framed the lake. It was a blue jewel in the morning sun. Luke looked back for the last time and saw the top of the slide. It was the tallest edifice in Bodfish poking up above the tree line. It was visible from the road, just like Dean said it would be. He had to smile. He marveled at the morning sun dancing on the calm lake below. It was a great lake.

Darla drove Luke to the highway and stopped to let him out. "Take care," she said. Her eyes said goodbye. That was it. He got out, pack in hand and closed the door behind him.

"You too." he answered, full of longing but knowing it was the last time he would see her. When she was gone, he was faced with a choice. Head south back to Los Angeles or north to whatever might be waiting in that direction. He knew what was down south, he had lived there all his life. Heheaded north. He took out his harmonica and started playing a blues riff.

A half hour later a man in his twenties stopped and picked him up.

"Where are you headed?"

"North," Luke answered.

"Any place in particular?" The man was incredulous. How could anyone be going nowhere?

"No, just north."

"Well I'm going to Lake Tahoe. Ever been there?"

"Naw." Luke had heard of the place, but knew nothing about it.

"If you want, I'll take you there." He looked Luke over. "Place is packed with casinos. I bet you could get a job dealing cards. Ever think of being a card dealer in a casino? Lots of young women go to casinos to play cards. I'll bet you would be a hit."

They headed north in silence and he imagine what life would be like working in a casino dealing cards. He envisioned himself wearing a ruffled white shirt with cufflinks and a black vest. Perhaps he would wear a visor. He thought, why not? Maybe he should become a card player. He decided it was worth a try.

1

Made in the USA
Monee, IL
19 November 2023

46672385R00122